First Printing, 2021

YULE TIDINGS TO HELL

Yule Tidings to Hell

Lukas Allen

Lukas Allen

Contents

Part 2: Temperantia — 83

Part 3: Caritas — 115

Part 4: Industria — 153

For my grandma

Part 1: Humanitas

Kindness

1

Pants. Finally. *Pants!*

All the skirts and robes were so tiring. Endless, angelic, white robes. Or skirts. Some of the angels still preferred showing off their sexy side. Strange that they were allowed into Heaven half naked like they are, but maybe that tells you a little about our creator.

Nudity *is* the natural form. But as I put on my white jeans, I couldn't get over how comfortable and enveloping they were. I did a little dance in my pure white *pants.*

I suppose the color just sort of rubbed off on me. When I was alive I wore the most bizarre outfits, of all colors, ever changing. But when I got to Heaven we had a sort of color code, amidst the fluffy white clouds.

Now, as I walked the Earth, swaggering in my new pants, down the street in the white, white snow, I realized I missed the natural colors of the world. That beautiful green of the pine tree, that red, pink and yellow from those Christmas lights, the blue grey sky.

Ah yes… the sky. I wondered what they were doing up there? So far away from everyone?

Ah well. Doesn't matter. I thought I'd try something else I haven't had since I was alive… Get a drink.

I opened the bar door and a drunk passerby said, "Yule tidings! Merry Christmas!" and stumbled past me as I returned the saying.

He threw up into the snow.

I sat down at the bar and ordered a... hmm... The Blood of God wouldn't do. I suppose I'd have something common, like what people drink usually. I ordered a beer.

The bartender plopped a frothing mug of beer in front of me, then rushed off to fulfill the rest of the people's orders and requests. It looked like it was a busy night. It *was* the night of our Lord the Savior's birth.

You'd think more people would spend time with their families on this night, but I suppose when you're alone it helps being with other lonely people on such a night. And to be very, very drunk.

"Hoooow'd you get such... *white...* hair??" a drunkard said from beside me.

"I'm actually an albino." I said.

He hiccupped, and said, "Albinoooo? That some sort of rabbit? No wait... You're like Michael Jackson or something... I'm..." hiccup, "'Thaniel."

"Nice to meet you, Thaniel! I'm... Yule." I said, shaking his hand.

"Na-" hiccup, "-thaniel." he said.

"Well, Thaniel, what are you up to tonight? Know any good jokes?" I said.

"Iiiiii'm... wondering why your eyes are so red! That something with the rabbit thing? Wellll I do know this one joke... A priest, a minister, and a rabbit walk into a blood bank... The nurse asks what blood type they are. The priest says he's a type A, the minister says he's a type B, and the rabbit says... he's a typo. Get it? Typooooo?"

"HAHA! That's hilarious! My friend Luke had all sorts of typos in his writings, and a lot of things got lost in translation because of them." I said, and sipped at my beer.

"My work is a writer... normally... I mean that's what I prefer to do. Now I work on bloody house repair... Fucking roof won't fucking fix itself..." Thaniel said, and chugged at his beer.

"Well, Thaniel, I'm sure your wife and kids think the world of you. Keep at it!" I said.

"Howwww'd you know I have a wife and kids??" he said.

I pointed to his ring, and said, "I'm sure they're waiting up for you tonight."

He grew sombre, and said, "Well... maybe Julia, my youngest. I'm getting divorced. Not that... I had a *choice* in the matter... She kept on bitching at me... and I couldn't help but bitch back. We just grew apart, y'know?"

I patted his hand, and said, "Sometimes we just drift apart. Me and my father... he'd be furious to know I left. But this adventure is what I've been dreaming about for all of creation. I always pray for his forgiveness every night, but I'm not sure he can hear me..."

"Hmph. God can go suck a dick. If he cared... then why would he let me get so drunk on Christmas? God doesn't give a shit. Iffff... he cared... I would've been able to keep *at least one* of the kids..." Thaniel said.

"It won't be forever. Just make sure to keep in touch." I said.

"Suuure... Well, you take care, Yule. I'm going to stumble to the gas station and get some smokes... Take care." Thaniel said.

"Merry Christmas!" I said, as he was getting up to go.

"Merry-" hiccup, "-Christmas." he slurred, and stumbled out the door.

I went back home with a bit of a buzz, and was listening to this *fantastic* reggae singer... about jamming. Bob Marley? I just wanted to jam all night...

I didn't really have many possessions yet in my apartment, but I hoped to change that sometime. I still kept the Bible that St. Peter gave to me as I snuck out the gates. It didn't look at all like something from

Heaven, just an old, dusty Bible. Maybe things from Heaven are normal everyday objects.

Yet still, I took St. Peter's lasting words of advice, "Don't drink too much," and only sipped at my wine instead of chugging it all down...

I was having so much fun!!

Living after death is astoundingly dull! Sure... there's all the- and the- and sometimes- but still, I loved being alive all the more despite those things.

I mean sure, I guess I could die now... but what would happen to an angel that died on Earth? Would I go to Heaven, Hell, or just be obliterated? Ach, who cares. I'm sure I could sneak back through the gates before my mortal demise...

I did kind of miss the wings. Flapping around, being so carefree... The halo always got in the way, though. It shined so bright! I'm glad I could get rid of the damn thing. The other angels all made fun of me, in their light joking way, of me always trying to swat the halo away...

Then the college radio station I was listening to changed tracks, and I heard heavy metal.

Devil music. I shuddered when I heard it, but... it seemed to be reeling me in. Seemed to be drawing my attention with those guitar riffs, the bass pull, and the beats. I noticed my head was bouncing up and down to the music not before long.

And soon, the song was over, and I was listening to some jazz.

Wait... wasn't jazz Devil music at one point as well? Hmm... Maybe music is just all an expression of God's will and merriment.

I'm just glad I don't have to play a harp anymore.

Or sing in that blasted choir.

Or take lessons from my music teacher, St. Cecilia.

Falling to Earth was the best thing I've ever done.

It was scary, falling, down, down, down... As my wings burned to crisps and my halo flew away from me... falling through the clouds instead of on them, but when I hit the ground, my feet lightly touched Earth, and I felt like my true calling had come about, and not my supposed calling of... y'know.

My true calling was to live.

To feel joy, pain, suffering, happiness, all the many beautiful fantastically complex emotions of life.

My life had been cut short, one of the reasons I went to Heaven I think... a tragic accident. But I didn't have to worry about that anymore. I had a second chance.

I drank wine listening to the radio, and turned on the TV, letting the extra stimuli submerge my brain in sound and music.

Then I turned on all the lights, and danced to the music and the strange Christmas cartoon on the TV.

I was worn out from dancing after a while, and sat in front of the TV. My, these commercials sure were strange.

But I saw a powerful looking woman, with short, short hair, like a man's, but not shaved off completely.

I wowed at her, the president of the United States. She looked sort of like a punk rocker.

So I took out my hair cutting kit, and went to work on myself.

Hair cutting was one of the few things I was actually good at, and clipped all my long, white hair off.

I looked back at the mirror, at the star tattoo on my cheek, at my slightly scarred face, scars from the accident, and my short, white hair. I smiled back into my own red eyes.

Then I looked a little longer, and I could see my angelic side. My eyes letting loose streams of radiating light, as I ran a hand through my hair, the hands letting out streams of their own, and the wings and halo outline around me.

But then it seemed to fade away, and my normal human form stood before me.

Truthfully, I never believed an angel of war could look so nice and friendly. An angel of war destined to fight all evil, demons of Hell, even Satan himself.

In *pants!*

2

I went to the football arena all gussied up against the winter chill. It had a light dusting of snow on it and I was the only person there. I sat in the stands. So this is what it was like being a spectator. It felt peaceful, and safe.

Not at all like being inside the arena.

Fighting lions, bears, even other slaves.

I had only lost once, against the Castrator, but the Emperor was merciful towards me. He pointed his thumb up, when my enemy was about to execute me, and I was allowed to fight another day.

I had to learn how to fight fast, and fight well. I was from a lost Germanic tribe, and after Rome dominated my people, I was cast into slavery. But no matter how hard they tried to break me, I wouldn't give in. They quickly learned, after a few of the deaths of my would be masters, that I was too feisty to be a pleasure slave. So I was thrown into the arena, as a gladiator.

Brrr… the winter breeze was chilling me to the bone. It felt fantastic.

I wandered down to the arena, and I felt the flashes of battle, the smell of blood and carnage, old memories of the past. The breeze rushed past me, growing stronger for a second, like the veils of the living world and the dead had been lifted for a moment.

I saw someone approach from the other side of the field.

The Castrator.

I gasped, his great form covered in metal, with a net and a knife, ready to reel me in and… well, if I *had* balls, he would cut them off.

He pointed towards me, a challenge.

Would I flee? Could I walk away from the challenge of my past?

From my loss?

I accepted his challenge. This time, it would be different.

A sword, my old sword, now shining a bright angelic light materialized in my hand.

My shield, shining back at the sun, a reflection of my own internal radiance.

Let all the demons of Hell fear my wrath, and specters of the past cower before me.

The Castrator and I circled each other, and he threw his net. I dodged nimbly out of the way! I rolled, turned, and somersaulted from his relentless swipes!

I screamed, and charged him, swinging my sword.

And in that same way of the past, a move of great expertise, he deflected my blade with his dagger, and stabbed me in the stomach.

I felt myself collapse to my knees, the roars of the crowd cheering and jeering.

I dropped my weapons, with his blade at my neck.

"You fight well… but not well enough." the Castrator said.

There was no Emperor to save my life this time around.

But the Castrator mocked me, by sheathing his blade, and walked away.

I fell to the snowy ground, crying.

Why couldn't he have just killed me?

Why did I feel this… shame?

I wandered back home. So this is what it's like living in both worlds, a world of life... and afterlife. I still felt, like I did for weeks after the injury, the knot in my stomach where the Castrator had pierced me. I felt... so cold, in the growing blizzard.

I quickly hurried inside, took off my coat, and turned up the heat a couple of notches.

I covered myself in blankets, and just slept off the feeling of... humiliation.

My dreams were strange, unnerving, nothing like the blissful sleep of Heaven.

And I talked to another specter of the past, the Emperor himself.

"I couldn't kill... a *fantastic* specimen like you. An albino woman, still alive, still winning despite the one sided matches that were thrown against you. Many wanted to see you fall just for your reputation, to feel the bloodlust of killing such an endangered specimen like yourself. Even my royal consort wasted a good portion of her allowance on betting against you, when you beat the Twelve Brothers." the Emperor said.

"Why did you enslave my people?" I asked bluntly.

"Come, come, we are all enslaved eventually. I to my duties, you to your God. It was nothing but the show of the times." he said.

"You... You didn't need to! You could've made peace with us!" I said.

"We *did* make peace with you. By defeating you. You were savages, mongrels in human clothing. You stole and looted from every village in your area, you caused mayhem and destruction wherever you roamed. You caused havoc." he said.

"We... We were only trying to survive! If you gave us aid, we would've gladly served you!" I said.

But he knew I was lying, and said, "Your tribe will never serve, never surrender. Your motto, or something like that, I take it? Do not try to change the past."

And the dream changed, to one of me falling from Heaven, down, down, down… and I woke up.

Instantly I felt like I whammed into the bed, but it was just a dream. What was it about? I couldn't really remember…

I yawned awake, and looked cheerfully at the alarm clock, making chirping sounds like I set it. Birds were always the best to wake up to.

I took a shower, got dressed, and pulled up my pants and put on a shirt, then a sweater, then a sweatshirt. I walked outside to see the many beautiful things of the day.

I saw a few cold sparrows on my walk to the shopping mart. They cheerfully tweeted out a song to me, as I whistled to them. Like hearing birds tweet pleasantly, making bird calls was the best as well.

I pat a dog who just seemed like the cutest little furball of joy, a golden retriever, even though the lady walking him told him to shush when he only barked playfully.

The woman said, "Damn mutt… He should know better than to jump up at strangers…"

I crouched down and let the dog lick my face, saying, "Aww, he's adorable! What's his name?"

"Freckles. You like dogs?"

"I think they're the best! I can't wait to get one of my own, one day. I'm… Yule. Who are you?"

"Uh… Mrs. Nestor. You… wouldn't be open to a fair proposition, would you? I mean… you seem nice enough. Would you be able to walk Freckles when you can? I'd pay. A good five bucks a walk."

"I'd love that!! Here, let me give you my number…" I said, and wrote down my number on a pad of paper and gave her the piece of paper.

"Thanks. It's just… I *hate* this cold… Makes my old bones feel numb. Well, I'll call you. Thank you… Yule." Mrs. Nestor said.

"You're welcome! Have a good day!" I said, as Freckles and Mrs. Nestor continued their walk.

I bought a bunch of food from the shopping mart, and carried it home humming a song about angels.

When I got home, I made myself a grand feast of a breakfast/lunch, and slurped up all the food by myself.

Food! Not even manna from Heaven was this good!

Potato pancakes, bacon, ham, eggs, blackberries and blueberries, some strawberries with sugar… Mmmm…

I undid my belt, and ate as much seconds as I could.

And then I took a nap, feeling much lighter in my head, and had my blissful sleep finally.

3

Freckles was the cutest little guy! He liked to chase the squirrels, but other than that, was the most well behaved "damn mutt" on the planet.

I took him down to the park and we walked through the snowy paths, enjoying the scenery. We took a rest on a bench, and I fed him some dog treats I had picked up special for him.

A father and his son walked past me, the son staring at me the whole while, and the kid stopped to ask me, "Are you a boy or a girl?"

His father was saying that was impolite, but I laughed and said, "It's fine. I'm a girl. I just have short hair!" and ran a hand through my hair which he admired.

"It's like snow! You have a nice doggy." the kid said, as he was petting Freckles who allowed the kid to pet him.

"His name's Freckles. I'm Yule." I said.

The kid said, "I'm Mason! This is my dad."

I shook his hand and the hand of the father's, and they continued their walk as I did as well. The kid looked back to wave at me, and I looked back and waved back.

We went down a forested trail, through a dense path. Freckles seemed to know where to go, but this part of the park was unfamiliar to me. The wind rushed past me, seeming to get through every boundary, even that of life and death.

As the wind howled, I heard the horns of battle. The Romans approaching.

Freckles growled, and led me through the forest. The dense wild forest of the Black Forest of Germany.

I was put in another time, another place, and with my trusty hound by my side, we escaped the Roman pursuers.

We passed by the deer, bears, and wolves, who knew that death approached, and were fleeing for their lives.

A patch of sky opened up in the forest, and I saw the cloud of carrion birds following the Romans, an ever present aura of death.

My village was burned to the ground, and like a few of us who were out hunting at the time, I had escaped death with my dog. Freckles took me down through the twisty undergrowth, the overgrown paths that only he and I would know so well.

We got out of the woods, and the Romans were all around us, blanketing the horizon, everywhere, on all sides.

The flaming arrows stormed the sky, landing in the forest and burning it to nothing.

I got a call from my cell phone.

I answered, and the visions of the past dissipated, and Mrs. Nestor asked me if I was doing alright with Freckles.

Freckles was sitting down and panting.

I told her we were alright, and would be heading back to her house.

"Good, good. I'm just a bit nervous that you're doing alright. Come back home, and I'll make you some tea." Mrs. Nestor said. We walked back through the streets of the present time to her quaint little house.

I had tea with Mrs. Nestor and Freckles, and we chatted a bit. She mostly hated politics, but seemed to love talking about them.

"She's gonna blow up the Earth, mark my words, she's gonna destroy us all." Mrs. Nestor said, talking about the president.

I nodded politely, sipping at my steaming tea.

"Well, here's your money..." she said, taking out her coin purse and trying to pay me five bucks in quarters.

"No. You don't owe me a thing! Keep it. As long as you feed me those delicious... cookies? And tea I'll walk Freckles for free." I said, remembering that she said she had a hard time paying for everything with her recent donations to a parish in Uganda...

"Biscottis. Thank you, Yule. Here, take a bag with you home." she said, and offered me the cookies.

I thanked her, waved her goodbye, and walked out the door, biscottis in hand.

I snacked on another biscotti on my way home, enjoying the sunlight, the fresh air, the cool breeze.

It seemed like someone was following me, but when I turned to look, no one was there.

I shrugged it off, and walked inside my home.

When I opened the door to my apartment, I heard a clatter of the dishes, and the smell of... brimstone.

And then it was silent.

My sword materialized in my hand, and I crept through the apartment warily. My shield appeared in my other, and I held it raised in defense.

"Pst." I heard a voice say.

I slammed my sword at the coffee can, where the voice had come from, and spilled coffee all over the floor.

A little demon spilled out of the can, laying on the floor covered in coffee. I instantly raised my sword to smite him down, but he raised his arms, and... cowered.

I stopped, mercy my first instinct.

"Please don't hurt me! I just want to tell ya somethin'!" the little guy said.

My sword and shield disappeared again, and I picked the demon up by the tail.

"What do *you* want?" I said.

He looked at me wide eyed, dangling from his tail, and said, *"I just want you to know... We don't needa fight! I was supposed to burn your house down or somethin', to make you think better of crossing into the living world... but you really do have a nice setup."*

I sat him on the counter, and said, "Hmph. The denizens of Hell should know better than to be in the living world anyway. Hell was sealed an eternity ago, and demons were never allowed into creation ever again. *How* are you here?"

"Well, no one really notices me unless they want something from me... I was just sent to check up on you, and if you don't mind me sayin', we don't like it when there are angels mucking about in creation either, ya know!" he said.

"Well. I guess I gotta get rid of you now. I don't really know how to do that, though..." I said.

"Please! You don't know how scary it is in Hell! C-Can I just stick around for the afternoon?"

"Um... I don't know... Alright. Just for the afternoon."

"Thank you, thank you, thank you! You don't know how much this means to me!" he said, bowing a little bow over and over.

"Well, just so you know... I'm telling someone about this, straight away!" I said, wagging a finger.

"Fine by me. We've really been overstepping our bounds, anyway, but it was fun while it lasted. Can I watch TV?"

"Ok... but don't go anywhere! I mean it!"

He nodded quickly, up and down, then hopped off the counter, scrambled to the couch, and turned on the TV with the remote.

I passed him, as he was absorbed in a silly kid's show, and I went to my bed and kneeled beside it, then I prayed.

The first thing I did, like I always did, was ask God for forgiveness.

The second was to tell St. Sebastian, my master, about the demon in creation… in my living room.

Of course, they were silent, but I hoped they heard me.

I went back to the living room and the demon was helping himself to my biscottis.

I took them away from him, and told him it was time to go.

"Ok… I probably shouldn't be telling a stranger my name… but I'm Sax. I'll go back to Hell now…" he said.

"Good. My name's… Yule." I said.

He waved goodbye, and popped away from me, disappearing.

4

I had a glass of orange juice after I cleaned up the spilled coffee and thought.

Demons in creation? I suppose if I got into creation then certain other forces might have as well...

The orange juice was half frozen, because I stuck it in the freezer after running out of places to put it in the fridge, and it was hitting the spot, delicious, like condensed sunlight in a cool glass with ice.

Demons in creation...

We were trained by the many saints of battle, by the valkyries, archangels, and veteran angels of war, in case this ever happened. We were supposed to know what to do when something like this happened.

But I didn't have the faintest clue. Well, if anything, demons aren't going to mess with *my* life. This was my second chance.

A valkyrie actually brought me to Heaven, when I died because of the accident. She told me it was my time to fight on, forever. She carried me in her arms up through the clouds, to the very gates of the Eternal Kingdom.

I had converted to Christianity from my pagan tribal beliefs, after I saw the death of a martyr. He held his head high, even as they burned him at the stake. He didn't utter a single scream.

I thought that I *must* have that strength, that will, that pure undefeatable hope. I *must*, so that my people may live on through me.

My parents, along with most of my tribe, were slain by the Romans. I was one of the last few left, destined to fight in the gladiator pits for as long as I lived. Their memories made me fight stronger, each and every one of my tribal companions and family.

But after I was beaten by the Castrator, I realized that I only needed to become even stronger, in any way possible.

I was baptized in the name of our Lord the Savior, Jesus Christ, in a hidden refuge for his people, for the downtrodden, the enslaved, the meek. And I lived again.

I mean, nothing *did* happen after I was baptized. I thought that at least I would feel holier. But I just felt like I had water poured on my head, despite the chanting.

But it helped center my will, and gave me hope.

The prayers, my mantra, to focus my mind.

The companionship of the other believers, showing friendship despite their suffering.

The promise of an eternal life, at the end of this wretched one.

I continued to fight, continued to win, continued to survive.

Then, one day, I caught the eye of a noble, who wished to free me, and me be his wife.

One last fight was scheduled for me, a little bet with my owner and the noble. If I killed another champion, then he would sell me to the noble at a discount, and if I lost I would remain his... or die.

The other champion, Maximus, my lover in our brief moments of solitude, who touched my hand and did not fear me, who looked me in the eyes and sometimes... even smiled.

Later in the evening, I went to a club, and someone who was flirting with me said, "Did you fall from Heaven or something?"

I laughed nervously and said, "No! Of course not!"

"Uh..." he said, "Cuz... you're pretty? Aren't chicks supposed to like stuff like that?"

I laughed, and said, "Well, women are all different. You should try approaching each on a case-by-case basis, instead of relying on a stupid line..."

"Oh. Damnit! Then why do they always use the same lines over and over on TV, and the girl just swoons into their arms?? Bloody unrealistic..." he said, taking a sip from his drink.

"You'll find TV to be a bit of a dated source of information. I mean, who ever heard of things like a 'whoopee cushion?'" I said.

"Ha... ha... I loved those gags, as a kid... I suppose only the Stooges use stuff like that, now... Old outdated crap..." he said, frowning.

"I love the Three Stooges! Whenever there's a Sunday special on them, I laugh until I can't breathe!" I said.

He smiled, looking hopeful again, and said, "Me too! I can't believe it... A woman likes the Stooges! I guess there's a first time for everything, huh? Say... I've got a whole VCR collection of them, wanna come over and watch them with me?"

I smiled, and said, "Would be nice, but let's just enjoy each other's company for a while, without the 'Whoo whoo whoo!' and 'Nyah nyah nyah!'"

He laughed, and said, "Sure. I hope to see you again. Next week, drinks?"

"Sure. I'm Yule. Nice to meet you." I said, shaking his hand.

"Max." he said.

Max. Like my old lover, Maximus.

I nervously said I needed to have a cigarette, and went outside to smoke.

I coughed a bunch at this strange… *tobacco,* but it did help calm my nerves and give me a little break from things.

This Max was nothing like my Maximus. Max was rather small, shorter than me even, and Maximus… he was *huge.*

But in between fights where he always tried to give his opponent a fair chance, by using showy moves and difficult maneuvers, he had the purest heart. A friend to all of us, in the pits.

He stood tall, when I went to fight him, and urged me to fight my hardest.

I flicked my cigarette butt, and went inside.

Max and I got into a thorough discussion on humor, and we found many things insightful about each other's comments. He made a silly joke, and I couldn't help but laugh my ass off.

Maximus was serious, albeit friendly. He knew that when he made friends with the lives in the gladiator pits, he may have to one day end them himself. We all kept separate, when we could.

But we couldn't help but grow so close.

Max accidentally touched my hand, and I was thrown into a memory of Maximus touching my hand, briefly, close, in our short hours. Maximus held my hands when he could, Max quickly drew away, embarrassed.

I punched him on the arm lightly, and he rubbed his arm in a farce. I said, "Well. It's time I go. It's been swell, Maximus… I mean- Max."

"Maximus! Never heard that before! Sounds swell!" he said.

"Just Max. Have a good evening!" I said, waved him goodbye and quickly left, embarrassed.

5

The next week I went to the old man's bar I went to on Christsmas, and saw Thaniel slurping down his sorrows. I invited Max to come visit here today, as I thought the people here were rather nice.

I drank with Thaniel, and he was as drunk as ever. He said, "Iiiii'm a single man today. A lucky, young, old, bastard… Iiii've got nothing to live forrrrr…" and slumped in his seat.

I said that he has a lot to live for, and that he can still do astounding things. I said, "Who needs to be married, anyway? When I was about to be married… Er hem… Never mind. Let's get another drink! I'll buy!"

He cheered at me, and I bought the next round.

Max nervously walked in, trying to saunter in like he was the coolest man alive, then quickly noticed me and shuffled beside me in the booth across from Thaniel.

"Whoooo's this, Yule? You're boylyfriend?" Thaniel said.

"Uh. I'm Max." Max said.

"Nice to meet ya, kiddo. Say! Did you ever hear the one about the horse from Germany?" Thaniel said.

"He got a condo and they all lived happily ever after?" Max said.

"No, no, no… He was… what's it… He was a Nazi… and… when he got a mustache like the furor, everyone called him… a Charlie Horse! Like Chaplin." Thaniel said, grinning a drunken smile.

"HAHA!" I laughed, "I never really understood the Nazis, but I do love Chaplin."

"That's… That's not a very tasteful joke…" Max said.

"Bah. Jokes don't have to be tasteful… If you can laugh at them. And boy, those Nazis… *should* be laughed at. Ridiculous people, all killin' each other because of a goofy little man with a goofy little mustache… If we fear someone because of what they did, then they win. If we laugh at them, then we make them a little bit smaller in comparison. It's alllll durastics…" Thaniel said.

"Uh. Do you mean 'drastic?'" Max said.

"Durastics! A strong or far reaching effect! Like drastic, but a noun." Thaniel said, and slurped on his beer.

"My mother was a durastic. The whole village we lived in would either scrape on their hands and knees to do her bidding, or would cower in fear from her. And boy… her arms! She sure had a reach! Could never escape those long durastics of hers." I said.

"Ok. You two are just making up words now." Max said.

Thaniel and I laughed, and I bought Max a beer. He tried to pay for it himself, but I just told him he could get the next round. He nervously accepted, even though a woman just bought him his first drink. But, I think he was learning that manly pride can't pay for everything.

In fact, pride can't pay for a single thing. Sometimes we must swallow our pride, when we have nothing, when we are imprisoned, enslaved, forced to fight. No matter all the pride I had, it could never have bought me my freedom in the pits. The higher pride raises you, the harder you fall when it is stripped away from you. I learned that much from my fight with the Castrator.

"Oh. Yule," Thaniel said, "I'm getting back into my old routine again, y'know, writing for fame, fortune, and pleasure, and I'm putting together a collection of my short stories. Wanna read one?"

"Sure! I'd love that! As long as it's got 'durastics' aplenty!" I said.

He smiled, and took out a wadded piece of paper from his pocket, an old newspaper clipping. He straightened it out, and handed it to me, pointing to a piece he wrote when he was still a young kid, a short story called "The Bees of Ferdinand." I folded it nicely and put it in my pocket, saving it for later under a warm blanket and with a sober head.

We drank and chatted some more. Max was finally starting to loosen up, and soon was laughing in drunkenness with Thaniel and I.

Max and I walked down the street, and Max said, "Thanks for showing me that place. I usually go to stupid clubs where women don't even bat an eyelash at me, places that look happy and lively, but it's all a show. That place… it felt warm, and friendly."

"Sometimes the best things are where you'd least expect them. Places in the sky, in the pits, tucked away down a lonely street. Sometimes, we just need a little help finding them." I said, as we looked into each other's eyes.

We looked a little too long, and then broke our gaze.

"Well! This is my corner. I'll see ya later, Yule. Call me!" Max said.

I smiled, waved him goodbye, and walked down the street to my apartment.

While I was walking down that snowy path, it felt like someone was watching me.

Getting annoyed at this feeling, I turned around my position, looking at every hidden corner.

I heard a clatter from an alley, and I yelled out, "Max? Is that you?"

A little cat poked his head out around the corner. I squat down, and he hid again.

"It's ok, little guy. I'm Yule. Who are you?" I said to the cat.

The cat peeked around again, and sauntered over to me, then quickly rubbed against my legs, purring.

I pet him. He was a meek little thing, all black and grey, and was making these adorable little mewling noises.

And then it hit me. This cat was the same alley cat that I befriended in the gutters when I was a slave. The exact same hair, the same eyes, the same mewl.

He quickly was killed by street urchins and eaten, unfortunately.

But this was him! I know it! Did cats really have nine lives?

"You're like a little Rasputin, aren't you? C'mon, I'll take you home and feed you." I said, picking him up gently, and let him purr in my warm embrace in the winter chill.

After I had fed him with some leftover beef, Rasputin sat on my lap with me under a blanket while I read the Bees of Ferdinand.

I laughed with delight at all the silly things! But strangely... it was so profound, not like a simple fluff piece for a newspaper, it had this deep quality to it, and then the main character makes another joke! I read through it one more time, enjoying the first ride and wondering if the next would be just as fun. I caught a few little details I had missed the first time, so it was worth it.

Then I took my little cat, Rasputin, to bed with me and we slept until the morn.

I woke up from a nightmare of things I've never seen before... battles with demons of Hell. I quickly calmed down as the sunlight streamed through my window, still remembering the dream of the demons killing all my friends and even usurping Heaven.

Rasputin sat next to my head by the pillow, sleeping softly. He winked an eye open at me, and I pet his soft fur.

I stretched, yawning, and got out of bed to make breakfast.

It was my day to walk Mrs. Nestor's dog, Freckles, and I ate a light breakfast and read the newspaper, anticipating a nice walk in the cool.

I scanned the obituaries, just in case, and prayed a silent prayer for every one of those faces. Thankfully no one I knew had died, yet.

But they could, at some point.

After death you don't really have to worry about these sorts of things, friends or family dying. In fact, most of the time a death on Earth just meant that you'd see a brand new face in Heaven.

But now… if they died, would I ever see them again?

I prayed I would, if anything.

I had never seen Maximus again, after our fight in the arena, even though after I died I searched everywhere in Heaven for him. He was a Roman gods believer, always praying to Mars to give him a swift victory, and his enemy a merciful death. I wonder if we went to different places, after we each died?

Would he have- No… Surely God would not have cast Maximus into Hell, would he?

With my blade at his throat, I wondered these things, as well.

He was the strongest, fastest man alive, and fighting him made him seem even stronger and faster, when he could actually use these qualities for purpose instead of just practice.

But when I fought him, I prayed to my new God, and something seemed to be guiding my hand.

He slashed! I parried and blocked! We clashed blades, dancing our last dance, the only dance we ever danced together, the dance of battle.

We accidentally locked eyes, and I felt all of our special moments that had come between us. When he snuck me some food and water when they were starving me for speaking out of turn, when they lashed him because of it, demanding to know if his food was given to me, and he would not reveal this action for me.

When I had killed that boy who was a new slave, pitted against me, and Maximus consoled me as I bawled my eyes out.

When I kissed Maximus, taking a huge risk, as we were not allowed contact with each other.

When we made love in that holding cell, each being taken to different quarters and accidentally, perhaps because of a miracle, put in the same cell between transfers.

And he faltered in battle, and I disarmed him.

Maximus knelt before me, and the Emperor put his thumb downward, commanding me to kill the loser, to kill my love.

I couldn't do it, with my blade at Maximus's throat, freedom beckoning to me from the sidelines, if I would only do this one, short action.

We would both be killed if we defied the Emperor's will, so Maximus took out his knife, and rammed it into his heart.

It felt like I had died as well.

I left and walked Freckles. He seemed to be in an extra good mood, but I was still remembering Maximus. If Maximus had fallen to Hell, then I promised myself I would save him from an eternity in the flames.

We passed through the graveyard, as I was feeling melancholy and wished to be somewhere that accentuated that. Strange, how sadness is drawn to sadness.

I looked across the many gravestones, with names of people I would never know, would never love, only in passing. A few of the crosses had already sunk deep into the earth, defiled by time itself.

We got out of the graveyard, and I took Freckles back to his home.

Mrs. Nestor was grumbling about her dead husband, saying if he died decently then he would've at least had cleaned up all the empty bottles of booze he left in the basement. I offered to do it for her, and she accepted, grateful because she couldn't get down the stairs as easily as in her prime.

I threw the bottles in a bag and took the bag out to the garage to the recycling bin. I wiped off my hands on my pants from the dust and filth that had accumulated on the bottles after years of sitting around in the basement.

We had tea, and Mrs. Nestor asked me if anything was wrong. "You just look... er, a little depressed. Usually you're a ball of sunshine!"

I smiled, and said, "Oh, nothing... I'm just remembering old heartaches... It's nothing to worry about."

"Ah. Boy troubles. Men are only about half of what they think they're worth, and more than half the time that's hardly a pittance! You'll find a good man eventually." she said.

"I mean, I meet nice people all the time... Good men, with good hearts... but I don't know how they could ever measure up to the love of the past... We loved each other, but we were separated because of... conflict." I said.

"Conflict, eh... Be thankful you didn't marry the sod, or else you'd have gotten ten times that conflict. Like me and Mr. Nestor, we'd fight all day and night... but I hardly regret a thing. If only he didn't have such a weak heart, and had to die because of it, then we'd still be arguing today. I don't miss the fights... but it's too quiet nowadays." she said.

Freckles whined up at her, and she patted him on the head.

"I mean, I *tried* to love again... nearly got married, too... But it felt like I had a weight in my chest, pulling down my heart, and the more I tried to get rid of it, to ignore and forget about it, the heavier it got." I said.

"Ah... The sinky thing. That's called grief, dear. A love lost can bring all sorts of emotions, but you should just let it be instead of wallowing in it, or even trying to ignore it. Simply notice it, accept it, and be thankful for the love you had." Mrs. Nestor said.

I smiled and thanked her. I realized I had been grieving for Maximus for a long, long time.

I accepted it, I let it be, and let Maximus pass.

It felt like he was looking down on me in Heaven.

6

I volunteered at a hospital, because they needed a few extra hands, and set to work cleaning and fixing the place up.

When I walked into a room, intent on cleaning the basin, I saw a little buddy of mine. Mason, the kid who liked Freckles and my hair.

He was all hooked up to tubes and wires, and was looking at me sleepily. He said, waking up as he remembered, "You're the lady with the doggy! Hi!"

I quickly sat beside him, smiled, and asked him how he was doing.

Mason said, "I have to get an operation because of my bones. It's... kinda scary."

"It'll be alright, Mason. We're all looking out for you." I said.

A woman walked in, and tried saying that Mason needed some rest, but Mason said, "C-Can Yule tell me about her doggy? Our doggy... died. He was a good doggy."

The woman looked back and forth between Mason and I, and said sadly, "Alright. But you need your rest. Fifteen minutes, ok?"

"Ok." Mason said.

I told him all about Freckles, the little things he did which showed how smart he was, like walking on the other side of me away from the street, to big things, like keeping Mrs. Nestor company in her house and protecting her.

Mason smiled as I told him of the dog, listening in relish.

Soon our fifteen minutes were up, and Mason asked me if I could come visit again some time.

I smiled and said of course.

The woman, Mason's mother, thanked me outside of Mason's room and said, "Mason has leukemia. He's being treated with some of the best procedures there are… but the leukemia is showing to be aggressive. We may have to put him through chemotherapy and other treatments soon. Thank you for talking with him. Sometimes hope and friendship is the best medicine."

I nodded, a teardrop in my eye.

I said an extra prayer for Mason, that night.

But worrying wouldn't change anything, so I continued my life. I kept Mason in my hopes though, a little kid, just starting his life. He didn't deserve sickness, suffering, and death.

No one did. And when your life is cut short, you die confused, wondering why you had to leave life.

At least I did.

I sent a condolence card to the parents, and they thanked me and sent me a picture of Mason, hoping that goodwill could change their son's ailment.

I put the picture up on a shelf, Mason with his friendly looking bulldog.

I eagerly visited Mason whenever I could, and got him a stuffed animal of a bulldog one time. He gingerly accepted the toy, then grasped onto it tightly, never letting it go.

I told Max about Mason when he was walking with Freckles and I, and Max said, "Ah… Poor kid. I'm sure he'll get the aid he needs. The healthcare system has never been better in America, thanks to that Mrs. President."

"I'm sure God will smile on him, and he will be able to walk in the sunshine again." I said.

"God? You're... a religious gal? I... didn't really expect that. I mean, I kinda figured, you just have this sorta super hopeful attitude... but... *religion...*" Max said.

"What? What's so bad about religion?" I said, as we were passing the frozen lake.

"It... kinda screws people up. At least in my own experience. My sister was indoctrinated in this super weird church... and she's never been the same since. I miss her, but she's like a different person now."

"Well, wanna come with me to my church tomorrow? I can show you it's not so bad."

"Uh... er... alright. Sure. As long as they don't try to perform an exorcism on me."

So, on Sunday, we went to church. I wore a nice skirt for the occasion, as I figured God would like it if I dressed a little more angelic than what I normally dressed like, and Max wore a grey hoodie, albeit with some nice dress pants.

He opened his eyes wide at me, as he was admiring the expertly put on makeup and the skirt, and said, "Uh... Damn! You... sure look nice! I-I-I don't look like trash, do I? I didn't expect people to dress so fancy here! It's not some sort of holiday, is it?"

"It's a few saints' feast day, but no. This will just be a normal ceremony, even though the normal priest is sick, and a replacement is filling in for him. He's doing a swell job, even though he's rather young and has just been ordained. Took him forever to get over that stutter." I said.

"Ok... let's do this." Max said, breathing in heavily a few times, pumping himself up, and then we walked in through the big red doors of the church.

Max was silent as I sang the verses of the hymns, but I nudged him and he tried to follow along. He actually had a rather nice singing voice, even though he was only just starting to learn how to praise the Lord.

The priest did a rather... interesting sermon. It seemed like he was just making it up as he went along, but in the end it all wrapped together perfectly, and everything he said made perfect sense.

"Huh. Never thought of it like that." Max muttered as the priest finished.

I donated my ten bucks to the church when the donation basket came around, and Max nervously put in some of his pocket change.

When we held hands for the Lord's Prayer, Max was sweating slightly but held my hand firmly.

I shook his hand in peace, and he smiled and shook it back, as we did to the people around us.

Then I got up for communion, and I whispered to Max that he didn't have to do this part if he didn't want to. He breathed a sigh of relief and remained seated, and I walked in the single file line to where the priest was giving out the Body of Christ.

"Amen." I said, as I received the host, put the little wafer in my mouth, and stepped aside so the next person could receive Christ.

I sipped on the Blood of Christ, and... I think I had that wine before. It was cheap wine, if rather good for the price.

But that didn't matter, as it was now consecrated, it was holy, a part of our ritual and worth more than the most expensive nectar of mortals.

I sat beside Max again, and he was starting to twitch irritably. I told him it was nearly done.

We sang the closing hymn, and walked back outside the doors.

Max looked like he had just been through a hard fought battle, and I asked him if he was alright.

He said, "It's just... If I'd have known it was going to be so long... I would've gone to the washroom beforehand..."

I laughed and laughed, and Max smiled and laughed too.

After saying goodbye to Max, I walked back home and... even just outside the door, it smelled like brimstone.

I carefully opened the door, and the TV was on.

I peeked through the opened crack, and a *huge* demon was sitting on my couch and watching TV. It looked like he had just eaten all the food in the apartment, with wrappers and empty bags of chips littering the floor.

He noticed me, and said, *"Oh. Heya, Yule. Could you get some more of those biscottis? I had a few, but it was never as good as that first one."* I noticed the empty bag of biscottis on his lap.

"Sax??" I said, "What- Why are you here?! *Why...* are you so big?!"

The demon shrugged, and said, *"I think it's got something to do with the growing malevolence in the world. Or maybe it was just all the food and souls I've eaten..."*

"Souls?? What- Who- I need you to leave."

"I would if I could... but I can't fit through even just the front door anymore."

"You need to leave. Now. Or else... Or else I'll smite you! I'll send you back to Hell or wherever you came from with my sword if I have to!"

He smiled, and said, *"We both know that's not going to happen. You let me in, and I like it here. I like you too. I think you're a nice angel."*

I grew very, very frustrated, angry, furious. A demon was sitting in *my* apartment, acting like he owned the place! I rose in fury, as I've never felt so angry. Show someone mercy, and they should learn from that, not take advantage of it!

My sword and shield appeared in my hands, and the light was rippling from me in my anger, sending out streams of radiance, enlightening every dark corner of the apartment.

Sax put a hand over his eyes as I blinded him with the wrath of Heaven.

I took a step forward.

He quickly got off the couch, saying, *"C'mon, Yule! You don't need to do this! W-We can have fun together!"*

I took another step forward.

He cowered back, saying, *"I know someone who's perfect for you! Yeah, a swell dude! I could set you to meet with him!"*

I took yet another step forward, and said, "Satan has no heedence here. Go back to your pit, vile fiend, or I will chase you back to Hell myself. And if I catch you…"

I ran towards him and he scattered away from me, opened a window and squeezed through it to run down the street.

I let my anger pass, and the light faded again.

I sighed, turned off the TV, and cleaned up the mess left by the demon.

7

It was clean in my apartment, but… was it clean in the world?

What had Sax done, as I failed in my duties to destroy him the first time? What villainy and wickedness did that little demon, now an overgrown parasite, do after the act of my mercy?

I prayed for courage and fortitude, and went down through the streets, sniffing out the smell of brimstone and corruption.

I saw a little hole in a slightly broken window, about the size that Sax was when he was tiny, in my neighbor's house.

I knocked on her door, and introduced myself to her.

She looked kind of like she was crying and I asked her if she was alright.

She said, "Whatever it is, I don't want any!" and slammed the door in my face.

I continued down the street, and saw another hole in another house, and another house, and yet another. They were hardly perceptible, but they all stood out because they were points of breakage, and not just wear and tear or a flaw in the design.

I followed the trail of holes into town, to a rather larger hole in the back of an Italian restaurant, boarded up from the inside.

I walked inside the front door, and it looked rather gloomy and… empty.

The manager was frowning at a list he was making, and I asked him what was wrong.

"Oh… You didn't hear? I'd rather not tell you, but half the town already knows… Some sort of big rats got in the back and spoiled almost all of our supplies. We only figured it out on the day of the health inspection, and we were shut down for a while… Then a prissy little reporter made an article on us… 'Rigatoni and Rats' was the name of the article… That woman… I hope she burns in Hell, one day…" the manager said.

I asked who was the reporter?

He handed me the paper itself, with the reporter, my neighbor, a woman named Nevaeh Shinto, standing out front of the restaurant. I skimmed through it, and she was unduly harsh, scathing, but still I had to note she had done her research well…

To cheer the manager up, I said, "Er. I'll order… some pizza?"

He did a double take at me, and said, "Right away, miss! It's a shame she named the article what she did. The rigatoni dish was one of our best ones, but one pizza, coming up!"

He asked me what I'd like on it, and I told him I'd let him surprise me. He smiled, winked, and said, "I know just the thing. Nothing with rats, I assure you."

And they put pepperoni, sausage, green peppers and mushrooms on it, with Canadian bacon arranged in a smiley face for me. It was still the price of a normal pizza.

I walked out with the pizza, and the manager called out, "Tell your friends!"

I went home and chomped on the pizza. I don't know why, but the crust was extra good on this pizza. I read the article on the restaurant again, and it said that the restaurant makes a lot of the bread by hand, letting it rise early in the morning and baking it for the pizza and other breadstuff later in the day.

Nevaeh then went on to criticize this, by saying that it was an unsanitary practice, and with the building overflowing with rats from the vents, you could only imagine how dirty the hands of the bakers were and what must go into the bread itself.

Her words did kind of turn me off from the pizza, but I shrugged it off, remembering that I've *eaten* rats before, starving in the streets.

When I was freed by the noble, the very first thing I tried to do was escape. The death of Maximus was still fresh in my mind, and I actually had a chance at true freedom for just a moment, and not one as some noble's wife.

I vanished into the streets, running away from one who wished to call me his beloved.

I was dirty, lost, casteless, a previous slave and gladiator, but I kept on running through the streets, hiding from Roman patrols. While I was hiding in an alley some thugs cornered me, intent on raping me, but I kept a shard of glass I found, clutching it harder and harder so that my hand had cut open from squeezing it, and I slew the thugs who wished to take me.

The streets were mazy and impossible to navigate, and it was a huge city. I thought I'd be trapped in that hellish place forever, but I listened to the sound of a bird singing and followed the bird through the streets, past a fountain, through an alley, up to a rooftop, and I saw the way out.

I ran as fast as I could to that freedom, to the countryside opening before me.

A guard stuck his foot out and tripped me to the ground.

They immediately grabbed me, intent on imprisoning me or using me for some foul purpose, but as I was being marched back into captivity, someone called out to them who was riding a regal horse with an entourage of soldiers.

The noble, my future husband.

The noble had the pristine qualities of all things Roman, he looked exactly like one of those marble statues that are now famous art pieces of Roman sculpting. He looked like some sort of demigod, in truth, like the grace of his Roman gods descended down into his features.

He called me his betrothed in front of the guards, and they immediately took their hands off of me.

He held a hand out to me, and I slowly approached him, took it, and rode with him on his horse.

We rode out into the countryside, finally, and he took me to his villa estate.

I finished some of the pizza, and kept the rest later for tomorrow's breakfast. I walked outside to the park, alone without Freckles. Mrs. Nestor said he wasn't feeling very well of late, something with this new dog food she got...

I sat on the bench, listening to the birds and the roaring wind rushing through my hair. Then the bench changed from a wooden bench to a marble bench, the snow seemed to evaporate instantly, and it was summer in the villa of the noble's.

He was working on a gardening piece of his, and I watched him in anticipation as he trimmed each and every detail carefully. He snipped a last little twig sticking out of the shoulder of his piece, and I walked up to him and looked back at a form of myself in plant life.

"There. What do you think? Ever since I saw you walk out of those gates in the arena, with your shield seeming to blaze with brilliance, I have been captivated with your features." he said.

"It's wonderful. If you don't mind me asking... what made you so set on buying and freeing me? For me to be your wife?" I asked.

"You show this certain mortality in you, despite your seeming immortality in the ring. You never sought to feed off the crowd's roars and cheers, in fact you were very professional. It was all business, your dance between life and death, yet you did not prolong this dance if it was not necessary. You showed your mortality when it was trying to be taken from you, as a slave, as an object used for entertainment. In the crushing maws of the arena, you held strong and were not consumed. You seemed to have all the qualities I was looking for in a companion. And, like I said... your features are set eternally in my mind. It's a shame this piece will wither and die, eventually..." he said.

I held his hand and said, "I like it. We all must wither and die eventually, and this is much better than a cold statue. Feels more alive, like our growing love."

He smiled to me, and said, "I will work on improving these pale replicas of your image. Our union will make the world shout in joy. We are already making ripples in society, as it was previously unknown of a man of noble lineage marrying a female gladiator. Our children will become great lords of men."

"Yes... our union..." I said, frowning as the vision passed, and I was standing alone in the snow.

8

———

Rasputin had somehow gotten to the roof, and I was telling him to stay put as I tried to climb up there.

I had figured out how to shimmy up there from the gutters, and Rasputin was mewling over and over. I crept over to him, and he walked over to me in the snow…

Then a piece of the snow fell, and Rasputin fell with.

"Rasputin!!" I yelled out, quickly getting off the roof to help him.

He wasn't moving. He lay there in the snow.

Then, like nothing, he got up and rubbed against my legs.

"Awww… you damned cat!! C'mere, and don't sneak out ever again!!" I said, picking him up and cradling him in my arms, against my breast, never letting him go.

I fed him again, even though he had just gotten breakfast, and stared at him hard for a second. He didn't seem hurt at all, and seemed to actually be in a better shape than this morning. This morning he was limping for some reason, and now he seemed to have shrugged it off. I guess that was another cat nine live gone?

I let Rasputin sleep on a blanket, and left the apartment to remedy what Sax did.

I saw Nevaeh smoking from her front porch, watching me, but then she flicked the cigarette in the snow and went back inside.

I decided to interview a few people at the restaurant, after I checked in with the other houses that had Sax holes in them. Some of my neighbors thanked me for being a good neighbor, and told me of their problems. Others ignored my knocking and doorbell ringing. They had all suffered minor, insignificant tragedies, that they would get over eventually. It seemed like the restaurant was hardest hit.

When I got through the doors of the Italian restaurant, the manager was begging one of his workers not to leave, a swarthy Spanish man who cooked a lot of the pizzas and made bread.

"It's done, Mike. I need to pay to have my family returned back to me. I'll work in construction if I can. All of them were deported, except for me. Está... done." the swarthy Spanish man said, and left the building.

Mike the manager put his face in his hands as he muttered.

"You ok?" I asked.

Mike put his hands down, tried to straighten out his distraught features, and said, "Oh! You're the girl from yesterday! Can I interest you in anything?"

"I just wanted to do a little interview for the restaurant. I figured, if a bad review made everything fall under, then a good review should do the opposite." I said.

He smiled, and said, "That's... one of the kindest things I've heard in quite a while. I don't know how much good it'll do, since our chief baker just left... The owner knew him from a past life of travelling, but... I suppose that's not enough, when your family is on the line..."

"Uh... why don't you jump ship, too? Surely you can find other jobs?" I said.

"The owner is my dad. He put his entire life into this restaurant, but he's a bit too old to continue this sort of thing. This place... it's kinda like my home. I'd hate to see it... fall to the rats..." Mike said.

"Well that's not going to happen. Why don't we set up some inter-views with your remaining workers, and you can show me a little about what makes this place tick?"

"Great! I'll get our sous chef, May, to talk to you for a bit. She's been just antsy waiting around, and this will give her something to do."

So I talked to May, a blonde woman with scars all over her wrists and arms. She looked kind of surly, but answered politely and intricately whenever I asked her about the inner mechanisms of the restaurant. She had a Russian accent.

She said, "Most people come here… I mean, *used* to come here for the fantastic bread that Angelo made, but we've got all sorts of Italian dishes that'll make you froth at the mouth just with a whiff of. Some go back to even the Roman period."

I smiled, thinking nothing could top the grand feasts that me and my soon to be husband used to have. We had moonlit feasts to the playing of bards from around the country, the moonlight shining down on us onto the terrace, with delicate, delicious, most exquisitely prepared, real Roman food.

I asked her why she got into cooking.

"I studied it for a spell. People don't understand, good cooking is the heart of any meal. Of course, company and atmosphere play a part, but it all comes down to food. Even if you are in a bland, boring atmosphere, and are having a meal where your lover just broke up with you, nothing soothes the soul like a well made pasta dish with homemade sauce and garlic bread just baked that morning." May said.

She went into a talk of her studies in a cooking school in France, but kept on rubbing her scars, and got a bit distracted looking at them.

I told her it was alright, holding her hand, and that her scars didn't make her any less of a woman. That she was strong.

She looked into my eyes as I smiled nicely at her, and she slowly smiled back.

She said, "It was in my harsh teenage years… But I've grown past that now. I just worry new people will see my scars instead of me."

We broke hands, and I said that her scars make only a part of her, and are not to be embarrassed of. That they are only a small part of the whole.

"…Thank you. I noticed you have scars on your face. I won't pry, but I want you to know you're very pretty even with them." she said.

I thanked her, and said it happened in an accident.

I had gotten a good bit of interviews from the staff of the restaurant, taking notes in my notepad, even from the dishboy who said he loved his job, but asked me discreetly to not tell anyone. He told me people take him more seriously as another hateful cog in the machine, but he winked at me and said that May has been checking him out recently, and he hoped there was something there.

So, I struggled to type something out for the restaurant… but when I saw that big blank space supposed to be filled with words, all my ideas seemed to vanish into nothing. I decided to go talk to Thaniel, since this was obviously writer's block.

I sat across from him in the bar, and he was remarkably… sober.

He sipped on his beer, a beer he's been cradling all evening, and told me about writing.

"The most important thing is just getting down some of that black ink on paper. It doesn't matter if it's good or bad, hopefully you can change it later, the most important thing is getting started. Like Mark Twain said, 'The secret of getting ahead is getting started.'"

"But… I really want it to be a smack out of the park! A homerun! If I can help this restaurant, then people will see that what that reporter said is just hateful and misguided!" I said.

"Hmm... Sometimes we're seeking to be too 'perfect.' I've found whenever I try to make something that is astounding, in depth, phenomenal, and just plain amazing, at least to other people, I get caught up in my words. Nothing is as perfect as we want it to be, it can always be just a notch higher, in our own eyes. Try settling for what you think is adequate, at least. If you feel strongly about it, it won't matter if it's 'perfect,' it'll be good on its own merit. Some people may like it, some won't, but that doesn't matter as long as you put your soul into your work." Thaniel said.

"Hm. Thank you. Can I ask you... are you feeling alright? I mean, it's a good thing, but... you seem different." I said.

He laughed, a sober, musical laugh, and said, "Just been talking to an old friend of mine. She's a great gal, and we haven't seen each other since high school. Just makes me feel young, in my prime again, seeing her pretty face."

"Oh! That's nice. How are things with the kids?" I asked.

He smiled, and said, "I see them on the weekends now. The boys are still rough young bastards, if you ask me, but Julia is the sweetest angel ever. I'm planning on a camping trip with them that my ex sanctioned."

"Good. I'm glad things are working out for you." I said, and sipped at my drink, "I found the Bees of Ferdinand to be astounding, in depth, phenomenal, and just plain amazing, by the way."

He laughed that musical laugh, and said, "Good. I got a lot of inspiration from this 'honey' I had been courting... The birds and the bees would always be a buzzing and a chirping, whenever we went out... I'm glad I get to see her again."

"So you mean the woman you're seeing... she's *her*?? That's... fantastic! *My*... Ferdinand must have really gotten more than he bargained for, with his trained, dancing bees!" I said.

He laughed, and said, "So you did read it. Be ready for the whole collection soon! If you don't mind me askin'... How are things with that one kid? The one who had the silliest little laughter?"

"Max? We're alright. Just seeing each other on off days. He's actually pretty cute. Nothing like any man I've been with before, and that's a good thing."

"Yeah, if you can find something unique in someone, it instantly makes up for anything you may wish to have wished for in a person. It's like... snowflakes are all different, but we get used to those differences, we see them, notice them, and soon learn to ignore them. But when you really look at a snowflake you'll find you'll never see it again, and when you *really* notice that snowflake, then you'll marvel at it, be astonished by it, and love looking at it. And then it's gone, melted on your finger." Thaniel said.

"Yeah... I hope no one I know gets melted..." I said, "This one little kid, which I met purely by accident, has leukemia. He's like the purest snowflake ever. I kind of regret meeting him, just because if I didn't, I wouldn't have had to worry about him..."

"Hogwash. Humanity worries, it's as simple as that. We wouldn't be such a marvelous specimen of apes if we didn't. Have you considered donating bone marrow?" Thaniel said.

"Wait, what? You can do that?" I asked.

"Well, you have to be compatible, but it's worth a shot." he said.

I got up, thinking that if I could save this child's life, then I must.

I thanked Thaniel, intent on leaving, and he yelled out, "Oh! And remember to cut your nails if you type! It's annoying having long fingernails at the keyboard!"

I smiled, nodded, put on my coat and rushed out the door.

9

I went to the hospital in the evening and said I'd like to donate bone marrow for Mason.

The lady looked at me surprised, and said, "The man who was donating just backed out of the procedure… We'll do a few tests on you, just to see if you're compatible. But really, you couldn't have come at a better time."

They tested my health, my blood, my bone marrow and proteins, and said I was compatible with Mason.

I prayed thanks for this miracle, and the date was arranged for the operation.

I went home, and whacked out a whole, phenomenal piece for the restaurant, even mentioning the Romans and how they would be proud to have this restaurant continue their authentic cuisine.

Rasputin jumped on my lap, as I reread the piece, and while it may not have been a one hundred percent perfect masterpiece, it got my point across, and showed the restaurant in a glowing light, despite their recent misfortunes.

I sent it to the newspaper, hoping I would get accepted for their paper.

I picked up the newspaper in the morning, and saw the piece written by "Yule Tidings."

I smiled as I reread it again and again. Take that, Nevaeh, Sax, all forms of evil.

I walked out of the apartment to Mrs. Nestor's, going to walk Freckles. Nevaeh was glaring at me from her porch. I smiled to her.

She flipped me off.

I was a little peeved about that throughout the day, but as I walked cute little Freckles I forgot about it for a while.

We walked down a street, in the blustering wind, and I felt like I was walking through the noble's huge villa instead.

Each room could've been a street, in actuality, and I got lost again and again my first time there.

But my future husband walked out of his study, and noticed Freckles, saying, "You got a dog! How… quaint!"

"He's rather well behaved…" I said, offering an excuse.

"It's fine. As long as you don't *insist* on taking him hunting every full moon… I don't know what you did in your tribal life, but remember we have dinner to go to in the evening." he said.

"What? What do you think I did in my tribal life?" I asked.

"Er… Just tribal things. I'm not really sure, to be honest. Which makes it so much more disconcerting. You are the epitome of any woman of the north, but still I worry that you're having a hard time adjusting to life here…" he said.

"Well, if that damn lady of that governor didn't tell me to go drink out of a trough, I wouldn't have had to pour that gravy on her and let the hounds chase her all night! I don't know… Are you *really* sure you want me to be your wife?" I said.

He said, "Yes. You are very important to me. And your dog too. I don't know why… but it seems like he's been smiling at me this entire conversation."

Freckles smiled at him, then looked up at me.

I patted Freckles on the head, and said, "He's a good dog. Alright… I'll go to dinner, and not show any 'tribal impulses…' I'll be the epitome of Rome."

"Good. And don't forget! We wed on the morrow! This last bit of political extravagance will be all we need to do! Then, you and I are each each other's, and we never have to put up with this ever again."

I smiled, kissed him on the cheek, and said, "How could I forget?"

I took Freckles to dinner with me.

The people were all aghast, looking at me with my huge dog, but seemed to shrug it off, just thinking of me as "another barbarian of the north."

It made me furious.

Freckles was very well behaved, and I even showed the nobles some tricks he could do. They clapped, and one mentioned something about me being "a beastmaster."

I singled him out, asking him what he meant, and he started sweating, looking into my eyes to the form that had killed countless people in the arena.

But my soon to be husband saved him from my wrath, bringing me and Freckles away from them.

He told me to relax, and that as soon as the Emperor made his appearance we could leave.

The Emperor. I suddenly thought of the hand that pointed downwards, the hand commanding me to kill Maximus. I wanted to chop it off.

But my soon to be husband and I ate politely, waiting for the Emperor to finally, if ever, appear.

The noble, the one I was bound to wed, who I was just starting to love, surprised the people and I by showing us a masterpiece he created. He took us down through the halls, and revealed the huge naked statue that he had sculpted for me, of me.

It was marvelous, breathtaking, it looked like me to the very little bits. Like he said, my features had captivated him.

I stood before it with Freckles, and a drunk woman accidentally knocked into it.

It started swaying downwards, towards me.

I didn't want to remember this part.

Then the statue fell onto my face, my body, cracking apart and cutting me with hard marble pieces.

I looked outwards, wondering at this strange feeling of death.

Freckles, howling, my despairing soon to be husband, and the Emperor himself, finally showing his wretched face, watched me die.

Then angel's wings took me away, far away to the Kingdom of Heaven.

But I walked on the Earth, and took Freckles back to Mrs. Nestor.

I fed him a few extra dog treats before we got to her, thanking him for being there with me.

He smiled up at me, after he had devoured the dog treats, of course.

I shivered at the cold and... from being *alive.*

I let my heart beat, I breathed in and out, let my muscles stretch as I walked back home.

It felt wonderful.

But I saw a form in Nevaeh's window, watching me, but Nevaeh was taking out the trash...

I approached her, and asked her if we could make peace.

She said, "Yule whatever, I don't know *what* game you're playing... But you need to quit sticking your nose in things."

"It was unfair of you to strike at the restaurant when it was wounded. Those people are just trying to live their life, like you and I." I said.

"Fuck you. I'm just doing my duty, enlightening the people… Maybe my next article should be about a bitch albino donating her time at the hospital…" she said, staring at me with such… hate.

"You know I volunteer at the hospital?"

"Ohhh yeah. I also know that the hospital has been firing people left and right, because they can't pay for everything since one of their higher ups stole a huge bunch of money, and the police were unable to recover it… Would be a shame, heh, if your name showed up in this scandalous piece…"

"I don't fear you, and I don't know why you're doing this."

"You really should fear me. You've sealed your fate! 'Misappropriation, Mismanagement… and Albinism.' My next masterpiece!" she said, and cackled.

I let her walk off cackling, just staring at her in pity. What happened to her that made her so cold and heartless?

The form watching me in the window shut the shade.

10

My surgery was tomorrow, and I invited Max over to spend some time with me. I was kind of nervous. I had died because of an accident, a completely random misfortunate event, could it happen again?

We watched TV on the couch for a while, but I shut it off because the sound was starting to grate on my nerves.

Max said, "Everything'll be alright. You're doing a really great, really cool thing, by the way! You're helping give that kid a better chance."

"Yeah... I mean, I wouldn't have it any other way... but... if I die, I want you to know it's been great living again..." I said, staring at my feet, "All the people, the friendship and companions, the colors, sounds and life... You especially, Max. You've been a great friend."

He was silent for a second, and I looked up at him, and was surprised to see him wide eyed... and starting to cry. He tried making a joke and said, "Live again? You some sort of zombie? Next time we go somewhere we should try the brain pâté." and tried to laugh, but quickly frowned, "I don't exactly know what you mean by living again... but... you're not going to die. I don't know much about God, but I'm sure he won't let you leave life yet. You or Mason."

"People die all the time, for no real reason. Sometimes we just need more faces in Heaven."

"Stop it. I know death just happens… but it's the living that makes up for that. Maybe we should do something special, just for you, to help take your mind off life's inevitable end? Anything."

I slowly held his hand, and said just being with him was enough for today.

He coughed, grew very nervous, but squeezed my hand back as I squeezed his.

I turned on the TV, and surprisingly, the Stooges were on the old channel. We snuggled together and watched Moe beat the crap out of Larry and Curly.

With his free hand, Max pet Rasputin, and I was starting to feel comfortable and relaxed again.

We watched a few other shows after the Three Stooges had ended, but Max said he should probably go, and told me to be well rested for the surgery.

He was staring back at me from the doorway, so friendly, hopeful and nice, and I stared back into his eyes, and slowly, he kissed me, and I accepted his kiss, and kissed him back.

We parted lips, and he cleared his throat, a little red, and said, "W-Well, goodnight, Yule. Stay safe."

I smiled at him, waved him goodbye, and he smiled and waved back.

I heard him whooping as he walked down the street.

I went to the hospital in the morning and they prepared me for the surgery.

It was over in no time, just a light sleep, and I was still alive after the procedure.

They thanked me for the donation, and even gave me a card from Mason, a big, pink heart with a smiley face on it, just for me, thanking me.

I held it to my chest, against my heart, prayed, and told myself everything would be alright.

I got the paper in the next few days, with Nevaeh's angry, spiteful, hateful piece, which was rather well written… but as I read every little mean thing she said, backed by supposed credible evidence, I just wanted to burn that stupid paper.

I stared back at her getting into her car from my window. She grinned malevolently and flipped me off again.

I sighed. Was there any way to change Nevaeh's wicked heart?

Did we just get off on the wrong foot? Or are some people destined to dislike each other for all their lives?

I just walked off the anger and went to breakfast with Max.

He kinda kept staring at me longer than usual, and I asked him if he was feeling ok, as we drank our coffee waiting for pancakes, bacon and eggs.

He blushed and said, "I-I-I just think you look really nice t-today…" then he breathed in and out once, straightened up, and said, "I was wondering if, y'know, you'd want to be… my girlfriend? If you're not too busy! I know you're all out there saving the world by helping people and st-stuff… but… I really like you."

I looked at him for a second, cocked my head to the side, and said, "I've never really had a boyfriend before. Would we have to sign forms or something?"

He had his mouth agape in surprise, and said, "What? You've never… had a boyfriend? That… surprises me the most! Back when we first met you had guys checking you out in every direction! It took all I had just to walk over to you!"

"I did court someone… a long time ago. I nearly got married, actually. And of course I've been paired with other tribal boys in my village… but that didn't last too long. And I... loved someone very deeply before, but he... died." I said.

"Oh. Sorry. I just want you to know, I think-" he started, but was cut off as the waitress smiled nicely and set down two big plates of food for us.

"Thank you!" I said to her, "It looks delicious!" She winked at me, and refilled our coffee. "What were you saying?" I asked Max, as I was already stuffing my face with food.

"Um... Nothing... It doesn't matter..." he said, and started picking at his food.

"Well, I want *you* to know... I think having a boyfriend would be pretty fun. It's a deal." I said.

He accidentally dropped his fork to the table, and said, "Gr-Great! Y-You're my girlfriend!" and he smiled really happily, and we both dug into our food, enjoying the syrupy, fluffy pancakes, the bacon and eggs, each other's company, and our new arrangement.

It was his turn to pay for our meal this time. We got up, put on our coats, and I locked my arm in his. We sauntered out of the restaurant, feeling strangely really happy, as I laughed and talked with Max. I could tell he felt just as happy as I did.

But for some reason, a car pulled down their window and someone called out at me, "Thief!" and sped away.

Max was staring back at the car inquisitively, and I pulled Max down a side street...

"What was that?" he asked, "I must look like somebody they know or something..."

"They weren't calling you a thief... They were yelling at me. This reporter- My neighbor, she wrote this whole horrible piece about the hospital, and made the suggestion that one of their volunteers, me, was a crook..."

"What? Isn't that against the law or something?" Max said.

"She never actually 'said' I was a thief, just put the pieces there for anyone to figure out… She actually starts off by praising me and the hospital, but quickly throws us into the mud, and makes it look like we're bloodsucking vampires."

"That- That really burns me! Goddamnit… Stupid- people…" he said, "Want me to talk with her? I bet she's just jealous of you or something…"

"I'd rather you didn't. She's maybe just lost in life, and thinks this will help her find her way. She'll get bored of it eventually." I said.

"Yeah. It'll come back to bite her in the butt, eventually. And isn't that what Hell is for? She'll get her comeuppance some day…" he said.

I smiled, and said, "I'm sure Nevaeh will find her way to Heaven eventually."

We walked down the streets, and before we separated on a corner, we kissed each other goodbye.

I checked in with the Italian restaurant, and while I'm sure they did much better before, I noticed they actually had a few customers as I peered in through the windows. I saw the dishboy wave at me on his smoke break, talking with May.

I opened the door, the little bell jingling, and I looked over to the wall and saw my newspaper piece framed and hanging.

Mike quickly dropped what he was doing, sweeping up behind a counter, and went over to me and smiled. He said, "Anything I can do for you, Miss Tidings?"

"Just checking up on you guys. I just had breakfast but I'll take one of those little pastries."

He said, "Right away! My dad is helping out when he feels up for it, and even Angelo can't measure up to his baking. When they worked together… they could've probably ran this place just on their own… but you're in for a treat!" and boxed up a little pastry for me, tied up the box with a ribbon, and gently handed it to me. I paid for it, and I heard a voice from the back say, *"Mike!* What- What did you do to the mixer??"

"Just got the new model, Dad! I installed it just a second ago! It's great! You don't even need to-" Mike called back.

"You get the old mixer back right now, and sell this piece of crap the first chance you get!" the voice said.

Mike shrugged to me, smiled, and said, "Duty calls. Please, come visit whenever you like, Miss Tidings. You are always welcome."

I waved him goodbye, and he rushed into the back.

I had tea with Mrs. Nestor after a short walk, since it got rather too cold for Freckles, and Mrs. Nestor was staring at me.

I asked her, "What's up? Do I have something in my hair?"

"No… in your eyes. You tell me, right now, did you steal from those sick kids in the hospital?" she asked.

I opened my eyes in shock, and plainly told her I would never do such a thing.

She stared hard in my eyes, but seemed to be satisfied and said, "Good. I didn't really think you would, I mean what kind of thief turns down free money for walking a dog? But… you could just be trying to earn my trust… and then rip me off as soon as I'm not here…"

I started sniffling, then bawling my eyes out, which Mrs. Nestor was surprised at. Freckles went up to me and put his head on my lap as I cried downwards at him.

"Uh… Sorry, Yule. There, there… I- I didn't mean it…" Mrs. Nestor said.

"It's… just such a mean thing to say! Calling someone a thief when all you've ever done is try to help them! I-I even just donated bone marrow, and she flips me off, and calls me a bitch! Even *you* think there's stock in her words! I-I-I… maybe I should move…" I said.

Mrs. Nestor patted my hand sadly and said, "No, dear. Running away won't solve anything. I truly think you have a good heart… it's just some people will do whatever they can to break that heart, to show to themselves that you're as bad as they are… I truly think you're a wonderful girl… I'm sorry I said such things."

I thanked her, and my tears seemed to be receding. I said I needed to nip this in the bud, before it grows out of control. I was going to confront Nevaeh head on, and if we couldn't make peace, then she would at least know not to keep hurting me, or at least not keep hurting other people.

The restaurant, the hospital, they were struggling, hurting, and Nevaeh just throws salt in their wounds. How many other people had she done this to?

I wiped off my tears and said goodbye to Mrs. Nestor. She told me good luck.

I knocked on Nevaeh's door. She opened up on a crack and glared at me, saying, "What do you want?"

"I want you to stay out of my and other people's lives. To not cause them pain and suffering with your hateful, vindictive words. If you don't… then all of Heaven won't stop me from putting an end to your evil."

"Heaven??" she exclaimed, and laughed, *"Hell* is what you're supposed to say. Whatcha gonna do? Plant flowers in my yard? *That* will show me…" and she laughed again. "Well… I've never had this much fun before! A little bitch thinks she can take on the big dog! Please. Come in. I'd love to laugh at you some more." and she opened her door wider, inviting me inside.

I nervously followed her through the door… and I smelled it.

She said, "There's a little leak somewhere, probably a crack in the pipes… but it's nothing to worry about. Just stinks like shit."

That odor wasn't anything from Earth. That was brimstone from Hell. It felt, and smelled, like I walked into the bowels of a snake.

We talked for a minute, and she kept on writing things down in a notepad. I asked her what she was writing.

"Oh. You always say the stupidest things! Thought it might be good to have a reference of them. Ha!" she said.

I looked into her eyes. They looked clouded.

I tried to tell her that it could be gas, that smell she was smelling, and she should probably leave this house.

"No... I've already had them test that. And the Devil knows... I sure as shit am not going to move back in with my controlling parents..." she said.

"Uh. I saw someone in the window here... Do you live with someone?" I asked.

"Hm? I used to live with an asshole ex of mine... but that was a year ago. Fucker left me for some idiot old milf. I hope they both get hit by a truck." she said.

"Is... that why you're so angry?" I asked.

She laughed, and said, "You've never seen me angry before. *If* I was angry, you'd be mush, and everyone, *everywhere,* would hate your guts. I think your new boyfriend will be my next target..."

"What? Leave him alone. Don't do something you will regret." I said, getting a little angry myself, "How did you know of him?"

"That little midget came over to my house and tried telling me to back off. But that was only for a second... Because he fell... like *that.*" and she snapped her fingers.

"What? What do you mean?"

She laughed evilly, and said, "I got the fucker into my panties in no time! See... See look here! The idiot even left me his number! As if I wanted a midget in my pants twenty four seven..." and she handed me a paper with… Max's number, and the words, in his handwriting, "Call me."

My heart sank into my stomach, but I said, "You're lying."

She laughed and laughed.

I quickly left the house, as she laughed and laughed at me, sounding like Satan was laughing at me instead.

11

I felt like my heart was about to break. But she must've been lying. There's no way... Would he have? *Could he have??*

The thoughts kept racing around my head in a circle, and the more I tried to reason them out, the faster I went through the loop.

I had to break this cycle, and I needed some answers.

I... didn't have the heart to talk to Max. I declined his call and left my phone in the apartment, intent on... just being alone.

I decided to find that demon who was infesting the world. I'd find him, and I'd kill him.

At least then it might relieve some of these... feelings.

I wasted a good half of the day searching for a demon, intent on getting some sort of revenge. I just wandered around town, looking for evil. It became nighttime, and I still kept on searching.

I smelled that wretched smell coming out of a dark alley.

My sword and shield instantly appeared in my hands... and I crept through the alley, shining light in the darkness.

I heard the smacking of lips... as if someone was eating a corpse.

I turned a corner, and saw Sax, even bigger than before, chowing on... a dead cat.

I instantly thought of Rasputin, and I felt angry... This looked like a dead pregnant cat, probably run over by a truck... and dragged into the alley by Sax.

"Stop, creature of the Devil. You will die for your wickedness in creation." I commanded.

Sax turned, and wiped the blood off of his lips.

But... It looked like he was crying.

"Yule!" he said in a deep voice, no longer a pipsqueak, *"I'm so glad to see you! I'm so sorry for messing with you like that... You don't know how lonely I've been!"*

"Your vileness ends now. For the people you've corrupted, for the things you... ate. You pitted someone against me, everything you touch turns wicked." I said, sizing him up, planning my strike to kill this demon.

He sighed, and said, *"I... thought we didn't need to do this... but I suppose it's just in our natures... Hell and Heaven have been at odds ever since... well, ever since creation. I want to live, and I don't care if you want to kill me. I want to live."*

"I... I too, want to live. But you cause death with every breath you breathe."

"It's not my fault! I swore that she would have a better life! Even introduced her to my boss... so he'd take me back... or maybe give me a real life... but... Satan is a cruel master..."

"Enough. You will die *now*." I said, and swung my sword, but he seemed to slither away from me. From the shadows he kicked his foot at me, and I flew against the wall.

"I told you. I want to live." he said, picking up a dumpster, about to smash me over the head with it. I rolled out of the way as he smashed it against the wall, creating a large crack in the foundations.

I stabbed at him, but he was unnervingly fast, slithering around me and punching me here and there. In the stomach, in the breast, whacking me in the cheek and making my head snap to the left.

I called on Heaven's aid, and the light around me grew ten times brighter, blinding everyone, burning anything it touched.

But Sax had hid, and some policemen were running down the alley. Sax slithered down a manhole, and I was about to jump after him, but the policemen grabbed me by the arms, holding me back.

"Lighting fireworks in the city? You know you could set this whole area ablaze. We're taking you in." one said.

The policemen dragged me with them, as I stared back down the manhole where Sax had disappeared, escaping me yet again.

I was brought to the station. One recognized my name, as the thief, but the other... recognized my paper for the restaurant. They argued about what to do with me, but the one who liked my paper said, "C'mon... She's got a clean slate. Let her keep it. You know old Antonelli has been really having a hard time, and well, this Yule Tidings gave him a second chance."

"The law is the law. It's illegal to be setting off fireworks in the city like that." the other said.

So they argued some more, and the chief walked in, a shorter woman who asked why the two weren't on patrol.

"Chief! We've caught a lawbreaker, and are going to give her the proper serving." the one who disliked me said.

The one who liked me said, "Ahh, she's just a kid. Surely we can just give her a warning. We've all done idiotic stuff when we were young."

"She's old enough to be prosecuted to the full extent of the law. We *should* give her an attempted arson and jail her." the cop said.

The chief motioned them to stop jabbering. She looked me in the eyes as I was sitting at the table, and said, "Fireworks? Is there some sort of celebration going on?"

I said, "I... No... I just... found out my new boyfriend has been cheating on me... and he's my first genuine boyfriend ever... I just... needed to let off some steam..."

"See! Young hearts, young problems." the cop who liked me said.

The other cop said, "Hmph. And young criminals grow up to be old criminals. Can't change a cat's stripes."

"Are you sure your daughter feels the same way?" the chief said to the cop who didn't like me.

He grew embarrassed, then said, "She... just- You know it's not her fault! It was all that bastard's fault."

"That 'bastard' has a statuatory rape charge because he couldn't wait a few months. And he was so young... They were even in the same grade..." the chief said.

"I don't need to hear this. Let's go, Dave." the cop said, motioning for the other to follow him. They left out the door and let the chief deal with me. She reviewed my case that the other policemen had left for her.

"They didn't find any sort of fireworks in that alley... But they testify that they saw lights and even a box burnt to a crisp. You know playing with fire is dangerous, so I'm going to have to give you a fine... but you won't get any sort of arson charge. Lighting fireworks in the city... That's all. Nothing to worry over, if you've learned your lesson." she said.

I nodded. She gave me a ticket, and walked me back out through the doors.

I walked back through the door of my home. I pet Rasputin who was mewling at me and rubbing against my legs, and fed him dinner. I looked at my cell phone and saw the ten missed calls from Max.

I didn't listen to the voicemails and was about to go to bed... but it rang one more time.

I sighed, and picked up.

"Yule! Are you ok?? I've been so worried when you didn't answer!" Max said.

"What do you want, Max..." I said.

"...Are you mad at me for something?" he asked.

"I don't know. Did you do something?" I asked.

"...No... But I talked to that one reporter... I know you told me not to, but I found the piece she wrote... and you told me she was your neighbor... It just made me so frustrated!! I couldn't stop myself from- But she slammed the door in my face, and I left my number in her mailbox. You believe me- If she needed to be mean to someone, she could be mean to me, and not my girlfriend. I'd have served her with ten times what she throws at you, me, or anyone."

I smiled, thanking God and Max ten times over silently, and said, "I was served with a fine today."

"She insulted my height! And she- Wait, what??"

"I talked to Nevaeh too... I won't repeat the awful things she said, hearing it once was enough, but I got so angry... and lit fireworks off in the city."

"Haha... Really? That's ridiculous, Yule, but I understand. Sometimes when you're all burned up, it's nicer seeing something else burn for a while. They gave you a fine for *that??*"

"Could've got an arson sentence, if God wasn't looking out for me."

"Really... Yeah, cops are all assholes. Well... if you ever do feel so angry that you feel like setting something off and watching it explode, talk to me first, alright? There's other ways to let off steam." Max said.

I giggled, and said, "Of course, Max. Next time we get angry, we'll be angry together, and let off steam by exploding all night."

"Ha... Ha... Uh, mhm. Yeah. W-Well, goodnight, Yule. Sweet dreams." he said, and I said goodbye and hung up.

Hmm... I wondered if that was adequate flirting? Been forever since I actually *did* flirt.

But I felt so much better, and hugged a pillow, thinking that I'd hug Max like this as well.

12

Max and I went to the bar and talked with Thaniel.

We said we were sorry for Nevaeh's latest misdeed.

But Thaniel laughed, and said, "Are you kidding?? This is the best publicity I've ever gotten! Who cares if she didn't like my book? She got two hundred more people to read it, with one, lame, overly critical article that even had a spelling error! That chick... she's like a blessing in disguise."

"Well, the spelling error was for a made up word... Spelled 'durasstic' instead of 'durastic...'" Max said.

"Eh, we're all fallible... I can't wait for her to read the next one! I was honestly getting a little worried, thinking that it's been too long since I last put something out there... but I've got a new hope now." Thaniel said, sipping on his beer.

"I'm just glad the hospital is doing better off now. They're getting some funding from the government, and the layoffs have halted. Maybe Nevaeh's article showed people how bad it was getting..." I said.

"True, true..." Max said, "And I hear that restaurant you wrote for is celebrating its fiftieth anniversary soon. They said Antonelli was going to shut it down before that, but maybe he and his son have a new fire in their hearts... thanks to you, Yule."

"And I would've never written that piece without Nevaeh. Hmm... Maybe we should all get together and send her a thank you gift..." I said. We all started laughing.

"Not a bad idea. Here, a copy of my book... signed to my biggest fan..." Thaniel said, and signed his name, "Nathaniel Hamburg," on his book he was going to give to me.

"Oh! And let's get her some champagne! So she can celebrate the turning point in our lives properly." Max said.

I nodded, smiling, and said, "I've got the perfect thing for her, a Bible that... someone important gave to me. Her name is Nevaeh, after all."

"Hm? Oh! Duh... That's Heaven spelled backwards... I honestly thought it was something Japanese." Max said.

I laughed, and Max and I bought some champagne. We put our gifts in a basket then put the basket on Nevaeh's doorstep, rang the doorbell, and ran away laughing.

We watched her open the door. She crouched down, picked up the basket, and looked around herself for a second. We hid again before she could spot us.

We looked back, and she popped the cork off the champagne, took a sip, and took the basket inside.

Later, Max and I were hanging out outside my apartment, and we heard... crying coming from Nevaeh's house. Loud sobbing, wailing, and we walked over to her front door.

We rang the bell, but she didn't answer. I knocked on the door, and it crept open, unlocked.

"Nevaeh? Are you alright?" I asked.

"G-Go away! I-I'm fine!" she said. She had never said she was fine to me before, ever.

I heard some strange whispering coming from the brimstone smelling house... so I crept in, saying, "I'm coming inside, ok? I just want to check up on you!"

But it was silent. Max and I looked around the corner, and saw Nevaeh crying…

With a pistol she was pointing at herself…

With the Devil whispering into her ear.

Then Nevaeh pointed the pistol at us.

She sobbed some more, and cried out, *"Why… Why?!?* G-Go away! I-I could shoot you for breaking and entering!"

I waved Max to step away. He got out of her line of fire and called 911.

"It's ok, Nevaeh. Don't do anything rash." I said in a calm tone.

"You know they'll lock you up for this. You won't ever see anyone again." the Devil whispered in Nevaeh's ears.

"I never see anyone! P-People hate me! Th-They think I'm some bitch… Th-They want me to die! So. I'll let them have their wish." Nevaeh said.

Then she pointed the pistol back at herself.

The Devil was urging her to pull the trigger, and telling her… just like her name… she'll go to Heaven.

I quickly said, "Please, Nevaeh. You don't have to do this. I always knew that something was hurting you deeply. I think you have a lot to live for, and that I or someone else can help you."

She said in between her sobbing, "N-No! You're just laughing at me! Y-You hate me the most! I-I singled you out! I tr-tried to make you suffer!"

"No. I do not hate you. I gave you that Bible because I think you're worth saving. Please. Put the gun down."

She was whimpering, crying, and the Devil told her to do it now, because the cops are at the front door…

The police rushed in.

Nevaeh, startled, dropped the gun and it went off into a policeman's leg.

The police pulled their guns and pointed them at Nevaeh.

I walked up to her and told her it will be alright. She was absolutely terrified.

I said, "I'm not going to hurt you. Let's get some air." and picked her up and walked with her outside. The police allowed us to pass.

The Devil crept away, as I lost track of him in the commotion, but whispered to me that he has an eternity to try again…

And that he'd even save a special place in Hell for me.

Nevaeh was being taken to a hospital for people like her, people who have suicidal thoughts, and I argued with the policeman who put her in handcuffs and put her into the back of the cop car. They said it was for her own safety.

They asked us a few questions, and we told them honestly what happened. "Giving her a thank you gift, eh? Kind of a mean prank, if she doesn't like you… But, if you weren't there who knows what could've happened." the cop said, and they left.

Nevaeh was looking down at her feet in the car, and I looked sadly at her as they drove her off.

Max and I went back to my apartment, and we just talked about things for a while. He said who would've thought?

I said I had a little feeling.

We just watched TV for a while. Max left late in the evening, and I went to bed.

A few days later, I got a call from Nevaeh's parents.

Her dad said, in his Japanese accent, "Er… since you two were such good friends and all… she wants you to pick up some things from her house that she can have in the hospital. She can barely have anything in that place, which just makes me angry… But she should be able to leave soon… Hopefully at the end of the month. She said the key is underneath the gnome out back."

"What did she want?" I asked.

"Hardly anything, really. Just a crisscrossing red and green blanket she's had since she was a kid, and a Bible from her house." her dad said.

So I went over to Nevaeh's empty house, picked up a gnome in the back which had the key under it, and unlocked the door.

Thankfully, the smell of brimstone had dissipated at last. It smelled clean.

I picked up the Bible sitting on a table next to Thaniel's book and the empty bottle of champagne.

I walked into her room, and saw pictures of her and someone littering the room. Of them laughing and having fun together, her kissing him on the cheek as she took the picture... This must've been the guy she was telling me about... She said she hated him, but I suppose she just hated him leaving her.

I found the blanket on her bed, picked it up, and took it with me.

I went to the hospital during visiting hours because Nevaeh said she wanted to see me.

I sat across from her. She was allowed to keep her black sweater and black pants on she left with, and not wear those teal gowns some of the other patients wore. The first thing I did was hand her the Bible wrapped in her blanket.

She actually looked, well, not *great...* but she didn't have those cloudy eyes anymore.

She said to me, "I want to say... Sorry. Everything seemed to spiral out of control... I... felt like I was being sucked into a pit, and the more I fought it, the stronger it got. I... didn't feel good, hurting you... but it made me feel... just a little bit less depressed..."

"You'd have to try a lot harder, if you wanted to seriously hurt me. I've been... through death, basically, and nothing could hurt more than that." I said.

She frowned, and said, "That's kinda why I targeted you. You seemed indomitable, like if I *did* shoot you, you'd get up again. Seeing you like that, made me realize how weak I was. So I tried harder... but... you just got up again."

I smiled, and said, "I don't think you're weak. Going through what you went through... Not all are as strong as you."

She smiled sadly, and said, "These last few months are the worst it's ever been for me. I... just kept having these horrible dreams... Demons, monsters, all sorts of messed up shit... then the house started to reek... and then... my old boyfriend... is getting married to that *milf...*"

"Mike's not a bad guy. I see why you attacked the restaurant. We maybe just love different people, over time, and he couldn't see that you still loved him." I said.

"Oh... you saw the pictures. I was going to get rid of them... over and over again... but it just felt like I was losing my old life... and if I did, everything I once loved would've been gone." she said.

"You have a lot to live for, and a lot to love. Maybe when you get out of here, you and I can hang out? Be friends? I know maybe we got off on the wrong foot, but when I knocked on your door the first time I met you, I just wanted to tell you about a little hole in your window that you might not have noticed." I said.

"Really. So that's why it was so fucking cold... Well, Yule, you've got a date." she said, and we shook hands in peace.

"And Thaniel sends his condolences, and eagerly hopes you can read his next book... He really was happy that someone, *anyone,* had the time to read his book and actually give it a review. He's aiming for something that you too can enjoy this time around." I said.

She laughed, and said, "That's ridiculous. That stupid piece was the hardest one to write, because I *did* like that one story with the silly bees..."

"Me too! I always liked the contrast of the bees, even though they all live in the same hive with the same queen." I said.

"I actually thought that was a rather nice comparison to writing. Every one of those bees live in the writer's head, and all have their own little voices, like characters in a story, but all live in the same hive. Although, that one drunk bee didn't really make much sense to me… talking about his 'durastics.'"

I laughed, and said, "That bee is probably a self portrait Thaniel created for himself."

"Hm. Alright. Tell your boyfriend I'm sorry I called him a midget."

"Ah, he's already forgotten about it. It actually showed his manly side when you harassed him. He'd take the brunt of the force, if he had to, to protect someone he cares about."

"Oh. Ok. Well… keep him safe. Nothing did happen between us. I just tried to get on your and his nerves… and it really irked you. If it hurts you so bad like that, you should probably just give up on him."

"Nah. People just worry, y'know? Makes us a great species of sentient apes."

"Ok… I'll keep that in mind. I'm worried that my parents are going to be smothering me when I get out…"

"It's probably for the best. If you don't feel safe alone, you should be with someone you know can protect you, even from yourself."

"I-I really love them, I really do, but… I hate church. And my parents are both devoted Catholics, who might drag me to one… I always hated my name… but I keep it because… I love my parents, and they gave it to me. I… know I have no place to ask this… but… you're like the best enemy I've ever had. Can I stay with you? I just… *never* want to go to church…" she said

"Sure. But just so you know, I too am a Christian." I said.

"R-Really? Never would've thought. But… you actually give me space, even if we hate each other…"

I laughed, and said, "Nah. I think you could be a great friend. Why did you ask for the Bible, then?"

"I just said I hated church. I… was raped in a church. I rather like the book of Genesis, though."

"Oh. Ok. Well, I have a spare room, and you're welcome to stay when you get out."

She smiled, and said, "Thank you, Yule."

13

Max knocked on the apartment door, I opened the door and accepted the flowers he got me. I invited him inside, and a voice said from the bathroom, *"Yule!* Where's my fucking razor? Did you tidy it away somewhere?? My legs are like a bear's ass!"

Max quickly stopped smiling as he heard that voice, looked at me in surprise, and said, "She's staying *here??* But- What if she tries to burn your apartment down! Or poison your coffee! Or... something! How can you trust her??"

I shrugged, and said, "She's fun to have around. It's by the sink Nevaeh! I just took it out of the bath when I bathed!"

"Oh! Thanks!" Nevaeh yelled back.

I took Max by the hand and dragged him to my surprise.

It had been a month since we started dating, and I hoped he liked what I got him. He said he planned a whole night of dinner and fun for me, and the flowers were just the start.

I put my hands over his eyes, walked him into my room... and revealed my surprise!

He looked around, and said. "Your bed?"

"No! What's on the bed! Look, look there, on the pillow." I said.

He walked over to it, picked it up, and gulped, saying, "You aren't... proposing to me, are you? Kind of a weird engagement ring..."

"No, damnit! Put it on! I want to see what it looks like on you!" I said. Max shrugged and put the ring on.

I grinned, and said, "You are now a proud member of the Ritz Society! Mason's father gave it to me! He actually owns that one club that we met at, and it's kind of... like a guild? A secret society? Something like that, but you are a VIP from now on."

"Oh! Damn! That's really cool! Always wanted to be in a secret club... of clubs! How is the little kid, anyway?" he asked, looking down at his ring and grinning.

"He says he feels like an angel, but is happier and more alive than ever."

"Well... must be because he got a little bit of angel bone in him now! You're- just- like God put you on this Earth himself..." he said, staring deep into my eyes.

"More like snuck back down to Earth, but let's go have dinner."

"Huh? Oh, yeah. It'll be great! Just you and I... We haven't been able to do this in a while!"

I coughed, and said, "Well... mostly just you and I..."

"What? No... You can't mean... Not her!"

"C'mon. She's having a hard time getting used to everything. They even took her off the writing team since they thought that was stressing her out... All she does is read Thaniel's book over and over again..."

"Hmph. Fine, but she better not ruin my romantic scene by the lake I had planned..."

I laughed, and said, "You take Valentine's Day too seriously. Just go with the flow."

"Alright. Well, let's get the most stressful day of the year over with, shall we?" he said, offering his arm. I took it, ready for a great night.

Nevaeh held us up, because she was still shaving her legs, but came out of the bathroom in a black hoodie and jeans.

"What was the point of shaving your legs then?" Max asked.

"Hey, I still have a chance tonight. Some loser is bound to get dumped, like always, unfortunately on Valentine's day. Let's go, you poor sods! I wanna get laid!" she cheered. Max muttered as we followed her out the door.

We had dinner at the Italian restaurant, and Mike sighed when he saw Nevaeh, but was very polite. Nevaeh seemed to be ignoring him, but always asked for more water whenever Mike came around, trying to talk to him.

The restaurant was booming tonight, and the owner, Antonelli himself, brought us the pizza. He glared at Nevaeh, and was about to say something harsh, but I smiled and thanked him for the pizza. He looked at me... shrugged, and went back into the kitchen.

Cupids littered the scene, a Roman thing, and I always wondered at those little baby angels. When Maximus and I made love, when he saw my naked form, he couldn't resist saying, "By Cupid!" and the noble had Cupids all over his garden. I guess it made sense that a god of erotic love would be a baby. Or did it make the least amount of sense?

Anyway, St. Valentine was always a friend to me. He actually loved to dance, and angels would line up to boogie with him when we had parties.

We went to a club, and I used all the moves St. Valentine had taught me himself. They took one look at Max's ring, and he was surprised when they let us past the line and into the club.

We danced and boogied! Max was a little stiff at the start, but I led him through the club, meeting his eyes as we touched each other in the dance, and I think he got his courage.

Nevaeh was sitting in a corner, not deigning to dance, but trying to flirt. Somebody said that she had pretty eyes, and loved her writing... saying it was like the Devil had written it himself.

Nevaeh stopped flirting, and asked Max and I if we could leave.

We did, and I asked her what was wrong, as she took out a cigarette and began smoking, offering one to each of us.

"It's just… writer's have many voices. When they talk about 'finding your voice' it really means finding you confidence. But… a writer needs to change her voice for the piece, needs to be flexible and adaptable. You can't say one thing in the same voice over and over, or else you'll be typecast. It's kind of like being an actor, but instead of being just a character, you're the entire scene as well.

"I just… found a different voice, when everything was going to Hell… It truly sounded like the Devil… but in the end, I realized it was just me."

I took her hand, and said that was over now.

She looked into my eyes, her eyes clear, and she said that's what she hoped.

We walked down to the lake for Max's romance scene, Nevaeh and I giggling as Max tried to recite poetry and be extra, extra romantic.

He gave up halfway through his poem, and said, "Eh, fuck it." He went to me from his romance pose, and we kissed.

I took Max to bed that night, and Nevaeh took Rasputin to bed with her, saying this warm body was good enough for her.

And I hugged Max close, just like I loved doing, and we made love.

I was admiring him in the middle of the night, in his boxers beside me, sleeping, and he suddenly woke up awake, sweating. He looked around frightened, then stared into my eyes for a second and calmed down.

"Oh. I just- thought you were gone. Like- Never mind." he said.

"It's ok. What is it?" I asked.

"I just had a dream… that you were taken away from me… not like just breaking up or something… but really, *gone.* Like you were never here, and didn't belong here. It was a weird dream."

"And the whole story turned out to be a dream, right? Those always pissed me off."

He laughed and said, "Yeah. I know you're not a dream. Maybe fantastically, unrealistically beautiful, but... not a dream."

I punched him on the arm lightly, then snuggled up against him again and he wrapped his arm around me.

Perhaps things were too good to be true... Perhaps. But when things finally turn up right for you, when your first life turns out terrible, it's nice to have a second go around.

Everything was finally great, at least just for now.

But there was a nagging thought in my head... something that kept on popping up, over and over again.

The Devil would always be around, perhaps, would always be whispering in people's ears and trying to ruin their happiness... and his minions were somehow on Earth.

Like Sax.

It wasn't that the Devil was anywhere near me... I knew that I would, unlike true mortals of Earth, see him if he ever showed his fangs.

He wasn't right behind me, was he?

Hiding under the bed?

Masking his foul stench, shifting into this world to cause suffering?

Nah... Probably not. I hoped.

But it was the whispering in people's ears that I wanted to stop. That hellish tormenting voice of evil.

I *needed* to combat this unholiness.

Nevaeh crept into my room, and it looked like she had been crying. I untangled myself from Max, and went to talk to her in her room, getting out of bed in my pajamas.

She said she was rather scared tonight, thinking of when she nearly ended her life. Rasputin mewled at me on her bed.

So I popped in a nightlight I got for her, knowing that shining brilliance helped keep the terrors of the dark, and of your own head, back in the dark. It was a smiling, little angel. Nevaeh stared at it, hugged me, and said that'll do.

I walked back to my room, as a draft got in through the apartment, and I had another vision in the hall.

But this wasn't a vision of the past, it was one of something I hoped would never be.

I hugged Max again and let the horrible vision of Hell pass.

Part 2: Temperantia

Temperance

14

Nevaeh and I had been out shopping, checking out an antique fair. Nevaeh plopped the big old typewriter on a desk in her room. She smiled at me, and said, "Loved these contraptions in the movies. Nothing like that old, antiquey type of a typewriter."

I said, "You'll be able to get back your mojo with this! It's a shame that you left the office, but maybe it was for the best."

"Eh. They were going to cut me back to part time, in the *mail* room... I hated shifting through those letters from all our crazy readers when I first started off, and I still hate it now." she said.

"We both found fantastic little treasures, didn't we?" I said, staring down at my... old Roman shield, that had the scratches, the battle marks, the same exact grip... as it did centuries ago.

"That's probably a fake, wouldn't have got it so cheap if it wasn't, but it does look cool." Nevaeh said. I held my stance, with the shield raised in my hand, and Nevaeh laughed. She said, "You look like an old gladiator or something. It's too bad there were no women gladiators. I'm sure we could've kicked butt in the colosseum."

I smiled.

Nevaeh and I had grown rather close. Our old fights seemed like the far past, and I'm glad I could call her my friend.

She clicked some keys on the typewriter, oohed, and said, "I'm... just gonna mess with this a bit. You have fun on your walk. Thanks for inviting me, but I'd rather not hang out with some crotchety old lady and a furry poop machine."

"Alright. See ya, Nevaeh!" I said. She was already posed on the typewriter, looking like she was about to write a masterpiece.

I hung the shield up in my room. Let it, like it did in the past, protect me from all danger.

The snow was starting to melt, revealing the trash and other refuse it had hidden. Freckles and I didn't mind. It felt like it would be spring soon.

I would catch the whiff of brimstone frequently these days, stinking up the town in random places... and the Castrator kept on following me, calling out to me with challenges.

I ignored him, and he didn't follow me into Mrs. Nestor's house.

We were drinking tea, and Mrs. Nestor said, "Bah... the town stinks, these days. Ever since that new plant opened up, everything smells like the Devil's ass..."

"Yeah... Makes me wish to be in the pure forests of Germany again..." I said.

"What forests? Germany has industrialized so much... You do a little travelling before?" she asked.

The Castrator was peeking in through the window. I turned my eyes away from him and back at Mrs. Nestor.

"Um... Kinda. Used to live there, for a while..." I said.

"Really? You're an immigrant? You speak perfect English though!" she said.

"I actually know a lot of languages. Old Germanic, Latin, English... And I've met all sorts of people from all over the world who taught me their languages." I said.

"Hm. Learn something new every day." she said. Then, Mrs. Nestor smiled, and spoke in perfect German to me.

I spoke back to her in surprise, and we laughed together. She said she learned German in school. She said that I had quite a unique German accent, like nothing she's ever heard before.

I eagerly told her about my life in Germany, about the tribe, my parents, leaving out certain details that would seem a little odd to someone in the present day.

She listened, saying she always wanted to travel there someday with her husband… but he had gotten ill from his heart and they never could do the trip they were planning.

I said I wanted to go back there someday, just to see how much it's changed.

She thought for a moment, and said in English again, "When you do visit your homeland again… please tell me all about it. Here, let me get something for you…" She walked out of the kitchen to a back room.

The Castrator threatened me from the window, but I just frowned at him and told him to shoo.

Mrs. Nestor came back with a camera and handed it to me. An old camera that used film.

She said, "Was my husband's… He took the best pictures with this thing, because it uses film and is not some fancy digital machine… Please, take it, and send me the pictures of your travels, your life, and whatever you think will please me."

I tried to decline, saying that I couldn't take one of her husband's last possessions… but I looked into her eyes, and she looked so serious.

"Please, Yule. I can't do things as easily as before. This will mean a lot to me, and I'm sure the pictures will come out better with my husband's camera. Let me see pictures of life, with what's rest of my life." she said.

I accepted the camera. It had a sort of comfortable feel to it.

I hugged Mrs. Nestor, and she hugged me back.

When I got home, I took a picture of Nevaeh typing, and she said to quit it. "You gotta see the world with your own eyes if you want to truly live it." she said.

I pointed the camera at her right beside her face, and told her to smile nicely this time!

She said, "Oh… fine. Here." and then she turned to me, giving me a cheesy, charming smile, and I clicked the button on the camera.

"Thank you, Nevaeh! How's the masterpiece?" I said.

"I got inspired by Thaniel. I'm trying to write a good piece… but…" she sighed, and ripped the paper off the typewriter, handing it to me and saying, "This one's… just boring! I made a classic fantasy story, of love and romance… but I'm sick to death of the prince and princess already! I just want to kill them both off and let the evil dragon rule the kingdom…"

"Maybe you should? Would be an interesting twist." I said, reading through it slightly.

"Hmm… yeah… and I can introduce the dragon's child, a half dragon, half elf… A sexy dominatrix who lashes that goofy prince and idiot princess to a stake, and let's the dragon devour them…" she said.

I gave the paper back to her, and said, "As long as it's got a happy ending! Maybe the dominatrix finds true love, one day? And the dragon gives his blessing, happy for his daughter?"

She giggled, and said, "True love… maybe… She's just gonna have some crazy sex at the start, though… I can't wait for the orgy scene with all the servants she frees from those fuckin' nobles…"

I stared at her, as she already began typing furiously. I shrugged, and left the room.

I looked outside. The Castrator had built a snowman, and then he stabbed it in the heart with his dagger. I guess he was starting to get bored harassing me.

It's just... It's not like I didn't *want* to fight him... but I already had fought him again, and had already replayed the battle over and over again in my head. Couldn't he just be satisfied with his win?

He saw me looking, waved, and threatened me again.

Huh. Maybe he was just a lonely, lost specter?

I took the shield off the wall, just in case, and went outside to the back to meet him.

He instantly was prepared for battle, and said, *"You come at me again, shield bared. Will you ever learn your lesson, pitiful wench?"*

"I'm not going to fight you." I said, "I just thought you looked a little lonely out here."

He faltered a second, then raised his dagger, and said, *"I have taken every man's pride who has come before me. Even you have fallen before me, despite your all powerful God."*

I sat down in a lawn chair that the snow had melted from, and started a cigarette despite present company.

I sat there smoking, shield raised between me and the Castrator, as he stared at me quizzically.

"Is this some sort of trick? You seek to lower my guard?"

"Nah. Just waiting for you to leave."

"I... must fight! I will never know peace, until I have conquered every foe in the arena! They must all perish by my blade! It was commanded of me! What I was brought up for!" he said, trying to get me to understand.

"I heard tell you were a eunuch, and that's why you cut off people's balls after you beat them."

"*Blasphemous! I- Does everybody know? I was even fitted with prosthetic genitalia...*"

"Old Roman medicine prosthetics. That's like, balls made of wood or something, right?"

He covered his crotch, and said, "*The codpiece isn't enough?*"

"I always thought it was a little crass, honestly, worn on someone called 'the Castrator.'"

He grumbled, and sat down on the lawn, legs crossed. "*I lived until I had won my freedom in the ring. No one loved me, but I had earned my freedom, and I was happy. I cannot remember how I died, only that I must keep fighting in the arena.*"

"Hey, you probably didn't die as bad as me. Squished by a statue of myself... Ironic." I said, taking another puff and blowing out a smoke ring.

"*I thought you had incredible skill, but you underestimated the reach of my blade, as most often do.*" he said.

"Yeah. I really thought I learned my lesson, but then I fought you in that football stadium and it was the same as ever... Pathetic, how we always repeat the mistakes of the past." I said.

"*Yeah... Well, I guess I'll see you later. Perhaps I may teach you! So you may learn to use the blade to the farthest reaches of your power!*" he exclaimed.

"It's alright. But if something bad does happen that I need help with, I won't turn down the extra help."

"Oh. Ok. Well, alright. Goodbye, Angel of the Pits." he said, and walked off.

I looked at him for a second as he walked off. He seemed to be different, somehow, but he vanished in the breeze.

15

I walked back inside, and Nevaeh was splashing cold water on her face from the sink.

She turned to me, grinning, and said, "That was... *such* a rush! I never thought... *writing* like that could make me... so *hot!*"

I looked at her quizzically, and said, "So the dominatrix had a good time?"

She just nodded up and down, water dripping from her face. "Can... we go talk to your friend, Thaniel? I want to thank him for this inspiration, and to bounce a few ideas off of him. I mean... I *could* just keep going like this... but I may burn up from the pure lust eking out of my fingertips onto those pages... And I'm not sure if I want to make a purely erotic novel, not yet, anyway." she said.

"Sure. It's a little early to be drinking, but hey, it's a Saturday and I'm sure Thaniel will be there." I said.

We walked to the bar, and Nevaeh told me of the erotic adventures of Hanatrix, the half elf/half dragon dominatrix, who slaughtered the boring prince and princess and was going to dominate the kingdom and every man and woman in it. Nevaeh blushed when she told me of the dragon slayer, a rough young vagabond who was set to vanquish Hanatrix and her father, the dragon. Hanatrix and the dragon slayer fought and dueled each other in an epic fight, but then in the middle of battle, where they were wrestling and their clothes had ripped off… they locked lips, and then the details got *really* interesting. Nevaeh stopped before she said too much, and kept what happened next a secret, and said it would be better if I read it myself.

Thaniel wasn't at the bar though.

We asked the bartender if he ever showed up, and the bartender said he was attending an AA meeting. The bartender told us all about it, which Thaniel was complaining about all night the last few nights… drunk to the gills. The bartender said we could catch the AA meeting in the act if we wanted to, and told us where to go.

So, we walked into the community center and found the meeting, open to all.

We saw Thaniel glazing over at the speaker, but he perked up when he saw us and waved us over to him. He had an attractive, older blonde woman sitting beside him, and he introduced her as Darcy.

The meeting wasn't, er, terrible, there was lots of coffee and the people were nice, but I preferred the friendly bar to this, even though I sympathized with the people who told us about their problems. Some seemed strangely hopeful, the others seemed rather depressed, itchy for alcohol.

We got out of the meeting, and Nevaeh asked Thaniel, "Are… you sure you wrote the Bees of Ferdinand?"

Darcy, the older blonde woman Thaniel was seeing, said, "Oh yes, he did. Won my heart when I first read it, but we grew separate, going to different colleges. Being sober isn't a bad thing, just lets you see life clearer."

Thaniel was twitching when she spoke, and said, "Yeah, Darcy… Nothing better! But, this woman… You're Nevaeh, right? And my pal Yule are going to interview me! I'll catch up with you later, Darcy."

Darcy smiled sweetly, kissed Thaniel on the lips, and drove away, waving to him.

Thaniel walked down the street as we followed him, walked into a gas station right before it closed, (it was a long meeting) and bought a forty ounce of beer.

He slumped down in the parking lot, and Nevaeh and I stared at him sitting on the curb, watching him slurp down the bottle.

"Ok, this is more like it. Secret scandal and drunken bees." Nevaeh said.

"You've gotta get me out of this!! Please... *Please help me!*" Thaniel said, clutching my hand.

"Um. It should be good for you... I thought you really had things figured out with alcohol?" I said.

"I-I did... but *Darcy...* I see why we broke up before... She's utterly terrifying!! She used to be *so* gentle... But now if she doesn't get her way... She just gets *this look.*" Thaniel said, letting go of my hand so he could grip the bottle with both hands and drink from it.

"Why don't you just break up with her, Thaniel? I'm sure she'd understand that the spark you were looking to reignite has been extinguished." I said.

"But... If I *did...* H-Her old husband... Disappeared! Poof! They found him murdered in Vegas! *Darcy and him were having a trip!!* A-And... he blew all her m-money..." he stuttered.

"I'm sure that's just a foul rumor. It shouldn't matter." I said, crossing my arms.

"You didn't... spend her money, did you?" Nevaeh said.

"Uh... well, she helped back my newest book... If I cut her loose, I don't know *what* she could... or would... do." Thaniel said, staring down at his bottle.

I sighed, and we sat beside him. He passed us the bottle and we drank with him. I told him to tell her honestly about... well, everything he could about their relationship. Nevaeh told him to skip town and go to Europe for a while.

We stumbled back home, after buying and drinking more bottles of beer, and Nevaeh and Thaniel were stammering about what specifically Darcy paid for and how he could write those off.

I shook my head, said, "Noooo... No, no... Y-You need to be hoooon-est! Iiiif Judas was honest... Then everyone would've been so much happier!"

"Ifff Judas was honest, you wouldn't have a religion to cling to, Yule." Nevaeh said.

"Pigwash. Juuuudas wanted to repent... but felt soooo bad... That's why he killed himself! We gave him chances over and over... but he never couuuuld look Jesus in the eyes after he died..." I said.

"Uhh... You shouuuld probably lay down when we get home, Yule... You sound a little drunk!" Nevaeh stammered.

"People... just need to tell the truth! If... you don't, then I will!" I said.

"You... think you could?? Just this once!" Thaniel said.

Nevaeh said, "Damnit... Thaniel, you need to be a real man! I knoooow you could..." hiccup, "Kinda phase her out... But whatever you do, don't let your drinking buddy break up with her for you!"

"B-But I'm sure Yule can take her! She's young, attractive, has a sorta light in her eyes... No one could fight Darcy like you, Yule!" Thaniel said.

"I vowwww to the Lord that I will help you out of thissss unfortunate arrangement..." I said, hiccupped, shook Thaniel's hand, and the thunder boomed from the growing rain clouds.

It soon started raining, and we rushed home. Thaniel slipped in the snow and rain, but I caught him before he could fall.

He was saying that he could find his way home and that the chilling rain was actually feeling kind of nice on his drunken skin.

Nevaeh and I looked at each other, and brought him inside before he could stumble away, saying that he'd probably catch pneumonia if he wanders around all night in the rain. He thanked us, and lay on the couch dripping wet, and soon passed out. His phone was vibrating over and over in his pocket, probably Darcy, but we let it ring. It would be prudent to not tell his girlfriend that he was drunk and staying at the apartment of two younger women. Let them sort it out in the morning.

16

Thaniel had left before we could wake up, but he left us a little poem of thanks by the coffee machine.

"Yule Tidings, you are as strong as the Vikings, please accept these writings…

Nevaeh Shinto, you are crisp and nouveau, a growing Van Gogh…

You are both great, dress snappy, and I don't want to make this too sappy…

But you could never make this old drunkard more happy.

(Thank you!)"

I made coffee, and drank off the slight hangover. Nevaeh was sleeping in.

I called Max good morning. He had gotten a new job and was put on the graveyard shift, even on a Saturday, but should have just gotten off work this morning.

He wearily answered, but seemed to grow more vigorous the more he talked with me. He said, "I just feel… ten times better when talking to you. I've been having a stressful time of late, this new job and things… My sister turned up missing lately, and it's been worrying me and my mom. Ever since Dad died she was getting more and more angry, different… and then she joined that awful church…"

"It'll be alright, Max. She'll be fine… Nothing bad will happen. You just sleep it off, and I'll come visit later." I said.

"I've been drinking energy drinks all night at work, so you think we can hang out now before I crash?"

"Alright… But you really do seem like you need a good nap. I'll head on over."

I went to Max's apartment and hugged him at the door. He was jittery from all the caffeine and made us some coffee to drink.

The energy drink cans in his apartment had a picture of a demon on it, albeit a cute little one winking at me giving me the thumbs up.

We talked a bit, and he thanked me for coming over. Although… he put his chin in his hand looking at me and trying to keep up the conversation, then slumped down with his head on the table.

"Max? You ok?" I said.

He bolted back up, and said, "Yes! Sorry."

I took him by the hand and we went to the couch. I snuggled up with him, with his head on my chest, and stroked his hair, singing him a song in old German that my parents used to sing for me.

He was soon snoring in my arms. I tucked him in under a blanket, kissed him on the cheek, and read one of his comic books as he rested.

He was an avid comic book collector, but said he didn't really have any super valuable ones, only really buying the ones he thought were interesting. I read one of a sexy looking, barely clothed female gladiator, and I admired her battles in the arena, critiquing it slightly here and there thinking that that move was rather inconvenient in the ring, or thinking that when her chest piece popped off she wouldn't cover herself like in the pictures, but rather go for the villain's throat as he was distracted by her naked breasts. The artist had a rather good way of drawing though, a bit different than classic comic books, and I enjoyed them despite the overly flashy storyline.

Hmm... I wondered if this was one of Max's fantasies? To be with a woman like this comic book character? He hardly had a clue he was living it in reality.

So later in the day after Max had rested up and I had gone to church, curious if I was right about this fantasy, I took him to the movies. We sat in the theater, after getting some popcorn and this one licorice I really liked, and watched the comic book character take up her battles in a live action film.

Ah... that damned Emperor... He looked almost exactly like the Emperor from my past, but acted way more ridiculous. The Emperor I knew was absolutely no one to trifle with, as he commanded armies of crack troops, held dominion across continents, and weighed your life in the palm of his hand, perhaps allowing it to slip away with a downwards thumb...

But I smiled as the main character, the female gladiator, defies him over and over again.

Max was enjoying the movie, with his arm over my shoulder, and during the romance scene I put a hand on the inside of his thigh...

And feeling clever with this, remembering something I saw in that comic book, I said, at the same time as the main character in the movie, "I will take you to Mount Olympus, with a kiss on the lips..."

I kissed him...

And Max clutched at his chest, unable to catch his breath.

He was having a heart attack.

I panicked, and called 911.

They wheeled him out on a stretcher, and I got into the ambulance beside him, him breathing through a mask.

I paced in the waiting room as they worked on him.

They allowed me in, and Max looked like he had been beaten up from the inside.

I asked him what happened. Was he alright??

He said, "It… was nothing… really… just, well this is embarrassing, too much caffeine… I should be better if I lay off the stuff."

I said, "You better. Why did you even start drinking that energy drink?? I had a sip, and it tastes foul!"

"Well, it helped keep me awake during working hours, and it's pretty cheap at the plant… since they make that crap… I hope they don't fire me for this…"

"What?! You're not going anywhere!! You just had a heart attack! Surely they can allow you a few rest days?"

He gave a halfhearted laugh, and said, "I… don't know… You've never met my boss, Saxley…"

"S-Saxley?"

"Everyone calls him Sax, although that's the closest you'll ever get to him actually being 'genuinely' nice…"

I felt the blood drain from my face, and told him firmly that if he doesn't get real rest I… or he, won't be around anymore.

"What? Oh. Ok… Al-Alright…" he said.

I smiled then, and kissed him… very, very carefully.

17

I strode into the factory, ready to tell this Saxley off, because they actually *did* want Max to go back to work. I kept Max in my apartment, not letting him have any coffee or energy drinks and let him rest. I'd chain him down if I had to, to keep him safe.

And this brimstone smelling factory did *not* feel safe.

They made me wait a good while, almost half the day, putting off our meeting for unnamed interruptions, but eventually I walked into one of the boss's offices.

He tried smiling, this big fat man with hair curled over his bald head almost looking like little horns… but the glamour faded fast, and I saw him for what he was.

A big fat demon, taking up half the room and squeezed in at his desk, Sax.

"I thought I told you to go back to Hell." I said.

"And I thought I told you that I was sorry. I'm doing something great for people here, on Earth, making great products with no equal." Sax said.

"And still… you want Max to come back to work after he had a heart attack! You're going to kill him!"

"He signed a contract to work through the month. He has to abide by these terms, or there will be dire consequences… But, I will be lenient, because it's you,

Yule... and I will ignore his absence today, and allow him to take a double shift tomorrow."

"What?! That's not lenient! That's slavery! I demand that you release Max from his contract!"

He grinned, and said, *"But then the poor kid's dreams... I believe he wanted to better his position in life, make something of himself, even do nice things for his girlfriend... How will he achieve that if I let him loose? There would be Hell to pay if he doesn't follow through... no one would hire him, he'd be in dire straits... I'm afraid not even God can get him out of this contract, let alone you, Yule."*

"I preferred when you were little and just watched TV."

He shrugged, and said, *"We all have to grow, change, adapt... It's called living. Should I call security to escort you out? Or will you leave of your own free will? Go back to Heaven, Yule."*

I stood there, furiously looking at his smug, demonic face, and stormed out, scattering the secretary who was listening at the door.

I thought about setting fire to the factory, anything to get rid of this horrible place. I was standing outside smoking a cigarette, staring at it from across the street, as they loaded energy drinks into a truck.

A thin little woman was getting into her car in the parking lot, but noticed me glaring at the building. She walked over to me, frightened, probably scared of my glowering hatred. I didn't care if she was going to tell me to leave, everyone in that building could go to Hell, and see if I cared.

She stammered something, but I turned and looked at her and she saw the look in my eyes. She shut her mouth and walked away again.

But she shook her head to herself, and turned around again to meet me.

"Y-You know Saxley?" she mumbled.

I flicked my burnt out cigarette, forgetting to smoke it and instead focusing on my angry thoughts, and took out another and lit it up. "Maybe. Why?" I said.

"I-I heard… from the door. It sounded like you two h-have a history." she muttered.

"Speak up, damnit."

She was scared of me, that much was obvious… but it looked like something else scared her more, if she approached me like this.

"I-I just wanted to say… We need help. My husband was roped into a contract too, and I joined him here to help him… b-but I can't get out. Please."

"What do you want *me* to do? Call the police or something."

She shook her head, and said, "That'd make it even worse. Th-The way Saxley looks at me… th-the way he talks to me… Th-The way he- I couldn't bear it if my husband's child… knew of what I have done."

I felt my heart skip a beat, as I read into her words. In shock, I said, "I'll help you, but I don't know where to start. I'll help you and I'll help Max."

"Thank you. Thank you so much. I-I go to church, I'm sure you wouldn't like to meet me there… but it's where I can actually feel safe. C-Can you come to the breakfast next Sunday?"

"Sure. I go to church every Sunday, and I was actually looking forward to that."

She looked surprised, but nodded quickly, and walked away to her car, then drove away.

I reluctantly allowed Max to go back to work. He thanked me and said it wouldn't be so bad. I would've made him break the terms of the contract if I hadn't made him dig out the copy in his drawers and look over it.

The fine print... the little bits that mortals couldn't see without looking at *just right*... mentioned that Max's soul was officially now on loan to Sax, Sax's master, their master and masters and etc., etc... All the way down to Satan. I reread it over and over again, trying to find some small, insignificant loophole, some smidgen of hope... but any crack of freedom was closed off by legal clauses. It was iron tight, and the penalties of breaking such a contract were bad enough in the living world.

I even had Nevaeh look at it, because she was good at wielding words, of forging them and reforming them to her purposes. But every time, she said stuff like, "Oh! This here- No... That wouldn't work... Or maybe- Goddamnit..." when she was looking at it. She said that he *could* just work off his contract...

But then he would have to sign another, to keep working, to keep... his soul. The contract was roped into another, just the start of it that didn't name "exactly" what the next one was... but I knew it wouldn't end for an eternity.

I had yelled at Max for signing such an obvious contract with Satan, but he said, "I-I... The pay and hours... It was just too good! I could finally get you that trip to Germany you were talking about! We could have a great time!"

I stopped yelling, realizing that *I* was sort of the cause of this desire the Devil was taking advantage of... and sighed, saying, "It was too good to be true, Max."

I just drank down my sorrows at the bar... alone, since Thaniel was at an AA meeting...

But as I left the bar, still sad and angry, albeit drunk, I saw him staring at it from just outside.

"Thaniel! C'mon, leeeet's get a drink!" I slurred, drunkenly happy to see him.

"I-I can't. The Devil is tempting me tonight, and I don't appreciate you being a part of his schemes, Yule..." Thaniel said, staring past me through the bar door I opened for him.

"The Devil? C'mon... It's me! Yule! You know the Devil is just a stuffed up chicken! Since when were you so religious?"

"I've... found a higher purpose. I need to remain clear headed... and Darcy told me to stay away from you and the bar... but... if you just... maybe... lose a beer by the bushes, I'm sure no one would mind if I found it... Wastefulness is a sin, just so you know..."

I rushed back in, ordered a beer, and walked out with it cheerfully. Thaniel was looking around, trying not to pay me any notice, and I set the beer in the bushes and walked a bit aways. He ambled into the bushes, looking like he was just interested in the shrubbery, licked his lips looking down at the beer and said, "My, oh my... what a waste." and picked up the beer and drank at it.

I said from the side, "Everything is horrible now, Thaniel."

He looked at me sadly, and said, "Tell me about it! Darcy is trying to get me into a marriage contract! God... and that whole wretched company of hers... I wish she just stayed back in the dark, where she belonged... Can't really blame anyone but myself, though. I did call the bitch and arrange the meeting."

"What... What company?" I asked.

"That factory that smells like shit. I thought it would be great if they set up in town, y'know, make tons more jobs available for people... but I didn't realize the cost was the air and my soul..." he said, slurping at his beer in the bushes.

"She literally is working for the Devil then, if she is part of that company."

"Was her husband's who 'disappeared.' I probably can't get you to talk to her for me anymore... but thanks for trying. And well, if you lose anything else, I'll be glad to help you find it again..." he said, finishing his beer and setting the empty mug back in the bushes.

"Hmm... Well, maybe you could help me... find something... just a few souls. I'm sure God is missing them, and they'd like it if you found... just a little bit of hope, friendliness... and excuses." I said.

<h1 style="text-align:center">18</h1>

I met with the woman who reached out to me, having pancakes at the Sunday breakfast. Her husband had to work today, but she brought her baby and she didn't seem so frightened as before, happy to talk to me with a good meal in good company.

I was playing peek-a-boo with the baby, who laughed in delight whenever I showed my face, and the woman, Tanya, said, "I'm so happy you like God too. I wandered away for a long time, but I really needed the hope."

"We all need the hope. I can help give you a little bit extra, if you're willing to stick your neck out a bit. Just tell people about the flu going on. It's not really as bad as the media is hyping it up to be, a reporter told me so who worked on it extensively, often embiggening the details in her news pieces, but if you… just do this one thing…" and I whispered how she could show the symptoms of this disease without actually having it, "They'll take you off work and maybe even replace you. My friend told me about it, when he was trying to escape from his girlfriend."

"That's… a bit immoral, but to free my husband and myself from working there, I will do anything." she said.

"Good. Can you… tell me anything about what happened with Saxley?" I asked.

She avoided my eyes and looked down at her baby. She said, "It started off as extra hours, just a bit here, a bit there... he promised he would give my husband an easier time, too... But- It was late... and- and- no one- no one stopped him. They turned their heads. Looked the other way, as his touches turned more aggressive. And soon... it's too much..."

"It's alright. You don't have to continue talking about it. I could tell someone... Make it public... but I would need you to admit this." I said, looking into her eyes seriously, "I could make sure it never happens again, to you or anyone."

"I thank you for the offer... but... I don't know what I'd say... and my husband's child... never needs to know about how their new sibling was conceived." she said, putting a hand to her belly.

I looked at her in shock. Tears were welling in her eyes.

I said, "Whatever you do, make sure the new one is baptized. Things will get better... You haven't thought of... abortion?"

"I- did, yes. But I could never do that to one of God's new children." she said.

One of God's new children... who was the spawn of Sax.

I thanked her for the company, and told her to remember what I said.

I walked down the street, just a bit confused.

How could God... How could *anyone* let this happen?

The days passed, and like usual, Rasputin watched me as I kneeled in my room for an hour, praying, for everyone like Tanya, for Max, for people who get caught in endless loops that they can't get out of. I asked God to help them.

I had this strange feeling... that really, the responsibility fell to me.

Nevaeh walked in, said, "Oh. Sorry, didn't mean to interrupt." and was about to walk out again.

I said, "It's alright. Was just finished. What's up?"

"I was wondering if you wanted to read my next bit of Hanatrix? It gets reeeally saucy... but in a way I think you'll enjoy."

I didn't really feel like reading anything right now, but I said sure, and thought maybe it'd do me some good.

So I read Nevaeh's new chapter... about a bardess named Evergreen. Hanatrix, after falling to the embrace of the dragon slayer, loses him when they were lustfully groping each other, rolling in passion, ripping off each other's remaining clothes, and he falls off a cliff. Hanatrix is changed from her evil ways, remembering a love that she will never have again, and soon meets a bardess called Evergreen. Evergreen instantly cheers up Hanatrix in most ways, when all Hanatrix thought would make her happy would be domination... and sex.

They go to a male brothel, almost losing themselves to their lust, but are saved by a man named Maximillian who wanders in by accident, and lusting after a man who would not fall to her advances for coin, Evergreen follows him out. Hanatrix follows suit, worn out from endless passion and hoping the two would find a sweet pile of hay for her to lie down in.

Then, Hanatrix realizes, as she is relaxing in the barn with the cows, listening to Evergreen and Maximillian recite to each other riddles and poetry, that she never really had this before, when she thought she had all in the world as the dragon's daughter.

She never had people she could call her friends.

I smiled to Nevaeh, and gave her a hug.

She said, "I thought the name Evergreen might point out too much that she's inspired from you, but then I thought about Max and named his inspiration Maximillian, so I said fuck it."

"I think it's great, Nevaeh. Keep at it."

"Oh, and I picked up the mail earlier and found this weird letter for you. It's over by the kitchen sink, if you haven't noticed."

"I did. Felt like I got an invitation to go to Hell."

"That bad, huh? What'd it say?"

"It was a job offering from the factory, by the CEO, Darcy."

"Yikes. Doesn't she know that you 'gave' nearly a quarter of their workers that flu?" Nevaeh said.

"Probably... but, what was worse... was the invitation to dinner from her with Thaniel."

"Gonna accept?" she asked.

"Only if you come with, Nevaeh, and if you have to, dominate the crap out of her."

She giggled, and said, "But then I'd have to use Hanatrix's famous whip! Hmm... Darcy, eh... I'll just call her the Succubus in my story..."

"Haha... Succubus?" I said.

19

I dressed up for dinner and brought... my shield, to show to Thaniel... and just in case there was a demon around that I didn't notice at first.

Nevaeh was looking rather well dressed, in a black dress with these old Japanese bits of jewelry bejangled all over her. I just wore pants and a blouse, something that would be easy to move around in... just in case.

Max had to work that night.

We knocked on the door, and Thaniel answered, looking very nervous even with a happy go lucky looking tie and dress clothes. "Hey, Yule, Nevaeh. Please, come in. Remember to wipe your feet off on the-Oh, fuck it, she can't hear me from over here-"

But Darcy appeared over his shoulder, smiling sweetly, and said, "Come in, dears." Thaniel seemed like he had his skeleton scared out of him.

We walked in, and I looked down at my shield, all polished and looking like a mirror, reflecting the scene, but Darcy wasn't in it.

She still smiled at me and led us to the table, right in front of me.

Darcy said she just had to get the food, and we all breathed a sigh of relief as she left the room.

"Nice shield, Yule. Looks good on you." Thaniel said.

"Thanks." I said.

Darcy came back in with lots of good looking food... but the pork roast turned me off, with the head of the suckling pig still attached, with a strange sad expression on its face.

"Uh. What? Do we eat its head or something?" Nevaeh said.

"The brain is the good bit." Darcy said. We were silent, but she started laughing and said, "I'm joking! My God you lot are serious... It's just an old family custom. My father showed me how to prepare it right. Don't you remember my father, Nathan?"

Thaniel said, "Uh. Yeah... Real military type. Killed over a score of men in some war..."

"That's right. A national hero. Taught me everything I know." Darcy said, sitting down, chopping me some pork and placing a thin slice on my plate with that sharp knife and pointed prongs on the fork. "No shields at dinner, dear! Please. Put that away." she said.

She looked me in the eyes, and for just a moment, if I looked *just right...* I saw something sinister look back at me.

I didn't want to put the shield down, but I put it on the counter away from the table, just close enough to reach if I jumped for it.

We had a silent dinner, but Darcy asked me if I thought about her proposal. Asking me if I would join the family.

I politely declined, saying having my boyfriend bound in their chains was enough for me.

She looked at me coldly, and said, "Dear. We're just trying to make the most out of life. I invited you here, and even gave you that offer, because I see something truly great in you. I think we can have peace."

I said, "Then release Max from his contract. And Tanya. And all the other people you've enslaved. It's immoral, it's wrong, it's just... hellish."

"People take what is good for them. Especially if that's a good deal." she said.

Thaniel coughed, and said he'd clean up the table...

But Darcy said, "You and Nevaeh sit back and relax. Watch TV while Yule and I talk. Turn it up. Loud. I'll need your help with the dishes, Yule. Cleaning up the filth."

Nevaeh looked me in the eyes, silently asking if I needed help, but I shook my head.

I brought the dishes, and my shield, into the kitchen.

Darcy was sharpening the knives and I asked why.

"Oh, you always need to sharpen whenever you use them, so they're in perfect condition when you next need to use them."

So she sharpened the knives.

Schlick. Schlick. Schlick.

The knives went schlicking on the grindstone.

"Are you even Darcy?" I asked.

She stopped schlicking.

She said, with a knife in her hand as I looked back and forth from her and it, "Who knew an *angel of war* could be fooled for this long... You're rather idiotic, Yule."

"What happened to the real Darcy?"

"She fell so far... so fast... and nothing could stop her. She simply got another chance one day... and I came to Earth." she said. I looked into her eyes. They were cold and dead, just like that pig's. "She fell... and Darcy's husband died... He stole all her money, fucked around for fun, and had a wealth of a company, free for the taking... If you ask me he *deserved* death..."

"So you took her place, after you killed him."

"I *did* kill him... and I ate his soul, too... I always hated him, and tasting the pure, evanescent nectar of his being was bliss... I always hated him... *because I am the real Darcy.*"

Then her demonic form revealed, a monster, a creature of evil, a succubus. The end result of Darcy's evil life.

She stabbed at me quicker and stronger than lightning.

But I raised my shield in defense in an old instinct, and she stabbed into it.

And it shattered, cracking into pieces and making a loud breaking sound.

"What the fuck are you doing?!" Nevaeh said from the frantically opened kitchen door with Thaniel peeking over her shoulder, "Stay the *hell* away from my friend!"

Darcy had turned back into a human, and looked like she didn't really know what to say.

"We saw on the news. That one woman you talked to, Yule, she just stood up, said she finally found the words that she wanted to say, and just revealed all the *fucking rapists* in Darcy's company… That fucker Saxley is going to jail, and the company is being sued." Nevaeh said.

"No one will believe her." Darcy said.

"I'll believe her. I'll believe Yule too, if she says you just tried to fucking kill her." Nevaeh said.

Thaniel had his eyes opened wide, looked at the knife in Darcy's hand and the broken shield, and suddenly… became furious.

He said, cold, sharp, and angry, "Get out of my house, Darcy. And don't come back."

"But Nathan-" she said.

"Just get out." Thaniel said.

Darcy quickly left, and took the bus… hopefully back to Hell.

Thaniel just hugged us each, and said he never could've done that normally… but seeing that she just up and smashed my shield like that, like she owned me too, really pissed him off.

"Toldja it was a fake." Nevaeh said, as we walked home.

"It served its purpose… I sure am going to miss it…" I said, knowing that the only reason my shield broke was because a truly evil soul had pierced it. Still, it saved my life, in its last act of life.

The whole, evil company of Darcy's had been shut down, as it was a festering pool of corruption. After Tanya came forward, dozens of other people did too, revealing sexual harassment, bullying, unsafe work environments… and all of the workers' contracts were broken, actually found to be illegal in some states.

Sax was taken to court… but had a real devil of a lawyer looking out for him. No one could tell, as he smoothly defended his client… but Satan is probably the best lawyer of them all. Sax was let free.

But I saw him on the corner one time, begging for change. I dropped a nickel into his cup. He was all thin and ragged, looking like he hadn't been getting much souls to feed on. He thanked me for the change, stared at me long, but didn't follow me this time.

I took a picture with Mr. Nestor's camera, of Max sitting on a bench with the sunshine on him, a free man again.

"Was that a good pose? Any more?" he asked.

"One more, and try not to overdo it." I said.

I sat beside him with the camera, we wrapped our arms around each other, and I clicked the camera at us as we kissed.

"I'm so glad that I'm still alive. I didn't want to tell you… but I was scared for my life when I had a heart attack." Max said, as we walked back home, holding hands.

"I'm glad you're alive too. Your soul deserves to walk around for quite a bit longer, happy and free."

"Yeah. I feel much lighter on my feet not working for that factory anymore. The only contract I'm signing from now on is if I give my soul to you, Yule."

"Nah. No contracts. I will give myself to you as you give yourself to me, freely, no strings attached."

"Ok. I have something else I want to give you, besides all my love for all you've done, for me and everyone, and for just being you, Yule. Here, look at this." he said, reached around in his pocket, and took out a small envelope.

I opened it, and inside were three tickets to Germany.

"The last one's for Nevaeh, since I *guess* it'd be nice to take her with. You both deserve a bit of a break from everything." Max said.

I kissed him a bunch all over his face, and said, "I can't wait, Max. Oooh… I can't wait to drink all those beers and eat every bratwurst!"

He smiled, and said, "I am so happy to see that look on your face again."

"What look?"

"Just… like you've risen up to Heaven. Happy."

I blushed, seeing him looking at me like that… just happy that I was happy.

Part 3: Caritas

Charity

20

Max and I were dancing in the bar to Irish music on St. Patty's day, holding hands and doing a little jig. Thaniel cheered whenever we swung around in a circle, and Nevaeh was petting Freckles and chatting with Mrs. Nestor. Mason and his parents were eating burgers and watching us, with Mason smiling in joy when I winked to him after the dance was done. I stuck up for Tanya, since some people had mixed feelings on her and the revolution she started, and she was now a server here and talking with her husband while he held their baby on her break. I saw May and the dishboy laughing drunkenly and flirting slightly, and talked with them a bit about the Italian restaurant. She said they had closed down briefly for Mrs. Antonelli's funeral, but that Mike and Mr. Antonelli send their greetings to me.

We ordered more beer! We drank and laughed, having so much fun. The trip was just around the corner, and I couldn't wait to spend it with my friends. The bar was as warm and friendly as ever, on St. Patrick's day.

Although, I do wish that bum, Sax, would pick a better corner to scrounge for change on.

He sat just out of the bar's reach, and I chased him away a few times, but gave up as he kept returning, again and again. I even called the police on him a few times, saying he was harassing Tanya, but whenever they showed up to take him in... he seemed to vanish, in an alley, up a fire escape, down a manhole...

No one saw him for what he really was, a skinny, starving demon. I was glad for his suffering on Earth, for the suffering he caused other people on it. I yelled at him this very thing, chasing him away again, but he said it was still better than Hell.

I went out for a smoke, just enjoying the solitude for a second, but someone sidled beside me. I didn't look at the source of the shadow that had covered me, smoking my cigarette, and said, "Go away, Sax..."

But the form chuckled, and whispered in my ear...

Saying, in his satanic voice... that he hopes I enjoy the trip.

I swung my sword at him, my angelic sword that materialized in my hand, but he stepped away, in darkness, shadows, and I followed the darkness to end it.

Satan needed to die.

I tried to materialize my shield, but I knew it was gone for good. All I had was my sword from Heaven.

I charged around a corner, and saw him watching Sax digging in a dumpster.

Sax immediately noticed him, and begged, groveled, for Satan to give him another chance... that he could really bring in ten times more souls, if he just had faith in him...

Satan whispered, *"I've given you so much... I've given you your dream... To be alive again. And you squandered it, wasted it, lost the chance at life... All the people you've hurt... tut, tut, tut. I never asked you to do that..."*

Sax whimpered, *"I know that's what you wanted, though! I know that would please you!"*

Satan laughed, that evil, horrible, menacing laugh, and hissed out, *"I only wanted one thing from you... for you to suffer. And I think I've gotten that... I gave you life again, out of Hell, and look at you... It really pleases my heart, seeing you brought lower than the lowest pits of Hell."*

Sax said, *"Wait... What?"*

"You thought Hell was the worst place? Nooo... It is being alive. Betraying everything you loved, everyone who ever believed in you, showed you mercy... even yourself. Enjoy your little slice of paradise... for it will haunt you for the rest of your eternity down below." Satan whispered.

Satan looked directly at me, and told me to remember his words too.

Then I blinked, and he was gone.

Sax just sat down from his groveling position, and just stared at where Satan was, dumbfounded.

"You got what you deserved, Sax." I said, and walked away.

He said, as I was going back to the bar, *"Kill me, Yule."*

I turned back at him, he was crying tears of sorrow, silently, tears that would keep falling for the rest of his life.

I said, "I offered you mercy before, take it again with gratitude. Live out your days as scum, repent, and maybe God will smile on you, for I will not."

I walked back to the bar, leaving him to moan in agony, from the pain he had inflicted on others.

21

Nevaeh had a big backpack over her shoulders, as I did as well. "Makes me nervous," she said, "Going out of the country... Never went to Europe before, although I nearly did for a foreign exchange program. What's it like?"

"I'm not really certain these days..." I said.

"Huh? The booze that good you forgot about it already?"

"Uh. Not that... It's just I haven't been there since I was a kid. I moved when I was young."

"Y'know, vague answers like that just make me more curious. I guess we have time to talk." she said, then crouched down and pet Rasputin in his cat carrier, poking a finger through the gate. He mewled up at her. "This little guy gonna be alright with Thaniel?"

I nodded, smiling, and said, "He says he'll like having another living thing in his house, since his family all moved out."

"Yeah, living thing... Darcy doesn't count as one of those. Heartless bitch." Nevaeh said, "I'm glad that they found her like that... all wonked out on all those drugs and walking naked in the street. Serves her right for all the hell she put everyone through."

"Yeah... I'm sure the sanitarium will put her straight... They said she lost her mind after she took all those drugs... Telling everyone she was a demon from Hell..."

"At least Thaniel is staying away from her... I'm sure he feels bad for her, but there's nothing he can do for her anymore." Nevaeh said, "Well. I see your favorite sex machine out front. Let's go."

I blushed as I followed her out, and said, "Haha... Max is at least ten times cuter than a machine for sex..."

"It was a compliment, Yule. I hear that bed of yours squeaking nearly every night! I'm glad for you."

"Oh! Damnit... I guess I gotta soundproof my room a bit better..."

She laughed, and said, "Nah, it's kinda hot actually. Although the first time I heard your loud moaning I thought a ghost had gotten in the apartment... OoooOOOoooo!!" and laughed some more.

I hit her on the arm, and we got into Max's car. Max and I pecked each other on the lips and I put Rasputin in the cat carrier on my lap.

I dropped Rasputin off at Thaniel's. He said he'd treat the little cat the best in the world. I thanked him and gave him a hug goodbye.

We soon got onto the highway, jamming to this great rock from the radio, ready for a great adventure.

We nearly got to the airport, got off the highway, and right after we got off, the car engine stalled. Max swore, and we parked off by the side... right in front of the Castrator who was waiting for us.

Max worked on the car, and I smoked outside of it next to the Castrator while Nevaeh read a magazine with her legs sticking out of the window.

"So how are you doing, these days? Figure out how you died yet?" I asked the Castrator.

"No. I get vague recollections of screaming peasants, but other than that it is my one mystery in death."

"Know anything about cars? I have no bloody clue what the heck Max is doing."

"I believe he's checking the oil right now. A good precaution to take if you can. Sorry, I only have watched a few mechanics work on automobiles. It's quite boring being dead with no challengers."

"So that's why you were drawn to me, eh?"

"I wished for some glory like in the old days... but I suppose there is no reason to fight and kill someone who is already dead."

"I'd kill all of these demons in the world, but I'm happy to know that they screw up their lives mostly by themselves. They get their come-uppance just with their wicked deeds, and usually get a fate worse than death." I said, blowing out some smoke.

"They did not reach their justice on their own. In every part of their villainy, you helped curb their corruption."

"Yeah, I guess. Max looks pretty happy, I guess he solved the problem. I'll see you later... Castrator? Is that really what I should call you?"

"When I was still a boy, before I was castrated, a friend of mine called me Felix."

"When was this? Before the Romans enslaved your people?"

"I was born a slave. I never knew freedom but the one I won for my-self after mutilating and killing every man who fought against me."

"Er... Ok. Well, see ya, Felix."

"Goodbye, Angel of the Pits."

I got into the car, and the wind seemed to blow him away as he disappeared.

Thaniel called me as we were waiting in the airport, basically crying. I asked him what's up.

He said, "Y-Your cat... I-I'm so sorry!! He got out, and before I realized it... I was al-already on my way to the store in my c-car..."

"Huh?" I said.

"H-He... I ran him over..." he said.

"Oh..." I said, getting a bit depressed. This did not seem like a good omen for the start of the trip.

"I-I'll make it up to you, in any way I can. I- Wait... The fuck??" Thaniel said, as I heard Rasputin mewling at him through the phone.

"Keep extra good care of him from now on, ok?" I said.

"...Ok. Er. H-Have a good trip!" Thaniel said. I told him goodbye and hung up.

Damn cat. If he keeps dying he'll use up all his lives in no time.

Nevaeh and Max were actually talking pretty friendly to each other. She joked about his height, saying he was taller than the giants, and Max laughed and said, "As cutting as ever, Nevaeh. I know you're just trying to be nice, but it's alright. I forgive you."

"What? I was trying to give you a compliment! I mean it! The birds probably hit your forehead as you stride through the clouds!" Nevaeh said.

Max laughed, and said, "We both know that's not true. I appreciate the effort, though."

"Hmph. People seemed to like me better when I was nasty with everyone. Or maybe they just feared me... Yule didn't, though." Nevaeh said.

Max said, "You're definitely *much, much* better trying to show your 'heavenly' side. I could see a happy future for you as a therapist one day."

"Pft. Everyone knows that someone who tried to kill herself is probably not the best person to talk others out of such an act." Nevaeh said.

I said, "I think you have an experience you've lived through, and probably can offer other people solace if they too feel those creeping feelings of depression. How's the medication?"

"It's alright. I don't really feel as happy as I'd like... but I do feel just a little bit more content. I've tried other stuff before, but the side effects and crap were just awful. One... One even made it so I couldn't orgasm! It's nice this one just hit a homerun the first time around." she said.

I nodded, and we waited some more. I watched as Nevaeh drew me a picture of what she thinks her medication could look like as a human being, and he was a handsome guy, with big muscles to push back the thoughts of death.

We ate our sandwiches from home, ignoring the expensive airport food, and after a good while of waiting, we got into our plane, ready for liftoff. Max had said he hated flying, but that it was a necessary evil.

The turbulence made us rumble, as the three of us sat in seats by the window side, with me looking out on the Earth passing away, up into the cheerful clouds.

I wondered if I'd see demons up here, so close to Heaven. Perhaps gremlins on the side of the wings?

Max threw up in a bag from liftoff, and then I held his hand and told him it'd be alright.

We continued on through the air, talking, reading, and getting excited for our plans.

"Blech. These throwup bags are the worst smell on Earth." Max said, as he had thrown up again in the flight. It was nighttime, and Nevaeh was trying to sleep in an uncomfortable position in her seat, fidgeting this way and that, then gave up and tried to read a book.

One of the flight attendants saw me, and said to me, "We have an extra seat available in first class. You look a little uncomfortable. Would you care to change seats?"

"Oh, no, it's alright. I'd prefer to sit with my friends." I said.

He paused, looked at me quizzically, and said, "Your seat was picked out special… A lucky number, we rarely ever do this…"

"Go on, Yule. There's only a few hours left in the flight. Enjoy yourself." Max said.

"Can't Nevaeh go? She could use a little more legroom." I said.

"…I believe it has something to do with your specific ticket." the attendant said.

"Take advantage of whatever special shit they throw at you, Yule. As long as it's not got some hidden fee." Nevaeh said.

"...Alright. I'll go to first class." I said, and shimmied out of my seat to follow the attendant.

The attendant showed me to empty seat number 66, just for me. Very close to 666... close to the number of the Beast, and close to the demon in the spacious seat next to me.

He didn't even try to use a glamour, like Darcy, and was muscular and looked like Earthen life had suited him, unlike Sax. When people talked to him they blinked for a second, had a brief smell of brimstone, and then fulfilled his commands. His head looked like that of a large bull.

"Hello. Molech, at your service. MISTER Molech. Can I offer you some champagne?" the demon said.

"Uh. No, no thanks. Should we do this now, or later? Me smiting you?" I said.

He laughed, a strangely charming laugh for a demon, and said, *"I think we can just enjoy the flight for now. It was wonderful that you got this special seat. I was getting lonely without an attractive female companion to talk to."*

"Did you rig this seat to get me here? To kill me or offer me some horrible deal?" I asked.

"Of course not! I am a firm believer that random chance can smile on you every once in a while. Happened to myself, when I won the lottery."

"And now you're binging and causing all sorts of suffering with that money, I imagine."

"Actually... No. I'm quite generous towards charities. The children's hospital I donated to has already made a plaque for me, that they are practically worshipping..." he said, drinking his champagne.

"Ch-Children's hospital?"

"Oh, I know... I was a pagan god of child sacrifice... but I know what you're thinking, and I'm not going to run around killing babies. Let my followers do that for me themselves..."

He grinned his bull grin, and I tried to ignore him for the rest of the flight.

22

We got off of the airplane and picked up our bags. I kept noticing Molech, and he didn't pay me much attention after I snubbed his offer to show me around Germany for a while. I tried to ignore him, but it was impossible not to notice a large minotaur looking demon walking around. That demon should be fearing me! He should know that I would smite him down without a second thought! Instead he tries to be a gentleman and offers me things!! I told my frustrations to Max about Molech, saying I just really didn't like that guy, no matter what act he was putting up, and instead of sympathizing with me... Max got a little frightened.

"That guy offered to show you around Germany? That guy who is getting in that limo? Wh-Why did you refuse?" Max said.

"What? I told you! He smells like brimstone, has the head of a bull, and is definitely up to something demonic..." I said.

Nevaeh said, "I think Max is a little worried someone just tried to steal his best gal away, Yule..."

Max exclaimed, "As if! Me and Yule... We got something special! ...We do, right? You're not going to sneak away with that guy... later?"

I glared at Max coldly.

"W-Well don't let that encounter spoil our trip! W-We're gonna have some real fun! Yeah..." Max said. I walked out of the doors of the airport.

Although I was frustrated that Max would think something... so *petty...* I got over it, as we walked down the streets of Düsseldorf, with its fantastic old buildings and people speaking my native language wherever you looked.

We drank these delicious big beers at a bar, and got into a conversation with some natives who pegged us as Americans, but I spoke in German to them, and they couldn't stop themselves from smiling in delight at my accent. They said I must've come out of an old fairytale or something. They offered to show us some of the best places in the city, the thin German man and his girlfriend.

We accepted, and after dropping our bags off at the friendly hostel, we went with them exploring the city in the night.

We walked down the Rhine, throwing stones into it, had dinner where I had my bratwursts I wanted, and stumbled along. Max and Nevaeh were smiling in glee, and I was happy I could show them my homeland, even if technically nothing was as I remembered it.

The German man said in his fractured English to us, so the others could understand, "It is great in Germany, no? If you wish to see something special... *wunderbar...* We can take you to the Blutfest. I warn you, you must be cool."

"Ja!" his girlfriend said, "Der Stier nimmt es mit dem Engel auf!"

I asked her what she meant, if what she said was what I was thinking.

"They are gladiators. Es ist blutig, and very, very cool." she said.

I translated to Max and Nevaeh, and they wowed and Max said, "An underground fighting ring?? That sounds... fucking sweet!"

Nevaeh said, "Shit! I didn't know they did stuff like this in Germany! Can we go?"

I said, "I guess..." hoping they would decline, and we followed the couple into the underground fighting pit.

We stood in the crowded stands, in this literally underground boxing arena. A man was sitting on a stool in the ring, with blue boxing gloves on, a tall, handsome blonde man... with a Nazi tattoo on his shoulder. He was the Engel, or Angel in English. He looked rather nervous. The crowd was cheering and roaring, and then started up a chant. "Stier! Stier! Stier!" they cried, over and over again, and the Bull entered the ring, waving his red boxing gloves in the air...

Molech.

I still wondered how no one saw what I saw... a demon with the head of a bull. The Angel stood up, and Molech and him bounced gloves off each other's, and the fight began.

The Angel was fast, that much was clear, but Molech blocked and dodged every swing, using amazing footwork for someone so large. A jab here! A swing there! But the Angel looked like he was getting tired.

But the Angel did something unexpected, and did a roundhouse kick at Molech, whacking Molech on the nose and making him bleed. The crowd booed.

Molech snorted, and grinned, wiping the blood from his bull snout. Then Molech pummeled and pummeled the Angel, smashing him to pieces with his fists. There was *no way* the Angel could stop his furious blows, and the more he got hit, the more he let down his guard, and the more he suffered. I was starting to feel bad for this blonde man who unfortunately was tattooed with a symbol of the Nazis.

And Molech kept beating him.

The Angel collapsed, and Molech put his foot on the Angel's face, pushing him down farther into the earth. Molech raised his foot, and it looked like he was going to smash his face, crush his skull, and kill him.

But Molech stepped away, and raised his arms in victory to the roaring crowd.

They dragged the Angel away, and Molech looked at me with a glint in his eyes, seeming to say...

That this is what will happen to me if I ever crossed him.

And he smashed his foot to the earth, stomping the ground.

Arranging how I would die.

I glared back at him, and I turned away.

Max saw me looking at Molech, and asked me if I was alright.

I walked up the stairs as Max and Nevaeh followed. Max asked me again.

We got out to the street, and Max asked me one more time.

I turned to him, yelled, *"I told you already! I don't like that guy!!"*

Max said, "...That much is obvious. I don't think you're going to run off with some stranger... I just worry a little that I don't have everything I should to treat you like you deserve. I only ask... because it looked like he was threatening you."

The anger passed almost immediately, and my furious expression left.

I sat on the curb and started to cry.

Max comforted me the whole walk back to the hostel, saying, "If that Molech ever does mess with you, you know I won't stand for it. No matter how... terrifying he might be."

Nevaeh said, "He sure did look cool though, beating up that Nazi. Why would he target Yule like that? Maybe he was just amped up from the fight?"

"He... just isn't a good person. Or even a person. You can tell by the bull head." I said.

Nevaeh snorted, and said, "You shouldn't judge people by how they look, Yule... I thought you would know that better than anyone, being an albino and all."

"Oh… I guess… I've just heard about him from the past… all those poor babies…" I said.

Max said, "Wh-What? What about babies?"

"Nothing. It's nothing. Let's just say hi to the rest of the hostel, shall we?" I said, and we went into the hostel.

A man whose name didn't come up and a woman named Lucy were offering beers to everyone. We accepted them and talked a bit. The man was rather mysterious, but they were both Americans. Lucy told my fortune with Tarot cards, and said I had a rather big conflict with the Devil.

"Yeah… he's a real bastard…" I said.

She said, "Well, it is not always the actual Devil. It means a desire for the material world and it's pleasures."

"L-Like if someone was dead… they wanted to be alive again? To walk the Earth?" I said.

Lucy shrugged, and said, "Maybe. I suggest you try to find the root of this desire, and do not become enslaved to it. Set your spirit free, like an angel on the wing."

"Thank you, Lucy." I said. The man and Max were gambling, playing dice poker which the man taught him how to do. They just gambled in sips of their beer, a drinking game. Max was slurring in no time.

Max hugged me goodnight, really drunk, and said, "Iiii think I loooove you… Yule… You're sweet, pretty, nice, friendly, aweeeeesoooome… and can really kick ass in the saaaack…"

I patted him on the back, and said, "Love you too, bud. Sweet dreams." and he nodded, smiling, and fell asleep in his bunk.

Nevaeh noticed and said, "Ooooh… Yule and Max sitting in a tree… K, I, S,S, I, N, G… in *looooveeee…*"

"Stop it. I hope he doesn't remember that. It would be a shame if the first time we said it properly to each other was when he was drunk and almost falling over in my arms." I said.

She shrugged, and said, "Probably wasn't properly then. You'll get another chance."

I slept in my bunk, still remembering Molech nearly killing the Angel…

I… had an odd dream. The mysterious man was beckoning me out of the door of the hostel.

I followed, wondering where we were going. I wondered if perhaps he was a demon? A spirit?

But he looked me in the eyes, and I thought I saw myself in them.

We walked down the street, as I asked him where we were going.

He said shouldn't I know?

I said I didn't have a clue.

It is your home, you know. His words seemed to appear in my head, seemed to be there, before and after he said them.

But I'm lost here. It is nothing as I remembered it… It's changed. Even monsters are stalking through my once homeland… And my own words materialized as well.

Who are you?

Who am I?

The world seemed to change… I felt like I was all of it, everything, connected together. Honestly it felt a little bit like Heaven.

But I felt a little more alive.

I heard Nevaeh's typewriter clacking out letters, and I then knew that this was a dream. I wondered how a dream could feel so real.

The man laughed, and said, "The reality of a dream is up to you." He then walked down an alley.

I woke up in the morning. I wanted to talk to this mysterious man some more, to actually know his name, but he and Lucy had left the hostel.

I had coffee and breakfast talking to a funny Algerian man who learned English in Dublin. He was actually an English teacher now, and had a thick Scottish accent. I bid him a good day as he left to tutor someone.

I had a cigarette outside, and I saw that path that I walked down in the dream. It was just sitting there, out in the open, with that alley the man left down in the dream...

I decided to have a little look.

I nearly walked past the alley instead, because it looked rather dark... like something would jump out at me from there. Like Molech waiting in ambush, ready to do me in.

But I calmed my breathing, and told myself that I shouldn't be afraid of demons. I was an angel of war, and it was my duty to fight them.

I crept down the alley carefully, as the wind seemed to rush out of it. It seemed to get darker and darker...

Until I was in utter blackness.

I started to panic, the way back out was darkness and shadow.

I tried running, but I hit a wall, and wherever I ran there seemed to be another hidden wall in front of me. The darkness was darker than any aid Heaven could give me, it felt like it was pressing down on my soul, shrouding me from my true self.

Then I saw a light in the dark, glistening far away, little shining rays of light beckoning me closer, and I walked carefully to it.

I saw a little, pure white flame in front of me, no tinder, no fuel, but still burning with brilliance. It looked like the remnants of my halo, after it had flown away from me when I fell.

I kneeled down before it, and as it shone back at me, as it seemed to move back and forth to the motion of my breathing… I realized that these pieces of my halo, this flame, was me.

My soul, my life, my essence, here down on Earth, where my body was.

I put my hand out to it, touched it, and then cupped it in my hand and picked it up. It felt hot, but did not burn me.

Then it burst into a blaze, engulfing me, wreathing me in the flames.

I thought that I would burn to a crisp… but I did not.

Instead I was consumed in light. Pure, holy, magnificent light. It shone all around me, on my head, from my eyes, bursting all around me and from behind the covering of my skin.

I thought it would overwhelm me, but instead I felt a magnificent feeling of strength, of my own will, and I used my will to calm it to a simmer in my hand.

I held the flame, and walked out of the darkness, out of the alley and back into the light.

My old halo shined bright, now a brilliant white flame in my hand.

I can't believe I hated it for all that time in Heaven.

For it was only me.

23

I hid the flame back inside me, where it would be safe, and walked back into the hostel where I found Max and Nevaeh asking around for me. "Oh! There you are, Yule. We gotta catch the train!" Max said.

We got to the train station, and we were in for a treat, as the train went just along the Rhine. We boarded as other people disembarked, and sat in our seats. Soon, the train rushed past the river… It was like I could put my hand out the window and touch the water going past me, if I wanted to.

We travelled some more, and got to a little village by the Black Forest. I definitely wanted to do this part, as my tribe was inside that dense forest before. The forest was definitely smaller than as it was in my childhood, but I learned that the Germans were good at reforesting, whenever they deforested they would replant again. They had to take care of their small country, not even a quarter of the United States.

Soon we were walking down a path in the Black Forest national park. I hoped we would see wolves and bears like I used to see, our rival predators hunting for game, and I told Max and Nevaeh this.

Nevaeh said, "I mean, I *guess…* Wolves are on the decline now in Europe as I've read, even though they're trying to bring them back, but bears… they haven't been seen in Germany for a long time. How old are you, anyway?"

"Uh… Just turned 21 awhile ago…" I said.

"Really? Damn, I'm an old bitch… I'm 24. I thought you must've been older than me, with those badass tattoos and things." Nevaeh said, "Strange, how I never really thought to ask. Just kinda slipped my mind I guess. And are you secretly a senior, Max?"

Max laughed, and said, "I'm around Yule's age, with a few months difference. Yeah, those tattoos really make you look like some sort of punk rocker or something. And that star tattoo on your face is just the start!"

"I mean, she's got those star sleeves too… Don't tell me there's *more?*" Nevaeh said.

"Ahem. I'm standing right here, guys." I said, crossing my arms as we got to where I wanted to go, "I can show them to you, Nevaeh. I kind of want to do what I did in the wild days… The old ages before my tribe was taken over by Rome…" They thought I was making a joke or something, and waited for the punchline, but as I stared into their eyes seriously, they saw the days of old Germany look back at them.

I thought I heard the drums beat the rhythm.

I had wanted to do this for a while. I wanted to reveal to my friends my heritage. I had been planning this for so long… and what better place than here? That stone that looked like my grandfather's head pointed out that this was the exact spot where my tribe lived… We were standing right where my family called their home.

The drums beat faster, readying my part in the ritual.

I disrobed, revealing the tribal star tattoos, starting from the star tattoo on my cheek, down my arms, down my body, around my breasts and going down the sides of my belly, down my legs to my feet. I then danced the ritualistic dance of my people, my last dance before I was taken away.

The tribe sang, as my father and mother gave me to the tribe, and they accepted me as their own.

I could practically hear the music all around me, filling me up and narrating my actions. The dance, like my past life, was soon ended, too soon.

The drums stopped.

I bowed to Nevaeh and Max, who were sitting on a log and watching. They clapped as I put back on my shirt and pants.

"Never seen anything like that... But I know just by watching you didn't make it up... What did it mean?" Nevaeh asked.

"It was a dance of a child growing to adulthood. There is little record of it these days." I said.

Max said, "What do you mean... by what you said with the Romans? Are you just trying to roleplay?"

I smiled, and said, "For once, I'm not. It is very hard to explain... and you don't have to believe me. I was just born in the days of old, old Germany... when we were only tribes. Oh... you think I'm crazy..."

"Hm... I don't think you're crazy or anything... I mean, sure, maybe with reincarnation or something... I don't really mind if you say... I mean, are, from ages past... Everyone's got their quirks." Max said.

Nevaeh said, "I think we need to have a longer talk later, Yule. But let's keep walking for now. It sounds harmless, but I just don't want you getting caught up in your head, ok?"

I smiled and said ok, and we continued the walk, leaving my village that was already gone before I came back to it.

I felt so depressed. You'd think it would be easier to come back to life and tell your friends you are centuries old, wouldn't you...

We had later bought a tent and camped for the night in the park. Max hugged me by the fire, and cutely told me not to run off naked in the woods and hunt all the wolves....

I laughed, and said, "Oh, quit trying to make me laugh. I can tell you stories of the past… that I made up. I made it all up…"

Max got a little sad, and said, "I… didn't want to ruin your fantasy… I mean, that dance was honestly the coolest thing I've ever seen. We all have dreams we cling to, some may be tangible, some not. But… Yes, please tell me about your past."

"The reality of a dream is up to you. Strangely, someone told me that in a dream." I said.

Nevaeh took off a marshmallow from her stick and made a s'more. "Mmm mm… Yummy German chocolate… So, Yule… Were you always a badass barbarian? I guess I have to change the character I made for you in my story from being a bardess…"

"I never liked that term… barbarian. It's almost synonymous with savage. Just because people speak and act differently than you does not make them lesser, does not mean that they should be ridiculed, imprisoned, or enslaved… Just means we're different." I said.

Nevaeh said, "I suppose you must get that a lot, with your skin condition… But yeah, some people think I'm some prissy Japanese princess, but I was born in the U.S., and I hate anime."

Max said, "We never really do talk like this. I guess we've been putting it off."

"I had to stay quiet… but it grates away at you… hiding details of your life… If I told you all the truth, you'd lock me up with Darcy and I'd never see the sunlight again…" I said.

Max held my hand, and said, "As long as you know where reality begins and ends… Even if you wish to be from old Germany, I don't think you're crazy. You've shown me parts of life that never seemed possible before, even in myself. You showed me courage, hope, given me some sort of belief that things will be better. Heck, I thought people who went to church were crazy for the longest time…"

Nevaeh said, "Yule is a bit odd, yeah, but not crazy. I think there are totally normal, crazy people out there... Even ones who go to church. That's why I was raped in that church. I mean, he seemed normal, good... but just thinking... just acting on that thought... showed how messed up he really was..."

Max and I were quiet for a second, as Nevaeh stared into the flames.

Max suddenly seemed to get angry, and said, "It didn't... happen recently? You never told me about this."

"I didn't want to. Some men get a little huffy, when I tell them... Like you're starting to right now. I told Yule though, but she never encroached upon my boundaries by prying." Nevaeh said.

"I thought you'd open up when you felt you could. You've already been through so much... I didn't want to bring on old hurts with what you went through." I said.

Max said, "I'll... I mean I wish... I could kill him or something. Or take it away. I wish you never felt-"

"Stop, Max. Please stop. I know you're trying to care, but I've heard all that before from so many people... It just gets kind of old when you can't do anything about it. Dude's in prison anyway, when I finally told my parents. I felt embarrassed, ashamed, like it was somehow my fault... that I led him on... or that maybe, somehow, I even deserved it." Nevaeh said.

"It wasn't some piece of shit priest, was it?" Max asked.

"Just someone who knew me, and took advantage of me when I went to pray." Nevaeh said, "But weren't we talking about Yule's past? How did you lose *your* virginity, Yule?"

"In a ritual, actually. We were set to be bound for life, but the next day I was enslaved. They killed him, and my parents, and my tribe. I ran with my dog and they caught me and killed my dog too. Everything died... and I was going to end up as a sex slave... but I killed him. And the next, and the next... until they thought, 'Hey! Let's make a sport out of this! Let's put her in a horrible bloody pit and watch her kill people for fun!' I can tell you, before I got a reputation, men in the arena thought I was their sweet reward for a battle well fought... so I killed them." I said.

"...I don't know if you're telling the truth, or just making up a story to make me feel better... But I sure wish I could've killed him, too." Nevaeh said.

I sighed, and said, "It's better you didn't. I only fought to survive... to keep some essence of myself still fighting. I thought I was doing just that... but in the end I realized that's what they wanted me to do when I fought. I was glad I could live a somewhat peaceful life without it... just for a little bit."

"Well, this little bit is gonna last a long time, if you ask me." Max said, "Fuck all the pain and suffering of the past... It's getting late. We have to go enjoy our future tomorrow! I'm going to bed." and walked to the tent, but turned back, and said to Nevaeh, "If you feel comfortable with it... I want to let you know everything will be ok, Nevaeh, and give you just a friendly handshake."

Nevaeh laughed, and said, "Oh, just give me a hug, you dweeb." They hugged, and Max smiled to her, and went to the tent.

"He better not be thinking he can get twice the action with two girls in one tent..." Nevaeh said.

I laughed, and said, "I'll sleep in the middle then. Goodnight, Nevaeh. Are you coming to bed?"

"Nah. Just gonna stare at the flames for a bit. It's kinda nice tonight. I'll be in in a minute." she said.

"If you ever don't feel safe, call me, and I will drive all the evil back. Believe that." I said.

"I will. And I do." she said.

24

We went to a few other towns, went to a few art museums and such, and as the three of us were wandering around the gallery of an art museum, I bumped into a tall handsome blonde man, beaten black and blue, who was staring at an art piece.

He looked at me, and said, "Es ist schön."

I looked at the picture, and said, "Ja ist es. Ich mag dieses Bild ... die Farben, das Thema, wie ein altes mittelalterliches Stück."

He said, "Das Bild ist nichts im Vergleich zu der Schönheit des Stückes vor mir. You are very pretty."

I blushed, and said in English, "You look pretty bad, Angel. Good you're still alive."

He offered a hand, and said, "Moritz. You saw that fight? I thought I would notice someone like you."

I shook it and said, "Yule. I did... I suppose it was hard to focus on anything but the foe before you."

"I fear that man. When I look at him... I sometimes feel as if I am looking at a rabid bull, gnashing its teeth and threatening its horns at me."

"That's exactly how I feel! I'm glad you can actually see it too."

He tried to smile from his bruised face, but lost the smile and said, "He will take Germany to Hell, if he continues his whoredom in our country.

Die Leute... sie verehren ihn. Sie würden Babys töten, wenn er ihnen sagte, dass das gut für sie sei. It reminds me of our furor of the past."

"Ja... I hope, like you said, it doesn't actually come down to killing babies..." I said, "I, uh... noticed that tattoo on your shoulder... You mean you don't follow the Nazis?"

""Nein! ...I mean, I've fallen away from them. In my youth I thought that we must keep our memories alive, when we made the world tremble with a breath. I thought if we could, we should learn from our strength.... But it became like I was only repeating our mistakes, instead of making a difference."

"And now you have a mistake on your shoulder you can't get rid of." I said.

"Ja... May I take you to dinner? Ich werde der Engel genannt, aber ich würde gerne mit einem echten wie dir sprechen, wenn ich könnte." he said.

I blushed... He had called me a real angel that he would love to spend time with... but I said, "I'm sorry, Moritz, but I have a boyfriend. Another time, perhaps."

We then shook hands, and he said if I could he'd like me to catch his next fight.

I politely declined, saying that I never wanted to see that violence again, but he said, "I wish to have the support. I believe if I saw you again it would give me courage and strength. Molech will be there... and he will make me tremor if I do not have the support of the angels. I am going to meet with him... to discuss terms."

Support of the angels? Support of someone like me... I said alright, I guess, if we have time.

Really I wanted to find how to stop Molech, because people were starting to like him, worshipping him, and if he made his people do something awful... then I'm sure Germany would remember it for years after.

We went to the Blutfest again, a lot earlier. No one was even there yet. I wanted to scope the place out, just in case... things get bloody.

Max walked into the ring, and said, "Wow. You can even see the old blood stains from before... Shouldn't they at least clean the place up?"

Nevaeh said, "I found out at the coffee shop we went to that this place is very unofficial... It would be illegal if they didn't pay off the right people. Most of the time it's just like this, an abandoned boxing ring."

"I'm gonna check out the back. See you guys in a sec." I said, and walked to the locker rooms.

I slipped on a pool of blood, falling into it. I got up, lit my flame, and saw... Moritz, bleeding out with a gash on his head.

"Moritz! Max, Nevaeh! Someone's hurt!" I yelled out, and rushed to Moritz.

He was wearily mumbling, and looked up to me. I asked him what happened.

He said, "Molech... I wanted to- But- He- Why is it so bright?"

His eyes were losing that brightness, he was closing them, and I knew I must be Moritz's angel of death.

My fire was burning bright in my hand, and I held his hand.

He looked at the shining brilliance around me, and saw my true angelic form revealed.

He opened his eyes wide, and said, "You *are* an angel. I did not know... I was flirting with Death... I-" and he died. I shut his eyes.

I picked his soul out of his body, a brilliant white flame itself. I felt all of his memories pass through me, the good and the bad, him and his childhood girlfriend sitting by a stream, when he joined a Nazi organization and got the tattoo, and even when he met me... then I released his soul to go to the afterlife, wherever he would go.

I wish I could've brought him to Heaven myself.

But moreso, I wish he didn't die.

We reported the murder immediately, and the police said that the Blutfest could be shut down now, with this sort of violence running rampant.

We were watching TV in the hostel, and Molech himself backed the police's investigation of the murder in the Blutfest... and donated generously to Moritz's family, to help arrange the funeral. One of the women that they interviewed, Moritz's mother, said, "Molech ist wie der Sohn Gottes." Molech is like the Son of God.

This sort of blasphemy... when I was certain that Molech had killed Moritz himself.

Could I assassinate Molech? Smite him with my sword and bring him back to Hell? I may be able to tempt him into attacking me... but I would have to make sure he was caught in the act. If the fault was not on his end then he would talk his way out of it, wriggling to freedom.

Max said, "Huh. You think he wouldn't be on TV, if he just killed someone... Why the fuck do people like him? Now that you mention it, he does look like a bull."

"...You see it?" I asked.

"I don't know... I guess. It's just... I just thought of what that guy did, what you said... He threatened you. From what you said, that Moritz was going to meet Molech. I just... don't really think all that money can buy you a soul, or a real human head." Max said.

Nevaeh was reading her Bible I gave her... and said, "Huh... there's a guy called Molech in here, too... What an unfortunate name..."

"His sins of the past will always follow him, if he continues to repeat them. I know he must have something that we can reveal..." I said.

I looked up "Mister" Molech on the internet, wondering what he could've done that wouldn't particularly be very good for humanity... Besides his acts of goodwill and charity, I found a forum where someone said he was involved in a murder in a sausage factory... and had the head of a bull.

Another comment said to stop believing that propaganda... and anyone who says stuff like that are ignorant pigs.

I said that there could be some truth to the rumor, maybe just slightly. I asked where the sausage factory was.

The forum quickly devolved into petty name calling, but I got the information I needed, that it was a sausage factory in eastern Germany.

Nevaeh, and Max, even though they were sick to death of Molech, supported me and we checked out the sausage factory.

"We have to go back soon, like the day after. If we really want to do something about this, then we should act fast. I really don't want to be stuck in Germany with Molech practically running the country... A candidate for chancellor is being heavily backed by Molech himself." Max said.

We snuck into the almost burned down factory. When we were looking for an entrance and Max and Nevaeh weren't watching, I slit a hole open in the fence with my sword.

We got in through a broken window, and looked around. The feeling in the air... it was a feeling of despair, perhaps past despair, but a broken, defeated feeling with no end to it.

We found the skull in a vat.

Nevaeh was freaking out, but Max calmed her down.

I went to the skull, put my slight flame to its forehead... and I saw whose soul this skull previously belonged to.

Memories flooded into me, memories of someone else... I saw Molech working as a worker, as an immigrant, and everyone called him "the bull guy." He was so fed up with it one day, claiming that they should all bow down and worship him... and he slaughtered one of the workers, this man's soul I was reading, albeit with only a few people actually suspecting anything.

I felt such furious anger coming from this spirit, as he told me that they were going to arrest Molech after they found the crowbar he killed him with… but then Molech won the lottery, bought the best lawyers in the country, and was now Germany's hopeful child.

The spirit told me that Molech had set the factory ablaze… leaving his hidden body to burn in flame.

I asked the spirit if he could testify to this.

The spirit laughed. He said Molech could tell me himself, if he didn't only spout lies.

I looked up, and saw a German man smoking a cigarette, the spirit himself.

He said, "Thank you for giving me some peace. I don't know what I would've done with all my rage. My family will never know how I died, besides base rumors."

"Go in peace, spirit." I said.

"Thank you." he said, and vanished in the wind that got into the factory.

25

We went to a club, on our last day here, one that Molech lurked around in.

I was dressed all fancy with rather sexy looking jeans and a shirt that was cut off and practically only a bra. I got a few lascivious looks, but I was saving this attraction for the demon I would slay.

Max thought this was a horrible idea, but he and Nevaeh were watching my back from the sides as I sauntered to Molech, swinging my hips slightly back and forth.

He had two barely clothed women fawning over his bull head, but he pushed them away to make room for me.

I sat beside him, and whispered in his ear, putting a hand on his thigh, "I'd love it if you could show me around now... I think it's time I fell properly..."

"What made you change your mind? I always... DESPERATELY... clung to the idea of an angel falling to me..." he said, subtly putting a hand on my ass.

"I just thought about your *sausage...* I just wanted some of that... Seeing you nearly *kill someone...*"

He laughed, and said that was just the start. I wondered why men, even demons, suddenly became so very stupid when aroused.

He took me to a back room, and I knew Max had followed. I thanked God for his protection and support.

As Molech was greedily undressing me, I stopped him with a light from my hand, putting the flame close to his face and blinding him.

"You killed a man. You killed another. How many more have you killed?" I said, threatening him with that fire which I knew that Molech feared.

He said, *"Men die so quick. You just think it's so easy... living. You just have it made... being blessed by God himself. People slew their offspring for me, made sacrifices in my name... I am a god, and I will never be just a man."*

"No. You are a cow. You will always just be an animal. The only reason people don't see you as one... is because they don't know what to believe... their eyes? Or your tongue. All you spit out are lies. Tell the truth."

"HA! The truth is what I say. People believe in me, they worship me, love my face... They believe every word on my tongue..."

"But not anymore." I said, and slammed my fist and the fire into his mouth, him screaming an animal scream. It smelled like beef was cooking. And I ripped it out.

I took my hand from him, dropped it to the floor, and walked away. Max had seen, heard, and he did not know what to say. But he saw Molech chase after me. Molech tried to speak... and Max was horrified.

Molech could only speak in the words of animals, as I had taken his tongue. People could see what he was.

They all stepped back in horror from this demon with the head of a cow, mooing at everyone.

Molech fled east, to Russia. People said it was a hoax, what happened to him, but the ones who saw knew the truth, that Molech was a monster.

It soon was found out that Molech had scammed and blackmailed numerous politicians, bankrupted companies with slander, and rigged every fight in the Blutfest as its prime sponsor.

The hardest heartbreak for people was the journal that Moritz kept... But his mother read Moritz's journal, and learned the truth. Moritz had said that no matter what threats were thrown at him, that he finally would stand up to Mister Molech.

So after first beating Moritz up himself in the arena, Molech had killed him.

They found the crowbar covered in blood, hidden in the old factory, after I gave them an anonymous tip on the place... With Molech's fingerprints on it and Moritz's blood. Molech had repeated the same sins of the past.

I suppose people just needed a different voice to talk to them, after they had heard Molech's voice for so long. They needed Moritz's words. But Moritz would never utter another one on Earth.

We sat in our crowded airplane seats, and flew back home.

We got out of the airport, and even though everyone living was busy and did not have time to meet us, Felix the Castrator waved at me and greeted me. I guess this was a normal thing now...

We drove back home, and I picked up Rasputin again. He actually looked a bit plumper than when I left him.

Max, Nevaeh and I were worn out... All we did was sleep and relax for a few days.

Max wanted to ask me about what happened with Molech, but whenever he tried to ask me, he'd get tongue tied. I told him to use that tongue for something else... and kissed him.

But he stopped kissing, and said, "I don't know what happened... and I want more answers... but I will believe whatever you say from now on."

I smiled, and said, "Then know I'm your guardian angel."

I didn't try to drag Max to church again, it was alright if he wanted to skip it, so I was surprised when he knocked on my door all dressed up properly for Sunday mass.

We got to church, and I noticed someone sitting in the very front row. Sax the demon.

I wondered how a demon got into the house of our Lord? I sat a bit aways and observed him.

"Yikes... That guy. Kinda makes you wish church was exclusive, when people like him show up..." Max said, talking about Sax.

"I guess we all deserve a chance at forgiveness, mercy, and hope. Let's just enjoy the ceremony." I said.

Sax went for communion, nearly spit the host out, and slurped down half the goblet of wine.

When it ended, wanting to talk to this demon who looked so much smaller than when he was fat and huge, he disappeared out the doors and ran down the street.

I had tea with Mrs. Nestor, showing her all the pictures I took in Germany. She marvelled at each one, saying that my boyfriend was really looking taller these days for some reason... and that Nevaeh looked as pretty as ever.

I told her of my whole adventure, of all the things we saw and did, even of the evil Mister Molech.

"You took on that hideous man? I heard about him in the news. Something about a bull? All those people's lives he ruined... I don't have a notion why." Mrs. Nestor said.

"Some people think we are in the Lord's shoes, and wish to make actions only he has the right to do. Some people think they're better than even God." I said.

"Yeah... I think that God is a little too judgemental sometimes, however. But maybe he needs to be, to separate the wheat from the chaff. I pray, I mean I hope, that he separates me with my husband, wherever he went." she said.

I put my hand on her hand, and said, "You will receive your just reward, I believe. I have faith in you and God."

"You alright these days? You seem to be talking... just a bit differently. A little more religious. Don't get carried away with yourself, dear..." she said.

I sighed, and said, "I realize it is my duty... to be like an angel on Earth. Maybe that's why I came back down."

"Hm... I think that people can do God's work without specifically trying to. I think we all have to act nice and holy, even without God, or any heavenly duty." she said, taking a sip.

"I suppose... but in these last few days, it feels like I found my soul again, when I felt like I had lost it. Heck, I wanted to lose it. But I've been too caught up in the material world." I said.

"Be sure to visit us back on Earth, when you're done doing whatever work God wants. We care for you, dear, and I'm sure you can just try to live a happy, content life without taking on people like Mister Molech all the time..."

"Thank you, I will... but I've been having these weird dreams lately too. One was with a man who showed me the way to my soul, and the one recently... was one with my old lover of ages past who died. He gave me a message... to come back. That he needs me... That they all need me..."

"Oh dear. You can go back to him when you've had your fill of life. Just take a rest day from smiting evil and wickedness and enjoy yourself." she said.

I said ok, and went back home, waving her goodbye.

I saw all the lost spirits around me, in the growing winds of spring. They were watching me, calling out to me, cheering my name.

I looked up, and saw the entire host of Heaven staring back at me, letting me know... that all of their faith was put in me.

Part 4: Industria

Diligence

26

I was sitting in the backyard on the lawn chair, bored, just throwing a soul fireball in the air and twirling it around my fingers. Felix was watching me, sitting on the lawn cross legged.

The other spirits left me after a while… After they were just waiting for me to smite down the next evil soul, or give them peace. At first I eagerly listened to all their problems, helping them figure out how they died and giving them solace from their anger, sadness, and unfinished business, but there was never an end to them! The spirits lined up down the block waiting to talk to the amazing angel of war on Earth! I angrily told them to all leave me alone, after they all started talking over each other, shouting at me their many problems…

They wandered off and I was left with Felix, the only spirit who wasn't afraid of me and my yelling.

I said to him, "What kind of spirit complains about his blisters… They're dead! They don't have any bodies to have blisters on anymore!"

"You remember those huge sores we all had from running around the arena in those awful sandals or even barefoot? I thought I'd give anything for just some foot cream." Felix said.

"Yeah… I had blisters on my ass from just waiting for the fight with that one guy who nearly escaped… It's a shame I had to kill him, broke his neck. He nearly got away from them too, all dressed up in that maid outfit…"

"A maid outfit? Never thought about that. I suppose it wouldn't have hurt to try."

"They groped him and were just appalled to find man parts instead. Really makes you think…"

"Think about what? Man parts under a maid's dress?"

"No… Just that women had it so rough in the olden days. Now we've got a woman president. Feels like we've come a long way."

Nevaeh came out back, going to her car, and said, "You just talking to yourself?"

"Nah, I'm talking to Felix the spirit." I said.

She laughed, and said, "Alrighty, Yule. I'm off to the store, need anything?"

"Get me some whiskey, please. I'll pay ya back."

"Drowning your troubles? I'll join you when I get back. Although, just because Max is visiting his mother, doesn't mean you have to get mopey and drink yourself to death…"

"Ach, shut it. I'm still sore from that. I wanted to go with him and talk to her… but he said they needed 'space' since they found his sister like that…"

"She'll get better. Those people she associated with… they turned her into some sort of animal. She didn't even recognize Max, right?"

"No… They were feeding her some low protein paste, just keeping her alive enough so that they could brainwash her…"

"This is why I think people who go to churches are nuts. Whether they like it or not… they turn into nuts because someone is pushing crap down their throat. If you ask me, an unorganized religion is better." she said, "See ya, Yule. Tell Felix I said hi." and winked at me and left in her car.

"She seems very nice." Felix said, "Like someone I would one day wish to have as a wife... Although, that would be pointless, as I'm dead, and couldn't have reproduced anyway."

"Hey, marriage isn't all about reproducing. You even like girls?" I said.

"Just because I don't have those urges like 'normal' men... doesn't mean I don't find something magnetic in the female counterpart."

"I'd set her up with you myself, but yeah, you're dead. Figure out why yet?"

"I was living in a village... I had a cow... no wait, maybe I had two..." Felix said, thinking hard.

"Forget I asked. You're not going to haunt the apartment forever if I invite you inside, are you? Or spread ectoplasm everywhere?"

"Ectoplasm? Is that even a thing?" he said, as we got up.

"Er... Just don't be a poltergeist and start stacking the chairs, kay?" I said, and he followed me inside.

Felix watched as Nevaeh and I drank whiskey, it burning down our throats and giving us a good buzz.

"Whooph, that's what I needed." I said, after I took the shot.

We clinked our empty shot glasses, and Nevaeh poured us another.

"Sooo... tell me about your 'Felix.'" Nevaeh said, "He your ghostly side action?"

"Not a bit. He was actually sort of a pest when I first met him, always trying to fight me. I'd kick his ass if he crossed out of line... but, he's actually a good fighter, and kicked my ass a couple times already." I said.

"Sounds like a strong man, if he could beat *you* up. What'd he do to get on your bad side?" Nevaeh asked.

"Um... He actually didn't do anything. We just fought each other because we thought that was what we were supposed to do. I wonder if we could've just held hands and sang songs of peace... probably have gotten tortured if we did."

"Oh yeah... that's right. You were a gladiator or something... Now you're talking to your old dead friends too. *Man...* I wish I had an imagination like you. Could really have written the crap out of that story then."

"Ever get around to finishing it?" I asked.

"I was thinking that I could bring the dragon slayer back to life... and they could get married and have kids and yada yada... but I think that's just a little unrealistic."

"What if you just made them fuck to death? And they kept on having sex even in the afterlife? To keep up the theme of Hanatrix's ever increasing sexual appetite."

Nevaeh giggled, and said, "That would be nice... but I get a bit lonely after writing like that. Makes me super horny whenever I do, but then I just realize I've got no one. Sure, I can just rub one out, but it's just not the same as having someone else do it."

Felix asked me, "Do women always talk about masturbation when they talk together?"

I told him to shush, and said to Nevaeh, "Well... the dragon slayer is just called, 'dragon slayer' in the story, right? What if you gave him a name? How about Felix? She could love him as a ghost, and then she would still have that old love without having to die or start up a family."

"Now that's *really* unrealistic... but I like it." Nevaeh said, and drank more whiskey. "Kind of like how old loves linger, and are never really gone for good. I wonder what a ghost would fuck like..."

I winked to Felix.

"Uh... But- I-" Felix stuttered.

"I want to tell you though... The Felix I know is a eunuch." I said.

"Really. That actually fits perfectly, since the dragon slayer... was *quite* good with his hands... and mouth... He actually never got totally naked in the story, as I was saving that part for him for later, but then I killed him off because I thought it was too good to be true… Should be a nice twist, when she has a vision of him in his astounding, ghostly nudity… How do you see ghosts, anyway? Just get really drunk?" she said.

"Hmm… I can see him because I'm an angel, but it might be worth a shot for you to try." I said.

"Angels now? An angel is getting drunk with me. Alright then, you're the boss, missus… angel woman." she said, and we drank some more.

27

We were slurring and talking about all sorts of stuff, some things profane, some heavenly, a little bit of both when talking about men.

Nevaeh accidentally looked at Felix, blinked, and took another shot.

"Whattttt if we got... *absinthe* or somethinggg? That makes you hallucinate, right?" she said.

"I think the whiiiiskey is working... gud. Good. Goooood..." I said. Felix wanted to join in our fun, and take a drink too, but his hand just went through the bottle... and then accidentally touched Nevaeh's, while she was reaching for it.

They both recoiled back, and Nevaeh blinked a couple seconds looking where Felix was.

"Heeeey..." I said, "Wannna see something cool? Watch this." I said, and burst my little fireball soul in my hand.

She looked at it, and said, "I think I'm dreaming... or need to lay down. I think I need to dream laying down..." and wandered to the couch. She nearly tripped and fell, but Felix caught her before she hit her head, and she said, "Thank you, Felix." and then opened her eyes wide, and said, "Y-Yule. I don't think I'm feeling right... Or am I? Felix is... *hot.*"

I did a little cheer, "Yaaaay. You're in *my* world now! I'm sooooo happpppy..."

She ran to the washroom and hurled up over and over into the toilet.

Felix said, "Are you sure you won't get in trouble for things like this? Breaking the bonds between the worlds of the living and the dead?"

"Pffffft… I broke that a long time ago…" hiccup, "And heck, I think God *neeeeeded* someone like me down on Earth… with all those motherfucking bullshit demons and crap…"

I heard Nevaeh spitting out the rest of her nausea, and she wandered back into the room.

She slowly sat down back at the table where Felix and I were sitting, and just stared hard at Felix, then at me, and said, "Everything you said was true."

"Yup!" I said, grinning like an idiot.

"…Then why did you let him rape me? If you're an angel. *Why did you let me suffer??*" she said.

My grin left. I didn't really know what to say. I started by trying to explain the whole theory of free will on Earth and crap, but Felix cut me off, and said, "It is very difficult in life. There are many challenges, many hardships. We can only keep living when they try to take everything from us… We can only continue. Nothing is happy forever, happiness is fleeting, like when I first moved to my village, and died. Like when Yule was about to be married, and died. But everything you suffered for has only made you who you are, and made you stronger, indomitable, and willful."

"Fuck you both. You're both dead… and I must have killed myself. I must be dead. What a shitty looking afterlife…" she said, and drank more whiskey.

"I thought you liked it here?" I asked.

"I *did*… but if this is all God's got for me in death… the fuck is the point of any of it?" she said.

Felix said, "You are still alive, Nevaeh. Yule is… kind of alive. I am dead and lost. My soul will never know peace until I have figured out *how* I died… I do not remember it, but I know that I felt the pain and loss of death."

"Must've been some sort of traumatic experience that you repressed…" Nevaeh said, "But… the thing is… here's the secret… *You always remember it.* You never forget. It's like it happened yesterday. I envy those lucky saps who can just wish it away and forget…"

"A trauma gets caught in your short term memory, and is not processed in the long term." I said.

"You sound like my therapist. All those bullshit EMDR therapy things she does with me… It's just idiotic! Can't even talk to her about it, because she thinks she's saving my life with her stupid buzzing machines!" Nevaeh said.

"Do you want to talk about it?" Felix asked.

"I- I don't, but if it'll make you feel better, then sure. If it'll get you pesky ghosts and fallen angels back to wherever you belong." Nevaeh said, and started a cigarette in the apartment. She continued, "I was a little girl, and I found faith. It all just *seemed to click* one day… Made me feel so alive, like I finally figured it out. All those sermons… all those masses… and they were all trying to get me to one point. To love myself. Simple as that, but I never really got it. Jesus is a metaphor for so many things… but he really just wanted all those lepers, possessed maniacs, and prostitutes he hung around with to just care for themselves, and then they can care for others.

"I prayed thanks for this miracle, this understanding, in that church, going to this one statue of Jesus where it looked like the lights were angel wings… Alone. And a man… a family friend who watched me sometimes… saw me there. I was pretty sure he had followed me, and he said he 'was just checking up on me.'

"He prayed beside me, sitting next to me… and then he put his hand on my leg. I tried to continue praying.

"Then he kissed me, forcing his disgusting smell on me.

"I wanted to scream, to run, but he told me to stay still.

"And he forced me down beneath the pew..."

She started crying.

Felix and I held her hands, and she yelled out between sobs, *"He smelled like peppermint! I lost my virginity to a rapist! To fucking EARL!"*

I felt very, very sad. I had nothing to say at this point.

But Felix said, "I... I am sorry. A woman was raped in my village... and the woman pointed me out. The peasants... already disliked me. This increased their anger and made them violent and aggressive.

"They quickly turned into a mob, and killed my one cow. I called her my prize... she was all I owned, in truth. She was my one possession that had value... besides my dagger.

"The peasants forced me out of the house I was staying at, an old abandoned place that the owner allowed me to live at if I would work his fields. He worked me as hard as a slave, like I always was, but I did not mind, and I was happy for the roof over my head. I thought I finally had a place on Earth.

"They burned it down, as I watched them take that place. I did not want to fight them... to kill them... to *castrate them...*

"They began beating me, stoning me, and I could not escape their wrath unless I fought. I always thought I would never take another life after my time in the arena was over...

"But I killed them all. I massacred the entire village. I slaughtered them with only my dagger. Their screams... it's like I can hear them now.

"I didn't care. If they wished me to be a murderous beast, then I would. And I mutilated them as well, as was my habit.

"Then I was executed by the Romans, as they laughed at me... calling me 'the Castrated.'"

"Wait." Nevaeh said, "Yule said you were a eunuch. You couldn't have raped that woman. Are you lying?"

Felix got up from his seat, undid his belt, dropped his pants... and revealed his naked form to her.

"Oh. I'm... sorry too." Nevaeh said.

Felix pulled back up his pants, and said, "I have figured out my death. I must leave you now... Stay strong, Nevaeh. Even if God has abandoned you... You will always be able to depend on yourself. Goodbye, Yule. Thank you for being... my friend."

Felix looked hard at his hands. He clenched them open and closed a couple of times. He clenched them hard, looked up to the ceiling...

And stayed where he was.

"Um. Why am I not disappearing? Surely at least I would be gone, my soul scattered to the winds? Is even Hell too much to ask for?" Felix asked me.

"Beats me. Sorry, Felix. I never did all the soul moving myself. I was trained for battle." I said.

"Doesn't *that* make you a useless angel... The fuck are you down here for, anyway?" Nevaeh said.

Felix said, "God is leaving me down here? *Forever??* I- don't understand... Why has your God abandoned me?? You must be some pawn in his wicked scheme!"

"Hmph. Like you said, 'You can always depend on yourself...'" I said, getting peeved that my friends were all ganging up on me.

"You leave him alone! Your stupid God is the cause of all our suffering, anyway!" Nevaeh said.

"You refuse to fight me, refuse to take me to Heaven, or even smite me to Hell! Haven't I suffered enough?? This excruciating... boredom! It's worse than being burned for a thousand eternities!" Felix said.

"I thought coming back to Earth was rather fun…" I said, looking at my drink.

"Fun?? You came down here for *fun??"* Nevaeh said, "What- What the fuck?! Shouldn't Heaven be more fun than anything??"

"It's- You don't understand… It's Paradise. It's- like someone gives you a present, and you open the present, and you find what you always wanted… but that gift is really another present, and you can open it up and reveal another new thing… and it never ends. I… just wanted to stop getting presents. I wanted to not have any presents, and find that something that I didn't really want, but got anyway, and just be happy for it. I wanted that extra sock, that apple for Christmas… just something that I could love even if it's not perfect." I said.

"Ohhh… I see. Like Max. Max is your extra sock. What? Your dead angel boyfriend too perfect? Not give you that little dick that you always wanted?" Nevaeh said.

"N-No! Max is great! He's like the only boyfriend I've ever really had, anyway!" I said.

"She loved another man, one of my greatest enemies… a gladiator who was the most obnoxious, stuffed up pretender I've ever seen. I can't believe they allowed you that time together… Must've been nice. They were trying to impregnate you, Yule, to make you breed like a dog. And then you even were *so lucky* to have a noble fawn on you… To think you were really an angel, when really you were his attractive curiosity… an albino gladiator." Felix said.

"What?! It was an accident, me and Maximus's time together!" I said.

"Maximus?? Little does Max know he's even a *replacement* sock…" Nevaeh said.

I was starting to get furious, and said, "What right do you two have to judge me?? You've never had your family taken from you! To be hunted like a beast and then pitted against other beasts! What right do you have to say my life had no value?? I've given up everything for life! For both of them! I lost everyone and everything! My tribe! Maximus! Even my future husband! Everything I loved either died or left me when I died young! And then God gave me a future, an afterlife! I don't even get a real life, and I'm stuck with a fucking life after death forever! But I left Heaven for all of you people! All you people, every little one, and you curse me and call me a useless angel!

"You think this place is bad, Felix? Have you *seen* those demons?? They're monsters! They're evil, awful, ugly, and want people to suffer for the satisfaction of it! And they'd be tormenting you forever down below. Be thankful you're not *truly* damned.

"And Nevaeh. When I saw you with that gun, do you want to know who was really whispering in your ear? The motherfucking Devil. He was trying to get you to kill yourself. Do you want to remember the last thing he said to you? The cops are at the front door.

"Then he whispered to me. Threatening me with eternal damnation, for helping to save your life. And now demons are stalking around, trying to ruin my second chance at a stupid, awful, pointless life! I've made so many mistakes... but falling to Earth still wasn't one of them. I've given a demon mercy, that one called Sax, and he spits in my face and causes more suffering! Well, not anymore. I'll kill them all if it makes you people content! I'll save each and every one of you from burning forever, whether you like it or not! Fuck you all!"

They were silent for a second, and looked down at the table. Nevaeh said, "I... didn't know that the Devil and demons were real... I didn't think God would let them exist, and always thought they were simply part of the story in the Bible. But that's exactly the last thing I thought I thought in that horrible voice."

Felix said, "I... have been sitting around, wasting my time in death. I didn't think I could do anything, truthfully. But Nevaeh can see me...

You have allowed me peace, Yule... May I join you in your battles? May I save all the rest of the souls on Earth with you from that truly horrible fate of Hell?"

"Hmph. Only if you say you're sorry. I'm sorry to you guys I haven't been able to relieve you of your suffering properly... If I ever go back to Heaven, then I'll take it up with the manager." I said.

"Will you go back to Heaven still? Are you trapped down here or something like Felix?" Nevaeh asked.

"I don't know... I may have to figure that out when I die again. So I'll be extra sure not to die." I said.

They laughed, and said sorry each in their own way.

Nevaeh was drawing Felix, just so she can keep his image around when she sobers up. "I probably will never believe this... probably just think it's a dream... but I don't *want* to forget this. You two are truly amazing, I mean that, even if you're not real or something, or don't really belong here."

I was sniffling at the thought, of Nevaeh forgetting, of people forgetting someone like Felix... and me.

I told her this, and then I burst out crying, and Nevaeh said, "There, there... I'm sure it'll be ok... Maybe this is like looking at one of those hidden images? Once you see it you always will?"

I held her hand, and said, "Living people shouldn't be able to see us... it would help them live easier. This was a mistake... this whole extra life of mine..."

"Maybe God, like they always are saying, put you down here for a reason? Maybe you just have to find your purpose like the rest of us?" she said.

"I don't know... I just want to forget about my entire life, and learn that one move I failed at from St. Sebastian... the one trick that you beat me with, Felix." I said.

"That? It's really a simple thing. The dagger's flat end is wider, and when parried with it can redirect a sword easily enough if held with enough strength. You just have to be precise... and not listen to any thought, any strategy, and be completely in tune with the moment. Relax, even." Felix said, "Now, I would've had a much harder time if you chose to use a spear or mace, or even a greatsword, but you always use that one sword, and I figured it would be easy enough to move the sword like redirecting water. That was a last resort though, and after I failed to entangle you in the net, I was met with that life or death move in the ring. If I failed, I know I would've died."

"Huh. You never boasted about your strength, but you *also* never said if you failed you would've died." I said.

"I guess I was just playing the part. We were all made to show our strengths, instead of our weaknesses... but I can admit my flaws. Unlike Maximus. I truly did hate him... He would use these bizarre, flashy moves in battle, even train on them when he could've done the same thing with far less steps. He acted as if his time in the arena, his life and death, was a game." Felix said.

"He killed himself because I wouldn't kill him." I said.

"Yeah... I remember them talking about that. Despite Maximus's obvious flaws and boasting, he never did speak badly of you. They would've killed you just because you didn't follow through... but like I said, the Emperor's son was quite fond of you." Felix said.

"I know... He probably did think of me as some sort of freak... but he made me feel special, in his own way." I said.

"Emperor's son?" Nevaeh said.

"Yeah... he was like a third or fourth son though, so I would've never been Empress or anything, unless my past future husband decided to kill off all his brothers perhaps." I said, "I'm not really sure what happened to him."

"Anything like your other Max? You two fuck forever in the afterlife?" Nevaeh asked.

"No. I didn't even see Maximus there..." I said.

"Yikes. Probably a good thing he's dead, then." Nevaeh said, "Y'know... if he went to the other place, or got stuck as a ghost. No offense, Felix."

"None taken. I probably deserve this lukewarm drink of an afterlife. I believe the Emperor's son died nobly in his old age, with his family surrounding him. At least that's what I saw when I haunted him for a spell." Felix said.

"Old age is what, forty six in the Roman period?" Nevaeh said.

"Something or other. Did you see what happened when he died? Did Satan reach out for him? Or did the angels of Heaven blow their trumpets and accept him?" I asked.

"Sorry... But I got rather bored at that point and walked out, and followed this one woman who always seemed to be missing her left shoe." Felix said.

"Oh... I was grieving for Maximus for a long time, and I finally accepted that grief, and it felt like his soul was lifted away from me... straight up to Heaven. I hope he's there... and I hope what he says in my dreams isn't true..." I said.

"What'd he say? Moaning and groaning in passion doesn't count." Nevaeh said, grinning.

"Haha... No, it wasn't some sort of wet dream... It was a serious one. One where he had angelic wings, magnificent, golden wings, not white like mine were, and flew down before me himself. He said that Heaven calls on me, and wants me to come back." I said.

"Hmm... Can we do a séance or something? We're already talking to a ghost." Nevaeh said.

"Sure. Let's try. How do we do that?" I said.

"We need something of your past loved one... Have anything?" she said.

"No... Not really. The only thing I had from Maximus in the past was a lock of his hair. His long, glorious, lustrous hair..." I said.

"Gross." Felix said, "Here, I'll just throw stones at the gates of Heaven or something… If I can even find it."

"Ok. Don't be long." I said.

So Felix got up, opened a window, and the wind rushed him away.

"I really like Felix, by the way." Nevaeh said, after she shut the window.

"I could tell. You two seemed to connect on a deep level." I said.

"It's a shame he has no balls. He seems very manly, if you ask me." she said.

"He's pretty lonely in death. All he would do before was follow me around and threaten me… like he thought I cared. It was the closest thing he had to a friend, I think."

"Hmm… Maybe he can do ghostly things with me, y'know, if he's still there tomorrow."

"What are 'ghostly things?'" I asked.

"I'm not really sure. Smash stuff with no explanation? Spook superstitious old ladies and haunt old hotels? Make muffled whispering sounds on the phone? Sounds kind of fun."

"I *guess*… If you're into that sort of thing. Maybe you two can help me sort out the rest of the distressed spirits…"

"What? There's more?"

"A whole army of them, all crying out about their past suffering. I don't really know how I could ever get through all of them… Because, as you know, there are lots of confused souls on Earth. More every day."

"I think… that would be the rush of a lifetime. I mean, this is crazy enough as it is… Who cares if I get a little crazier? Just an opportunity to not wear pants."

I laughed, and said, "You're pretty silly, Nevaeh. Want me to get Felix to hang out with you?"

"Uh… I'd prefer it… If he wants… for him to ask me himself. I think that would be really nice, since I have no place to ask a spirit to spend time with me. He should probably be going through Purgatory or something, so he can get into Heaven, and not be loafing about on Earth with a woman."

"Oooh… but you 'are' Heaven… Hopefully he can get into youuuuu…" I said, and stuck my tongue out at her.

She laughed, and said, "Goddamnit, I'm so happy you saved my life."

"I think the police did that, and not me."

"Fuck no. You actually talked to me, and the police pointed guns at me! If one of them twitched accidentally they would've killed me instead! Like Max said… I think I love you, Yule."

I smiled, and said, "I truly think he does. If he would just fucking say it properly… 'I love you, Yule.' Not that hard!"

"Then you must love him too. Sorry I called him your extra sock… But you truly think you would have it all, in Heaven. Who knew it was better on Earth? Makes me sad that I'm going to die one day…"

"Ah, don't worry about it. I'll show you around if we ever get there. There's this one place… just littered with cute, adorable babies! They say the unbaptized go to Hell, but God would never be that harsh. He grabs them up quickly, before Satan even has a chance at them."

"Babies? Nasty. Any place for the cool kids like us?"

"Hm… You wouldn't think it, but Jesus is very cool. I know that sounds just like some Christian girl talking, but he's like… he gets you. No matter who you are, what you did, he understands. You laugh and make jokes, and you feel like you've just talked to your best friend again. He has time for you, even if he's got a million bazillion other people who want to talk to him. He'll take the time."

"Oh… I always thought he was laughing at me in that church as that statue… Getting his kicks. But… maybe he just was a witness for me, like that little nun who saw Earl go into the church. Maybe Jesus stopped him from killing me, instead of just raping me."

"It is not 'just' raping you. I truly feel angry for what happened to you. But, if you think about it, Earl's probably being raped in prison now, so he is getting his comeuppance… right up the butt."

"Yeah. He was weak. That's why he had to single out a little girl." Nevaeh said, smiling.

Felix knocked on the window followed by someone, and Nevaeh let them in.

Felix said, as he was sitting back down, "Found him wandering the streets, looking for you… Fucking dumbass."

And Maximus said, *"Hello, Yule."*

<h1 style="text-align:center">29</h1>

I just hugged him right away, and he hugged me back. Felt like the old Maximus, even with his glorious golden wings. I asked him where was his halo.

"*It... got away from me. Damn thing kept floating up and down and around... Never could get it to stay still.*" Maximus said.

"Well don't let it go too far! I found my halo again, didja know??" I said, and showed him the halo fire burst forth from my hand.

"*...Really. That's marvelous! Maybe I can find the thing again if I looked hard enough...*" Maximus said.

Nevaeh introduced herself, and Maximus shook her hand in a gentlemanly fashion.

"*It is nice to meet you, Nevaeh. I want to tell you that you are doing a great job on Earth, and that you really stuck it to Satan... God told me all about your struggles.*" Maximus said.

"Really?? I'm glad. Although... he doesn't have to tell *everybody*..." Nevaeh said.

"*I only learned because I knew you were a friend of Yule's. Anyway... Are you ready to go, Yule?*" Maximus said.

"What? Of course not! I've got so much to do! What... is it exactly God wants?" I said.

"He wants you to fight Hell rupturing forth. We know that they are going to invade the Earth, making life into a living Hell... We need every angel of war we can muster." Maximus said.

"I... Oh. I... guess I'll get my things... I mean, never mind... I can't take anything to Heaven anyway..." I said.

"What?!" Nevaeh said, "She can't leave yet! And she's on Earth, so can fight back Hell here!"

"I really don't see the point of Hell going to Earth... and most of the spirits wouldn't take it well if their eternal limbo was encroached upon..." Felix said, "Me especially."

"We must all plan accordingly. It will be a long and hard fought battle... but we believe we can take down Hell permanently if we strike decisively. Forever. There will never be another awful place for people to go and become demons in... God would destroy it all with a wave of his hand, but I believe he is getting weaker over the millenniums..."

"...What? You think God is weak?" I asked.

"I... No! I think... he's very strong! If he just kept all the angels he could at his command, and not let them fall to Earth like you, Yule." he said.

But then I realized something... I had never seen a golden winged angel in all of Heaven. And his voice... it felt cold, hollow, nothing like the Maximus I knew.

He sighed, seeing that I saw through the illusion.

His wings revealed their true forms, shredded crisps of golden wings, like when he fell from Heaven down to Hell, and his true face... well, it didn't change very much, because as Maximus was beautiful, glorious, and handsome...

Satan was as well, a fallen angel, one of God's first, even if he was twisted, and corrupt, and villainous. Every handsome feature looked ugly, because of the truly awful soul contained beneath them.

But, I recognized him from when I saw him over Nevaeh's shoulder, from when I saw him in the alley... as this was how Satan always looked.

When he was not shrouded in shadow, concealing his form, and trying to deceive the innocent.

He cackled, a truly awful laugh, and we all stepped back from him. Felix and I drew our weapons, Felix his dagger and I my sword and halo flame.

"At least let me take Nevaeh." Satan whispered.

"Go back to Hell, monster." I said.

"Everything I said was true... Heaven really does need you. You should go back there, Yule. Kill yourself and ascend. For none can stop Hell as we come to Earth." Satan whispered, and the brimstone smell was overwhelming, and it got cloudier and cloudier, as he laughed and laughed.

I thought I would choke to death from the fumes, but Max had opened the door, as I gave him a key to the apartment, and walked inside. The fumes dissipated out the door, and Satan was gone.

Max walked through Felix, and said, "Hey guys. I got some pizza, if you like." He set down the pizza and I quickly hugged him. "...You alright, Yule? It smells a little off in here."

"I-I jus-just... Never mind. It's just a little scary sometimes..." I said.

Max said, "What? But you've got Nevaeh here and everything!"

Nevaeh hugged Felix, and Max stared at her oddly.

"...Uh... Yeah. Ok. Well... I'll stick around, maybe?" Max said, "You two didn't smoke something funny in here, did you? I mean... Nevaeh is hugging nobody..."

"He's not nobody... He's a poor lost soul..." Nevaeh said, "Who bravely defended my life as the Devil tried to take me..."

"...Um... I think you two need to sober up... I'll make some coffee..." Max said.

Max worked on the coffee, and I hugged Felix with Nevaeh as he hugged us back.

Felix said, "I'm so sorry... I found him... I truly thought he was Maximus... Had the same air of self righteousness and everything..."

"I'm sorry I let him in! The Devil seems like one tricky bastard..." Nevaeh said.

"I'm sorry I believed he was Maximus... I feel like such a fool..." I said.

We just hugged until Max came back with the coffee.

We sat down with him, and Felix said to Nevaeh, "I like this Max better. But I would like to talk to you for a second... if you like... Nevaeh, and we can let the lovers sort out their tangled hearts."

"You could really be a writer, you know." Nevaeh said to Felix as she followed him to the porch, "You just have this... deep soul."

Max was staring at her, seemingly talking to herself, and said, "...How are you guys doing? I see you drank quite a bit."

"That doesn't matter. How is your sister?? I've been dying to ask all day." I said.

"...She's going to a hospital to sort her out. I... just want to destroy that cult she was in... For that's what it was. Just some evil cult. They took advantage of her... used her... and she can never have the time back that she spent with them..."

"At least she'll get back her mind, eventually. She just needs a lot of warm hearts and good therapy."

"That's not the point. They'll... never let her have back her soul. They indebted her for so many things... We're getting a lawyer to help us out of it. But lawyers all end up in Hell... and I'm sure she'll take advantage of us too..."

"I think a few lawyers end up in Heaven, despite the jokes. Have faith. As long as you believe things will turn out right, they have a chance of actually doing so."

"What about that one guy who lost everything because Satan basically dared God that the guy wouldn't give up faith? Feels like what we're going through."

"Job. He is rewarded in the end, even just with an eternity in Paradise. I believe Fate will be ok."

"Yeah, but my sister… Fate… didn't even recognize me! *Instead… She drops her trousers and bends over!!* Like that was something normal for her!! I- I- I-" Max said, breathing heavily.

I looked him calmly in the eyes, and he seemed to calm down, and I said, "It will be alright for now. Your mother is watching her carefully, even with the hospital, right?"

"Y-Yes… I know nothing bad will happen to her 'baby girl' with her around… She'd fucking murder them all if anyone took advantage of her… Like I feel like doing. We actually got along when we talked about Fate… we actually connected. It's sort of bringing our family together… I just wish… the member of our family we're trying to save wasn't so lost…"

I shrugged, and said, "Sometimes hardship brings out the best in us. Ever have an Irish coffee?" and poured some whiskey in his coffee.

He shook his head, and drank his whiskey/coffee.

Nevaeh came back with Felix, and they were grinning to each other and giggling slightly.

Max said that whatever we smoked, he wants some too.

I decided to come clean, and said, "We've been talking to a ghost all evening. It's been really heartwarming, awesome, and fun."

"…Nevaeh too?" Max said.

I hit him on the arm, and said, "She's as crazy as me now, so get used to it." I then said to Nevaeh, "Sooo… What'd you two talk about?"

"We just… felt… that…" Nevaeh started.

"I'm finally seeing a woman! I may be dead, may be a eunuch, but I never thought I could enjoy such a thing so much!" Felix said.

"We're going to have our first date next weekend. Felix thinks he can get the waiter to stumble ten times, and I bet him ten kisses that he couldn't." Nevaeh said.

"...Who's Felix?" Max asked.

"He's the ghost I told you about, duh! Try to keep up. I'm so happy for you both!" I said.

"...I don't know if I just walked into the oddest prank, or like you said, are both just crazy now." Max said.

"How do we get him to understand?" Nevaeh said.

"You remember Molech, right, Max?" I said.

"Y-Yes... You ripped out his tongue... and he couldn't speak. It was very disturbing." Max said.

"But, do you remember what he looked like? The ball of flame in my hand?" I said.

"...That was just my imagination. Trying to make sense of it. I mean, I reasoned it out, it was found he killed that one guy you met with, and you somehow knew. I'd do the same, honestly." Max said.

"Do it, Yule. Do that thing with your hand." Nevaeh said.

Max covered his mouth and shook his head.

"No... Not that!" I said, "Just... see my soul burst into flame..." and I burst the flame from my hand.

Max looked at it for only a second, and looked me in the eyes, and said, "What?"

I sighed, and put the flame back down.

"That's disappointing, Max." Nevaeh said, "Say... wanna see my type-writer, Felix? I got it at an antique fair."

"Only if you let me try to possess it and make that tappy sound." Felix said.

Nevaeh giggled, took him down the hall, and I heard faintly her say, "You think you can possess me? Get over here and try this one thing first..."

"I thought you said you would believe me, Max." I said.

"I... just don't want to put too much faith in anything right now... that's what happened to my sister... I still think, heck I believe, that you are my guardian angel. That you care for me as I care for you... I just... don't want to get my hopes shattered." Max said.

We heard the typewriter clacking out and Nevaeh squealing in glee.

She rushed back in, and said, "He's doing it. Oh my God... I have a ghost boyfriend... who can possess my typewriter!" as the clacking continued.

"...How are you doing that, anyway?" Max asked.

Nevaeh urged us to follow, and Max and I walked into her room. He fearfully looked at the typewriter clacking out letters on its own and then it stopped.

Max took out the paper, read it, turned pale, dropped the paper, and said, "I think I need to go." and left the apartment while I begged him to stay.

I picked up the paper, and it said, "Max. Your sister just needs the right care. Let her remember you, in her own time and pace. Remember the blossoms in spring that she loved so much, let her walk in the tulips like she did when she was young."

Felix got out of the typewriter, nearly got stuck halfway, but Nevaeh pulled him out.

"What's that about tulips?" I asked him.

"Oh, it's just a guess... but I wondered if she was that little girl in the past who looked at me once. I believe she went on thinking I was her imaginary friend. I was truly happy to slay all the monsters she made up for me to fight... but it was just a guess. She loved tulips." Felix said.

"Hmm... You think it's just a coincidence?" I asked.

"Maybe an act of fate?" Felix said.

30

I devoured half the pizza, as Felix and Nevaeh talked and connected. She said to him, "You... don't have a place to stay, do you. Wanna stay here?"

"No, no, no." I said, "I told him not to haunt the apartment forever. I don't want to be taking a shower and have Felix come out of the pipes instead of water."

"Aww c'mon, Yule! Surely it must be better than letting him roam the streets all night!" Nevaeh said.

"Fine. Just for tonight, and Felix can get his own place tomorrow. He can haunt the attic, for now. I think there's actually a trap door in the hall." I said.

"Really? Never noticed that! Ok. Let me show you to your room, Felix! And don't worry, you can haunt the shower when *I'm* in there... but then you're going to have to suds me up yourself." she said, grinning at Felix.

Felix followed her to the hall, and said, "I get that you're flirting with me... and I don't feel a thing down there... but I do feel... very happy." Nevaeh giggled, and they found the trap door and soon were climbing up to the attic.

I burst my halo fire in my hand... and just stared at it.

I went to bed, and slept off the alcohol and pizza. The night was actually a good night, even if Satan popped in to scare our socks off.

I fell asleep, just praying that Nevaeh would be able to remember, and that I wouldn't have to go back.

I had another dream of Maximus.

He had no wings, and his halo was over his head, shining bright.

Gosh. The lobby in Heaven sure looked boring. It was like a giant DMV, if the most friendly and efficient one ever. The souls all talked and waited around, telling each other of their past lives and wishing each other a good afterlife. I had skipped this part, since St. Sebastian drafted me immediately into his corps of angels of war.

Maximus was looking nervous as he waited beside a woman who would've been a saint if she had caused a miracle. She took his hand and said he would have the time of his life.

"But my life... I never had a time to myself in all my life. I was always fighting and training." Maximus said.

"No special someone that you could spend some extra time on?" the almost saint asked.

"I did have someone, yes. A beautiful woman. I... died because I would not take her life." Maximus said.

What? I thought he died because I wouldn't take his life?

Maximus continued, "Her beauty... her care. I believed that I loved her, and it was my downfall... If I shoved those feelings down, then I could've slain her, and not have met my death."

The almost saint patted his hand, and said, "You would've died eventually, one way or another. Is it not better to die for someone you love?"

"I suppose. I had the time of my life when I and her made love. It felt the closest I would ever get to a paradise. I didn't want to tell her... in fact I nearly believed the accidental placing us together *was* an accident... but

I overheard that they wanted us to make children, to ensure our stock, and have more gladiators with our prominence." Maximus said.

I felt the blood drain from my face, even in a dream.

"I wanted to take her fully, completely, giving her what we both wanted… It was so tempting… just to even approach it. But I could never damn our children to lives like we had." Maximus said.

I smiled. I thought he was just being a gentleman… pleasing me in the way he did… and his seed had fallen to the earth, instead of in me.

"You did a good deed, son." the almost saint said, "Maybe just another reason you are here."

"Will my number ever be called on?" Maximus said.

"I believe so. You've just revealed your true feelings, your love and goodwill. What number are you?" she asked.

"759,375,801,102." he said.

"Really? I think you must have the wrong number. I'm the next one up. Here, let's change tickets." she said, and she snatched Maximus's ticket before he could protest, and gave him her own with a smile.

Maximus's number was called, and he nervously approached the counter, thanking the almost saint as she waved him goodbye.

There, he was fitted with wings, glorious, white wings, just his size, and he was accepted into Heaven.

I smiled as he flew in the clouds in glee, dancing and singing in his beautiful voice.

31

I yawned awake, pet Rasputin and fed him breakfast, and saw Nevaeh peek around the corner to look at me. She looked around the apartment, underneath the couch and in every nook and cranny, and said, "Where's Felix?"

"You remember!! I'm so happy!" I said, rushed to her, and gave her a hug.

"Yeah, yeah… cut it out Yule." she said, as I gave her a big smooch on the cheek, "He didn't ascend or anything, did he?"

"I'm so happy I'm not alone anymore!! I've been wanting someone to understand what I've been going through since I first came here! Have you checked the vacuum cleaner? Maybe he got ghost busted." I said.

"Nah. He wouldn't hide in somewhere so filthy. Did you notice his hygiene? Like a goddamn soap incarnate." she said.

We heard mooing coming from outside.

I burst my halo flame and held my sword, remembering Molech.

I peeked out the window, and saw Felix with a cow.

We went out to the backyard, and he said, "I have found my prize! The only thing I ever really owned! May I keep her here?"

"Uh… Felix, that's a living cow." I said.

"It is? Um… she looks the same as before… I guess all cows do look kind of the same. Is it too much to ask that you kill her for me?" he said.

Nevaeh burst out laughing, and said, "No, man. We're not gonna have beef for dinner tonight!" and she laughed some more, "I'll help you return it... Haha..."

"If we have to... She could make us some fresh milk..." Felix said.

"This is a boy cow, Felix." Nevaeh said.

"...Oh. Then let's quietly return her- him, back to the farm I found him at..." Felix said, and the two walked off.

I started a cigarette. Damn ghosts.

The blister guy appeared before me, with the rushing wind, and moaned.

"Stop moaning, please. I know you're a ghost but you don't have to overdo it." I said, sitting down on the lawn chair.

"But it hurts..." he said.

"Just walk it off. Or fly it off. However ghosts get around." I said.

"But... I can still feel it... I feel it now... I feel everything... hurting..." he said.

I stared at him, confused.

Then a giant hand reached forth from the ground, fracturing the ground in a fissure, nearly scaring me to death, and grabbed the blister guy downwards.

I saw through the crack. It was the most horrible thing I've ever seen.

And now a soul had been dragged to Hell.

I had dropped my cigarette in the grass, staring at the crack. I was sweating, fearful. Was it something I said to him? Something that made him join the damned? Was I just not caring enough??

A voice said, "You really should've talked to him about his blisters..." and I looked back at Rasputin staring at me, somehow getting out of the apartment. He smiled a cat's smile.

I just stared at the cat. I swore he just said something like a human. He started licking his paw.

I turned back at the crack, and the voice said again, "Doesn't dying hurt? You should know. Maybe you should've empathized with him, you know, shown a little understanding."

I turned back at the cat sneering, and stared at him with slit eyes. I said, "If you can talk, why didn't you say so at the start?"

He mewled at me.

I stared at him again. I shrugged, picked him up, and brought him inside.

I was making breakfast at the stove, with Rasputin watching from behind me… and that damn voice said again…

"This is fun, isn't it?"

I turned to him quickly while he was saying the words, while the cat's mouth was moving. He quickly shut it, and stared up at me cutely.

"…You trying to gaslight me or something?" I said.

Rasputin the cat said, "Maybe you're just crazy? First you're a gladiator, then you're an angel, now you hear cats talking to you. You should really get yourself checked out."

"Nevaeh can see Felix, too." I said.

"Nevaeh isn't real, Yule. She's just a fantasy… I'm sorry, but it's better you heard it from a talking cat." he said.

I stared at him with slit eyes.

"Mewl." he said.

"I do something to piss you off?" I said to the cat.

"Well… I do wish you wouldn't skimp on the cat food…" he said.

"I get you the best kind there is!" I said.

"Correction. Best in a can." he said.

I sighed, and flipped my egg. "I really don't need this right now, Rasputin…"

"Oh, it's not so bad. You're just like Max's sister, now." he said.

"You… Don't talk like that! Max and her need our support!" I said, and put the egg on some toast and made a sandwich.

"'Our' support? I honestly couldn't really care. Why do you?" he asked.

I sat at the table, offered him my sandwich which he shook his head at, and I said, "People should care about other people. They need to show support so that we can all live together peacefully. It's just the right thing to do."

"Just like you and Mr. Blisters?" he said.

"Grr… I didn't know he was so close to tipping! I thought that if he was dead he'd be able to push through it just a bit!" I said, trying to explain to the cat.

"What was I going to say… Oh, yeah. It isn't always obvious people are going to fall off the edge. There isn't always a whiff of brimstone and a suicide note on the counter. Sometimes we're just going through the motions, and then, plink, we fall into the brink." he said.

"I feel like you're trying to get me to a certain point, like you're staging me with your snide cat comments." I said, taking a bite of my sandwich.

"Then it really should be obvious." he said.

"What?" I said.

"That you're losing your mind." he said.

I threw the sandwich back on the plate, and stormed off to the TV. I sat in front of it and turned it on, and Rasputin tried jumping on my lap, but I pushed him off.

"Hey… I actually think you're very soft." he said, staring at me.

"I'll be hard as stone if you keep pushing me." I said.

"But Yule… it's me, your little cat…" and he rubbed against my legs. I tried to angrily look away, but I picked him up and put him on my lap. He got cuddled on me, and said, "Pathetic."

I pushed him off again.

"Why are you even watching this show?" he asked me, looking at the TV.

"Huh? Oh. I guess I'm not, really." I said, looking back at the flashing lights.

"But you still turned on the TV."

"Are you going to be critiquing every part of my life from now on?"

"Only 'til they throw you in the bin and fix you. Then I can go live with Thaniel... he feeds me half his dinner, after he's done crying at the table. Nothing like a good, home cooked meal... Too bad his wife left."

"But he ran you over!"

"I kind of asked for it... The sun was just, just right in that one spot..."

"He really cries after dinner?"

"Only if he's not drunk. Are you going to help him drown his sorrows tonight?"

"...I was..."

"He mentioned to me that he kind of thinks of you like his daughter... like little Julia..." the cat said.

"He talks to you too?" I asked.

"Calls me up every weekend." the cat said, smiling.

"...You're rather snarky."

"You're rather crazy. Yulia."

I turned off the TV, since that wasn't taking my mind off the talking cat telling me I was losing my mind.

"Wanna play cards?" Rasputin asked.

"I don't think playing cards with my cat will make me feel better."

"Then you're finally admitting it to yourself. You're nuts... It's a big step to take."

"If... you are me losing my mind... If none of this is real... then why does it feel so real?"

"The reality of a dream is up to you, right?"

"Then how come it isn't crazier? How come this isn't some nonsensical crazy bizarro life?"

"Maybe craziness... is just slight. Here and there. You barely notice it until the cows come home and the cat starts talking." he said, "I'm trying to help you, Yule."

"Then why... am I breathing so fast? I'm an angel come back to life. The cows came home, and the cat is talking."

"It probably didn't help drinking so much last night."

"Yeah... before I went to bed. I'll just sleep it off..."

I wrapped myself in a blanket... and the cat was quiet... and I was about to fall asleep...

The cat pawed at my face.

"Feed me, Yule." he said.

"Motherfucking cat! You just had breakfast! Every time, you do this!" I yelled out, sitting up.

"Good. You're awake. You can't sleep off depression, grief, or insanity."

I sighed, and said, "Then what do you want me to do? Go to a hospital?"

"If it'll make you feel better. But sometimes those places just seem to close you off even more, keeping you in your head, shove medication down your throat... It's really not the best for everyone."

"I'm going for a walk."

"That's the spirit. Fresh air and exercise is always good for the mind. We'll finish the conversation when you get back."

I glared at the cat, and went to walk Freckles.

It was a nice walk, I breathed in and out, and Freckles didn't talk to me.

I had tea with Mrs. Nestor, we talked, and she didn't meow like a cat.

I went back home...

Rasputin was sleeping on my bed. I looked at him, sighed in relief...

And he winked an eye open and said, "Feeling better?"

"Are you some sort of demon?" I asked.

"Am I speaking in italics?" he said.

"...Uh... What?"

"Oh. Sorry. No, I'm just a cat."

I sat on the bed and pet him, which he stretched and let me pet his belly.

"Cats sure are assholes." I said, as I pet him.

"Comes with all the dying..."

"Oh yeah... you always do seem to never die permanently."

"Want to know a secret? Cats don't have nine lives... We only have one. We're just like you. Well, maybe not you specifically, Yule, but we're like people. But only a short 10 to 20 years if we're lucky..."

"I really did think you looked a lot like that cat who I pet in the slums... That was the nicest cat I've ever met..."

"I thought you were nice too, Yule." he said.

I stopped petting him and walked away.

"What?" he said, following me, "Can't a cat give a compliment?"

"Are you immortal or not?" I asked.

"Well... I wouldn't say it like that... it's just a matter of speaking in a certain way... having the right rhythm... going through the flow... and I completely distracted you. What were you saying?"

"Forget it. If you're not going to tell me, I don't want to know."

"You can't solve *every* mystery... but I'm sure you could try. Why didn't you solve Blister's?"

"I... I'll help him, if I can... I don't want him to keep hurting, over and over... Gosh... those blisters must've sure hurt..."

"Aww... You're caring. What a human reaction. Too bad he's burning in Hell."

"I-I'll find some way to save him. By God almighty."

"I don't think that's how it works. Calling on God doesn't make everything possible, even for an angel."

"Then... I'll try?"

"Ok. Sometimes all we can do is try. At least that."

"What was that you were telling me about Fate before? Max's sister... I feel like she really needs the help... but I don't know how to help her... how to try to get her out of her head, out of that insanity..."

"You're already starting a zoo in your apartment. Suicidal Japanese women, ghosts, you yourself, an angel, what if you offered her somewhere to stay? To have a home? I'm sure she called that church a home, but it was taken from her."

"...She's not going to do something nuts if I do, will she? The apartment downstairs is empty right now after our neighbors left..."

"Something nuts? You're talking to your cat."

"Lots of people talk to their pets."

"But usually they don't talk back. At least not in your own language."

"Alright... Thanks, Rasputin. I'll let Max know."

"Anytime. You nut." he said, and walked off.

32

I called Max, but he didn't answer. I left him a voicemail, inviting him and his sister to move in below us. I said that if he did, we could really all care for her together, like a family, since I knew that just Max and his mom were having a bit of a difficult time with only the two of them caring for Fate.

He called me back in a minute.

"Sorry I didn't pick up... I really just didn't want to talk, but I listened to your voicemail. You and Nevaeh acting so... bizarre, and my sister acting bizarre too... It just really irked me. Like you two were making fun of me and her." Max said over the phone.

"We weren't... We were just having fun in our own way. So what do you think of my invitation?" I asked.

"I don't know... As long as you two *never* pull off stunts like that while my sister is healing. My mom thinks it's a great idea, since I've told her all those stories of you and things... Said there couldn't be a better person to help me take care of her. My mom only didn't take her back to her house because she always has to work and everything and wouldn't be able to watch her... It's tough, because the lawyer we got is charging an arm and a leg to get Fate out of her debts..." Max said, "My mom says that with you and me together, with Nevaeh, we should be able to give Fate all the love and care she needs."

"It's probably better if she gets fresh air outside, instead of stuck in her own head in the hospital."

"Exactly my thoughts. She's not dangerous... just damaged. I... uh... brought her some tulips, and she looked me in the eyes for once... and she said my name."

"That's great, Max! She probably- Oh. Are you alright?" I said, as Max began crying on the phone.

"I- I never thought..." he tried to talk as he was sobbing, as I comforted him and told him it would be alright, "That I would be able to see the real her again! I..."

"Just take it easy, Max. Nevaeh and I will handle everything."

I called up the landlord, who was a really nice guy, and told him of Max and his sister's situation. He was a bit wary of allowing such a person, who had been to a mental hospital, to rent a space, but was glad I checked in with him. He said, "You've been the best tenant I've ever had, so if you say nothing bad will happen, I'll believe you. Don't screw up, ok? It'd break my heart. I'll come over and drop off the keys."

Nevaeh and Felix had come back, laughing at their silly adventure. They nearly lost the cow as Felix accidentally spooked it again, but found it again in the fields of the pasture. The cow had gone back home... even though the owner had noticed it missing. Nevaeh and Felix watched as the owner was flabbergasted at how the gate had come undone like that, and the cow had reappeared... but shrugged it off, thinking he had just forgotten about it. I guess all those little random things that people think they themselves did on accident are really ghosts.

It's easy to shrug something off, thinking that you had just forgotten about it, imagined it, created it out of your mind. Really, all those unexplained phenomena can be explained... even though you will never actually know the exact explanation. Even if it is that a ghost wiggles the latch off a gate and a cow gets out, or a cat starts up a conversation, or an angel appears before you.

Max's sister, Fate, didn't have any wounds, no scars, no bruises, but it looked like she had been hurt. She was very quiet when we came to visit her downstairs. She didn't say a single word.

Although she loved hanging outside with Max, Nevaeh and I, just sitting at the extra chairs and table I got for us, enjoying the sunlight. We always talked to her, even though she didn't talk back. I tried to show that I cared, just tried, and I think that trying would succeed in the end.

She noticed Felix, smiled at him, and then sighed and looked away. Felix stayed away from her... didn't try to spook her or anything, but the wind seemed to blow a catalog page for tulip bulbs to her... Really, Felix had just handed it to her.

She looked at the tulips, sighed, and said, "C-Can... you get me some of these?"

I called up the number on the page and ordered the tulips immediately.

Fate worked on her garden after the bulbs came, and she just sat in her new garden. Just sat, and waited for the flowers to bloom forth. She had something to hope for now.

Max and I were watching her in her garden, as she smiled in the sunlight, and Nevaeh and Felix had come back from their lunch date. Nevaeh was kissing Felix, saying, "One... Two... Oh. I'll let Fate enjoy herself. 'I'll' go inside..."

Fate turned and said, "Can Pancho slay my monsters again?"

We were quiet, and Nevaeh said, "Pancho? Who's that, Fate?"

"The man you're kissing. My imaginary friend. I didn't know other people could see him." Fate said, "Can you kill my monsters, please?"

Felix came forward, and said, "I will drive them back. You've grown up, and don't really need me anymore. But I will always be there for you."

"Thank you, Pancho. I've missed you." Fate said, and the two hugged.

Max took her inside, saying it was time for her medication, and Felix, Nevaeh and I watched them go into their apartment. Max breathed out a long, worn out sigh as he shut his door.

"Probably wasn't the best to talk to her like that..." Felix said, rubbing his arm, "But she was a good real person to be an imaginary friend for."

"Thank you, anyway." Nevaeh said, "Now where were we? Three..." and she kissed him again. Felix smiled and accepted her kisses.

"I talk to my cat, and I'm crazy." I said, sitting on the chair.

"I'm kissing a ghost. Four..." Nevaeh said, and kissed Felix again.

"Are you even real? Am I even real?" I asked.

"I wouldn't worry about it. Debating reality is fun... but in the end, you don't really get anywhere. You get stuck in the same boring existence you always were in, so what was the point of it? I just try to live my life and stay grounded." Nevaeh said.

"Like how?" I asked.

"Eh. Think of every possible solution, every possible outcome, and then throw them in a box for later. If it's really important, you can always open it back up again and think about it. If it's not, bury it in the box." she said.

"Hm. Alright. I think I'll pray for a bit, that always helps." I said, and went inside.

"Five..." Nevaeh said.

I kneeled by the bedside, and Rasputin watched for a second. He didn't say anything. I asked him why.

He *tried* to look around the room and ignore me, but said, "I was going to give you some space for this. Just for your little ritual."

"You really do love to hear yourself speak, don't you? I can't imagine why you were quiet for so long."

"And you're getting cleverer. I can never resist a good conversation..."

"A mocking, sarcastic conversation. I'll pray for your soul too."

"Likewise." he said, and left the room.

So I prayed to God, for Fate, Max, Nevaeh, Felix, Maximus, Rasputin, Thaniel, Mrs. Nestor and Freckles, Mason and his parents, May, the dishboy, Mike and Mr. Antonelli, Tanya and her family, Moritz, my family in Heaven... and got into a long prayer for the blisters guy. I hoped he would be able to heal, like Fate.

"How can I ever stop hurting?" Mr. Blisters said from behind me. It felt like he had crept in from the hissing of the vents.

I turned to him, and he looked like he was covered in blisters, them littering his body.

I tried to approach him, but he flinched at my approach.

I said, "I can help... heal it, I think. With the warmth of my soul, through everyone caring for me, for you, from myself caring for myself. I will try to help."

He calmed down, and knelt before me. I let my halo fire burn calmly in my hand, a warm gentle light, and let them hover over Mr. Blister's wounds. He said, "*I feel...* just a little better. The blisters don't feel so bad with you actually admitting that you notice them. That you care."

I touched his blisters, like Jesus must've touched the lepers, and I healed him with the power of God, with the power of my soul. I mean, he was already dead from those blisters, when one of them burst and had gotten infected. I couldn't heal him from death... but I could heal his lost spirit.

The blisters healed, and he sighed in relief, crying tears of joy.

I let him disappear, ascending to Heaven.

Part 5: Castitas

Chastity

33

Nevaeh and I were practically a psychiatry booth for ghosts. We'd set up shop in the backyard and give them all solace from their past problems and future worries. Some worried that they'd be stuck down here forever, because most didn't ascend very often, even if they learned how they died and made peace with the past. Only a precious few that I had helped actually went to Heaven, namely only the blisters guy, and a ghost puppy.

Nevaeh offered them somewhere to relax for a little bit, while they adjusted to life in their permanent limbo on Earth, and showed them around our apartment to let them talk with each other and make friends. Felix was kind of like our ghost security, although he wasn't aggressive against his ghost brothers and sisters, but just in case that giant hand of Hell came forth again… Felix was there to grab them back to Earth. Just in case.

Felix also cleared out the ghosts when Max and Fate came home, so that we wouldn't disturb Fate. Max would just be getting home with her from taking her to therapy now.

Felix cleared the room and shooed the ghosts back into the air, and with a strong gust of breeze they had all vanished again.

Fate had left the car, and Max walked her to the apartment. Fate just went straight to her tulip garden, however, and sat amidst the growing sprouts.

Max looked at her for a second, then lightly took me by the arm so he could have a word with me so Fate wouldn't hear. We walked to the side of the house and Max started a cigarette.

"You started smoking?" I asked.

"I never really wanted to... but it's better than caffeine, right? Just helps give me a breather..." he said.

"What's up?" I asked.

He inhaled, coughed a bunch, and said, "Ach. I didn't expect it to be so harsh."

I laughed, and said, "First time, huh? I didn't either. I think you're doing a great job with Fate."

He said, "I guess... I'm worried about that therapist she's seeing... He came highly recommended for cases like Fate's, but she never seems happier after she has therapy... More depressed, actually."

"I think that happens sometimes. She doesn't have to go to that specific therapist forever."

"Yeah... I'll look around. Thanks. It's nice having someone to talk to about things like this. I think you're doing great making Fate feel welcomed. She's never really had a whole garden to herself before."

"We're all in this together, bud." I said, and punched him on the arm.

"So... the cigarettes... Do they make me look cool? I mean, you smoke, and I think you're like ice." he said.

I laughed, and said, "You seem to be frowning whenever you inhale."

"Oh. I guess that's not very cool... Unless frowning is cool? What about this?" he said, and grinned with the cigarette hanging out of the corner of his mouth.

I laughed, and said, "Like a goddamn polar bear. You don't have to smoke to impress me."

"Really? Dang, mind holding onto these for me then?" he said, and gave me the cigarette pack. He tried finishing the cigarette, but frowned and coughed from it, so I took it out of his mouth and put it out myself.

Max went inside to make lunch while we, Nevaeh, Felix, and I, watched Fate. We let Fate enjoy her peace with her tulips.

A ghost walked back into the backyard, saying he thought he forgot his wallet.

I sighed, and said, "You don't have a wallet anymore, Greg."

"Really? I was sure I did… Makes me feel lost without it. Before I died I had a big fat paycheck cashed and finally went out into town…" the ghost said.

"What were you going to do in town?" I asked.

"Erm… nothing. I was… going to enjoy the arts!" he said nervously.

Nevaeh said, "Strippers?"

"…That's an art." he said.

"You would've lost that money one way or another, so just be glad for the scantily clad women you have seen, and think on that." I said.

"I guess… but the only scantily clad woman *I've* really seen is my wife…" he said.

Nevaeh said, "Really. Maybe you should haunt her and apologize instead of looking for a wallet you lost to look at other women?"

"I hope she goes to Hell… with her damned yoga practices with 'Seamus…'" Greg said.

"Oof." Nevaeh said, "I'm sure less things happen in yoga than what women's husbands think happens."

"No… I don't think so. It was a special private teacher I got for her… They'd be 'stretching' and 'posing' and wouldn't even let me watch them…" Greg said, "And she would never give me the time of day anymore, always spending that time for Seamus. So, I thought, fuck it, and went out to the strip club. Then I got hit by a bus."

"Sounds like an act of God." I said, "I mean… if God actually did that stuff… Does he? I'm not sure…"

"Hmph. I thought one of his chosen could at least make me not feel bad for getting hit by a bus." Greg said.

"Sorry." I said, "How about this? You go to that strip club, enjoy those butts and boobs, and do the thing you always wished you did. It'll give you relief from your loss of your wife, and your life."

"Really?? I… was so lost… and I lost my wallet… but I suppose, it doesn't really matter if I'm dead and no one can see me. You could be an astounding therapist. I'd recommend you for a job, but I don't think anyone would take a dead man's word. There's an opening now, after I died." Greg said.

"You were a therapist?" I asked.

"Yeah. Helped a lot of people, I mean I hope… Even helped this one guy get out of a case where he took all these drugs and lost his mind. He was forced into therapy because of it, court mandated, and I always gave him a letter to the judge that he was doing well… I mean, sometimes he just seemed totally out of it, but I'm sure he would do better if I told the domineering courts he actually was. He went a long way, and I believe is writing books now, even though has been diagnosed with schizophrenia." Greg said.

Fate was watching him, and asked, "Could you therapy me?"

Nevaeh and I were trying to let her down, gently explaining, and I said, "Fate… Um… Greg has a lot to do, now that he's dead… and shouldn't you see someone living?"

Fate said, "I don't want to see anyone living. You're all talking to dead people and speaking to me like I'm some sort of idiot. I want to see who I want to see, and not be babied like I'm a rape victim."

Nevaeh was taken aback, and said, "Hasn't… Hasn't horrible stuff happened to you? We just want to make sure you're safe now."

Fate said, "By Calmaog, I swear if you don't let me talk to this therapist, I'll tell Max you all see him too."

"Defiance is a good thing for one who has been recently hurt badly." Greg said, "Means she's having faith in herself and not things like... Calmaog."

"Calmaog is the divine blood in us all. We all live through him, and I gave myself to him and his followers." Fate said.

"Yeah... It wasn't very fun, was it..." Greg said, sitting beside her in the tulips, "I never liked going to church, but I always did for the people I cared about. Who did you care about?"

"I... I cared about my family of Calmaog's... But... I just... liked... a friend of mine... Calmaog liked me... and me and her were his favorites..." Fate said.

"Did you like Calmaog back?" Greg said.

"He... loved me... and it would hurt to say that I did not love him back... but I did not love him back." Fate said.

"You don't have to explain. Please, we can continue somewhere you feel is safe and comfortable." Greg said.

"...Will you hurt me then? When I am safe and comfortable? Like Calmaog?" Fate said.

"No, Fate. It's actually impossible for me to. See, watch this." Greg said, and passed a hand gently through Fate.

She looked at the hand, and said, "...Ok. But I feel safest in this garden, or with my brother..."

"Then let's continue talking here. Yule, Nevaeh, Felix, please help Fate's brother with lunch. I smell something burning, and I think he could really use the help." Greg said.

We went inside, and let Fate talk with her new ghost therapist.

Max had burned his hand on the stove, making paninis for us, and was running his hand through cold water. I quickly took the pan off the paninis, and took them off the frying pan. They were nearly burned to a crisp…

"Sorry, guys… Fucking hell, that hurt…" Max said, "How's Fate doing?"

"She's just… enjoying the garden. She just wanted some time alone, so we're going to help you! Yeah. These paninis are great! Very salvageable, mhm." I said.

"Alright. I'm worried when she's alone… but I suppose she's gotta get some time for that. Let's set the table." Max said.

"You don't eat like animals like me and Yule? We just eat in front of the TV." Nevaeh said.

"Of course not! Every meal is a blessing! Or some BS like that. It's just a good time to chat." Max said, and took out the plates for the table. We helped him and set his table.

Soon, we called Fate back in, and she was looking strangely happy with Greg. I think they were just talking about jokes and stuff, but she was more the better for it, and waved him goodbye as he rushed away in the breeze.

Fate, Max, Neveah, Felix, even though he couldn't eat and Max couldn't see him, and I all sat down for lunch.

Fate enjoyed her paninis like nothing else. She said, "All we had was the milk of Calmaog. It feels nicer not eating that…"

"Calmaog can go to Hell." Max said, taking a bite of his crispy panini.

Fate grew tearful, and started crying. Max quickly said he was sorry.

Fate calmed down, and said, "I know you do not understand… but Calmaog was my life."

Max said, "Calmaog took your life. It- just makes me frustrated… You don't have to worship anything you don't want to."

Fate said, "Then I won't worship Calmaog… or God, or Satan, or anything. I'll just be a lost soul in the breeze. Is that what you want??"

Max said, "Well, kinda, yeah."

She started crying again.

Max swore and said, "I will do anything to help you. I just don't know why you cling to that church! They took advantage of you! They abused you! What the fuck do you see in them?? It's not like they're your family!!"

Fate just continued crying.

Felix calmed her down, by doing a strange dance that Fate seemed to enjoy.

"You remember our happy dance, Pancho." Fate said.

Max said, "...Alright. You're ignoring me and talking to your imaginary friend. Sorry... I just wish- I just wish it never happened to you..."

Fate turned to him, and said, "I'm just glad you're my brother... and that you care for me, and won't do things like my other brothers did..."

"I'm your only brother, Fate." Max said.

"...I know. Brothers of... Calmaog... and when they-" Fate said.

Max held her hand as she remembered and told us of what happened, letting her know she had a true brother.

34

I had listened to Fate tell her memories of the cult. It looked like she was still stuck there, even though she was safe in Max's apartment. And boy, like Max… I wish I could just destroy that stupid cult.

I looked them up on the internet, with their flashy website and "welcoming" words… They were still going strong, almost getting religion status in America. This seemed evil, demonic, awful, and I wondered if a denizen like that was this Calmaog…

Their god had risen on Earth, like Christianity's in a sense, but their god was still living and breathing, walking around and talking to people. I saw a "heavenly" looking picture of him on the website. They invited me or anyone reading to go to their meeting on Sunday, same time as around church for me on Sunday.

"I thought you already had a religion?" Rasputin said from underneath the chair.

"I do, but I'm just wondering… if I could destroy this one." I said.

"Religious persecution. How quaint. You could be an old crusader, screaming 'Death to the Saracen!' Will you be looting their coffers when you are finished as well?" Rasputin said.

He hopped on my lap, and I pet him while he purred.

On Sunday, I went to this demonic church. Just to check it out. Just to see what it was about.

They actually had a headquarters for their cult, a big friendly building, a sibling to ones around the country. I walked in dressed in pants and a shirt. No skirts for this church. This god didn't need to see anything heavenly about me. This'd be like eyeing my opponent in the arena, all business, and planning my sure, swift strike to kill them in one fell swoop.

I sat in the chairs of people dressed extravagantly rich, of all types. Old ladies, young men, old men, young ladies, no children though. It was frankly a rather boring ceremony, even with their over the top doctrines. I feel like they ripped a lot of things off of the Bible, just made their own little twists here and there, and accredited the acts to Calmaog instead of God.

Then Calmaog came out, to talk to his people.

I was sure I would smell brimstone, see horns and a spiked tail… but he was just a man, and he even stumbled on accident going to the stage.

"Brothers and sisters of Calmaog. Welcome to this holy mass. We give thanks for what we take, and we will take the world. You are all strong, holy, and will receive your just reward. We will all ascend to the mothership, together, and join as one in the fleshy mass of the nether.

"Do not take this life for granted! The Earth is sacred, as my birthplace. Let your loved ones not stride in strife, forever to walk the Earth as ghosts amongst the living! Take nothing for granted, and take what you deserve. For you deserve peace in the gates of the body.

"Believe in yourself! Believe in Calmaog. Love yourself, love Calmaog."

The saying was murmured back to him. I stayed silent.

"We thank you for your cash donations as you leave this church. If you do not have money for a donation, please help around our sacred sanctuary. Peace be with you." Calmaog said, and left the stage.

I was getting up to leave with the rest of these lost sheep, and when I got to the priest taking donations... *huge* donations were being thrown in the huge basket. It looked like hundreds and hundreds of dollars had been accumulated, after the first person left the building.

I had a dollar in my pocket, but I still wouldn't donate a thing to Calmaog.

I tried to sneak out, but one of Calmaog's faithful, the "priest," lightly took me by the arm to the side and said, "Sister. Please help with the church if you don't have anything to spare."

I shook my arm from his hand, and said, "I'm not going to help you with your blasphemy."

"Blasphemy? Please, we really need the help... The roof is leaking, and the other faithful need help in the garden... They haven't had a good meal in days because the crop has been ruined by insects. Please." he said.

I looked into his eyes. He looked desperate. He honestly looked like he was telling the truth.

I said, "Er... I suppose I can help you clean up the place a bit. Just for your followers."

"Thank you. Thank you so much, Sister." and bowed to me, showing me to the commune.

He led me into the inner sanctum, with walls around but the open sky breathing down on the people working these fields, dressed in bland white clothes, all the same.

Then the priest shut the gate behind me, and locked it.

I threw myself at the gate, telling the priest he better let me out *right now.*

"I-I'm sorry. It is Calmaog's will." he said... and it still looked like he was telling the truth.

I frantically looked for a way out of this commune, but there wasn't another entry or exit apparent. The workers noticed me for a second, but then quickly went back to working.

A big woman with two men came to greet me. I tried to call someone, the police, Max, anyone, but she snatched the phone from my hand before I pressed dial.

"Ah. Welcome to the commune. I am the Mother of Calmaog. Please, let's get you into something more comfortable." she said.

"Give me back my phone!! Just let me out of here!!" I yelled.

"You must lose yourself from Earthly possession and feelings tying you down. You must be free like the breeze. Please, take our sister to the indoctrination chambers." she said.

The two men grabbed me roughly. I thought about slaying them with my sword, burning them to a crisp with my halo fire, but… I could never use the power of Heaven on a living soul. I don't think that would even work anyway.

They threw me in a small concrete room, and the woman said, "Undress."

"Fuck no! Let me out of this hole!" I said, and swung a fist at her, but she took the blow, and didn't flinch. I whacked her again and again, but she still stood in front of me.

"I can turn the other cheek. Now undress." she said.

I just kept beating and beating her, trying to push her away, but she still stood before me, then the men came from behind her with a hose.

They blasted me with that water, like a fire engine's. I felt like my skin would burst off from the force. And they kept blasting me with that water.

"Undress." the woman said, and they blasted me again.

This was getting me nowhere, so I said, "Alright, alright, but I warn you, I'll kill you if you touch me."

So I took off my clothes, and they blasted me again with the hose.

"Undress." she said.

"...I'm not taking off my underwear." I said.

And they blasted me with the hose.

I refused! I did not need to go through this torture! Whenever I tried to beat the woman in front of me away, they blasted me with the hose.

So, angry and humiliated, I took off my bra and underpants.

And they blasted me with the hose.

They took my clothes and closed the door, locking it. I sat there in the dark, dripping wet and naked... I just prayed for hope, strength... and vengeance.

35

It felt like an eternity in that hole. I did not know how much time had passed alone in the dark in the wet and cold. But I continued the Lord's Prayer, over and over again…

After I was on my thousandth prayer, they opened the door and threw me those bland white clothes. I put them on, shivering, thankful for anything to wear.

They then let me into the commune, so I would work their fields.

The men led me to the fields, with that woman watching over the whole thing, overseers scattered throughout the fields shouting out Calmaog's teachings and mandates. They commanded me to work, and even though I just wanted to kill them all, I saw the bedraggled worker beside me motion to start working.

I picked beans, and placed them in a basket beside me.

I tried to whisper to the worker, "Do you need help? We can't stay here."

But the worker just continued working, even though he looked at me frightened for a second.

I picked beans, scanning for a way out. The gate was closed and locked with heavy chains. If only I had my wings… I could fly out into that big, empty sky.

I worked the day away, finding solace with the plants and other workers, even though they were both silent.

This annoying horn wailed, signaling it was time for another mass of Calmaog's. We filed single file into a small room… and the Mother of Calmaog played us a tape on an old TV.

There, Calmaog congratulated us on a fine day's work. He was smoking a pipe sitting in a luxurious cabin, and said that one of us will be ascended soon, a true believer, a lucky chosen. They would ascend to the mothership and become part of that fleshy mass in the nether.

I looked around the room, and these people were staring at the TV like zombies. They were totally absorbed in Calmaog's every word. I glazed over at him rattling on about impossible divine acts. Everyone knows Jesus didn't step aside for Calmaog, congratulating Calmaog as a true messiah! This utter blasphemy… Calmaog said on the TV, "I truly love each and all of you. Believe in yourself! Believe in Calmaog. Love yourself, love Calmaog."

The phrase was repeated back to the screen. I was silent.

They put me in a bunk bed, locking us in our shared room. It looked like a hundred people were here, all in this same room, squished together in bunk beds. There was no way out of here, and worse was the guard standing by the locked door.

He wasn't nearly as tough looking as my enemies of the past. Felix would castrate him in a second if he stepped foot in the arena.

I went to the bucket to relieve myself, then smashed the guard in the stomach with my fist, in the head with my other as he was doubled over, and beat him unconscious. It was nice to let out some anger.

I looked in his pocket for the key… but there was none. He was locked in here with us.

Someone started screaming for help.

I whispered out, "It's alright! I'm going to get you people out of here-"

But the woman kept yelling for help, yelling, "Help us, Calmaog! Help!"

The Mother of Calmaog unlocked the door with swarms of men.

"I pity your soul, Sister… Such violence. Take her to the indoctrination chambers." she said.

I kicked and screamed, even bit one man's ear off, but they overpowered me with sheer numbers, and threw me back into the hole.

And they blasted me with the hose.

It was days in that commune. It'd nearly be Easter soon, and I shuddered at the thought of spending it in this wretched place. The same boring routine over and over again, wake up, sit in front of the TV with Calmaog saying the same damn thing if in different words, eat this crappy mush that they made us eat, work the fields, and watch the TV again.

I muttered the words, "Believe in yourself. Believe in Calmaog. Love yourself, love Calmaog…"

They had thrown me into the hole again after I said, "Jesus is cooler than Calmaog." during that part… and blasted me over and over again. At least it was a nice change of routine being thrown into the hole and being blasted by the hose, because I could at least choose when that happened by acting out.

I didn't understand why these people didn't rebel! Why didn't they riot and fight! All of us together could destroy their people and smash that gate to nothing! While we were planting seeds, I tried planting the seeds of rebellion.

I whispered blasphemous things to the workers, explaining that we could defeat Calmaog. They quickly turned away from me, but it felt better hearing my own voice talk like that if anything.

And they kept fucking blasting me with the hose! I had bruises all over my body from that fire engine strength blast. I was black and blue, and a few blood vessels had ruptured underneath the skin, showing pulpy bits of red on me as well.

When they changed our clothes after a week, I was given another bland outfit of white, the same as what I had, if a bit too large. I always had to pull my pants back up because they would fall off my naked ass.

I was sitting in the cold, wet, dark hole, worn out from working the fields and being beaten by water so many times. I tried to sleep, shivering in my solitude.

I wish I had told someone about this... I wish I made sure someone knew where I was. I didn't want them to know I was poking around in this awful place... and have them worry about Fate, in case I made too big a deal about it. I realized that you should *always* tell someone where you are going, leave a record of it somehow, anything. The only one who knew I had come here was my cat who talked to me.

The only one who knew I left Heaven was St. Peter. I wish he could help me again... I wish he could send some sort of heavenly aid... but what could he do? Open the gates for me after I died in this awful place? I prayed for aid anyway.

I fell asleep... and had friendly chats with demons. It was definitely a nightmare, but I thanked the demons for not being so bad as living people. Satan whispered, *"We were all in your shoes once."*

I woke up in a fright. Was I the Devil in this church?

I whispered in the devoted's ears, I spread corruption and rebellion. And all I wished was to fall out of this sacred sanctuary and go back to my own place.

On the TV mass, Calmaog said on screen, "A lucky follower, a true believer will be called on today. Look at your tags on the inside of your shirts. The divine number of 36 will ascend and come to my side."

I looked at the tag on the inside of my shirt, and I was number 36.

36

Calmaog had entered the gates. I stood before him, looking for any demonic excuse to slay him. Any smell of brimstone, any little demon in his ear, anything. But I knew he was human, as he talked nervously to the people gathered in the fields for this "event."

"My daughter will ascend! Hail her as the chosen of Calmaog! Love her, love Calmaog!" Calmaog said, and the phrase was yelled back.

They took me out of the gates, the gates of this faux Heaven.

I would've ran, if I didn't want to beat the ever living shit out of Calmaog so badly.

His men and he took me to a back room in the church. He waved me into the room, after he had entered it himself. I went in and they closed the door behind me. "Are you ready to ascend?" he asked, "All you need to do is open the gates."

"What?" I said.

"The gates of your body. You must release yourself and become one with me." he said, and took a step towards me.

I stepped back.

"Just drop your pants and bend over. It won't be long." Calmaog said.

I smashed him in the face, and told him I would kill him.

He shocked me with a taser.

I lay on the ground, twitching, and he said, "Or lay there. That works."

He pulled down his pants, and then my own.

Is this what Fate felt? What Nevaeh felt? This horrible shame and anger? This awful... *rape?*

After he had finished I had regained control of my body.

I tore his dick off. Just wrenched the fucking thing off his body, with a sharp, swift snap.

He screamed, and blood spurted from where his genitals were.

The men came rushing into the room, and I dropped his bleeding dick to the floor.

"I'll kill you all if you don't let me go." I said.

They stepped back. I walked out of the room, out of the doors of the church, and ran down the street.

I was so happy that I was free. But I was crying tears of sadness and anger.

I called the police from a public phone with spare change laying on the machine, and told them I was raped. They took me immediately to a hospital and I told them of what happened. The semen was still on me, and they took a sample and helped me wash off. They took my disgusting bland white clothes, and even took a sample of Calmaog's skin underneath my fingernails from when I ripped off his genitalia.

I just shuddered in anger from this whole affair, as they got my whole story again and again. "You ripped his penis off? My, you've got balls- I mean, you're very brave." Dave the cop said.

They were treating me from my wounds, all those bruises and internal bleeding, and Max and Nevaeh came rushing in and hugged the crap out of me.

"We were so worried!! What happened? I've only heard rumors about it so far. Something about- rape. In that cult, with Calmaog- He didn't touch you, did he? If he did, I swear I will find and kill him this time. First my sister, then you- I just want to kill something." Max said.

"I… was raped by him. I don't really want to talk about it… But I hope he dies bleeding out from where his penis was." I said.

They just held my hands lightly, crying.

We watched TV for awhile, and fucking Calmaog was on it… but the picture shown of him was an awful, ugly one, of him being arrested in the hospital. His poor people… his idiot followers, who just wanted to love themselves, were being freed. Other ones were reporting cases like mine, but after they were raped, men and women, they were meticulously cleaned…

With the hose.

And only I had escaped, leaving an unmistakable mark on the rapist. No penis.

Calmaog's many lawyers he bought with the incredible donations, from people who were just like him and wanted idiot sex slaves, usually got Calmaog out of any legal jam, but my evidence was too damning for him this time. The Church of Calmaog was damned to Hell with my words, with the growing anger and hate for this sort of cult.

Families were reunited with their loved ones, and the world was just a little bit more free of evil.

I finally went home, and hugged Fate, saying I understood her pain. I asked her how she ever escaped. She said, "He let me go, after he couldn't get aroused from me anymore. Thank you for ending it."

Felix, who was giving Fate company, said, "You castrated him… and even then some?? We're like brother and sister now! We could've made an astounding duo! 'The Castrators…' I like the sound of that."

I laughed, and said, "If you castrated anyone like Calmaog, then I thank you ten times over."

Nevaeh and I went to our apartment back upstairs, and she just hugged and hugged me. She smelled nice, not like Calmaog at all.

I pet my cat, Rasputin, asking him how he was doing.

He said, "I kind of missed you. Nevaeh is a little more bony in the lap area." and jumped on my lap.

"Thanks, I guess." I said.

"So did you get what you wanted? You destroyed that religion, just like you said." Rasputin said.

"I… feel like I've been martyred. It sucks that people only realized how horrible something like that was after it happened to me." I said, petting him sadly.

"Jesus didn't die happy. No one likes suffering for their cause. But I think you've learned your lesson."

"What lesson is that?"

"Don't only talk to your cat about things."

I nodded, smiling, and continued to pet him.

37

Fate just had another therapy session with Greg, and she had cried a lot, but said she really needed to unload those tears. She said she felt like she was carrying them around for so long...

I just sat on the lawn chair, feeling and looking like shit. I felt like I could use a therapist as well. But thankfully, I had a boyfriend instead.

We went to Easter mass, and the choir was extra booming and joyous. They sounded like the choir of Heaven in truth.

People offered their condolences to me whenever they could. It was nice for a while, just that people cared, but I soon wished they didn't know me, or knew I was raped.

I had a little get together with other women who've been through the same thing. Tanya, Nevaeh, Fate, and I all met and had coffee in our apartment. We cried, we laughed, and gave each other support. It kind of sucks when you belong in the rape victim club, but at least there's lots of faces in there, friendly, supportive faces, faces that you even know.

I waved Tanya goodbye and Fate went back downstairs. Nevaeh sat in front of the TV and ate chips. She kind of reminded me of how Sax was, but was way more pleasant.

I wondered how that little demon who seemed to constantly be changing even got to Earth? We really didn't need demons, humans can be their own worst nightmare all on their own. Calmaog proved that. But still, there were demons, who perhaps all had been living and deserved their eternal damnation.

Like Darcy. She murdered her husband in cold blood, and somehow died, but that wasn't enough justice. No, she had to come back to Earth and cause more suffering, being a concealed succubus. At least she was locked in an asylum now, screaming at everyone and telling them she was a demon from Hell. And Molech had fallen from godhood, twice at least. People didn't worship him anymore, and soon learned that things someone tells you, especially a god of child sacrifice, may not be true. Thanks to me, he could never utter another lie.

But Satan would always live... and I played his part in a church all by myself. Everything he said seemed like something he would do... Like when he told Sax that betraying everything, like Satan did to God, would haunt him forever in Hell. Like how he said he was in my shoes before, being locked in Heaven or something.

He still tried to kill Nevaeh and tried to take me away as the guise of Maximus. He threatened me, and the entire Earth, with Hell.

Was it just a threat? He was the King of Lies... even if some of his words were true. And anyway, the best liars don't lie one hundred percent of the time... they throw in a bit of truth, just to mix it up, just to make you trust them a little bit, so that they can pull the wool over your eyes.

I began to wonder why I ever reentered this horrible existence. I thought of Satan's words, *"Kill yourself and ascend."*

It was awful to think of.

But I wondered about it just a little bit.

Max snapped me out of it, saying, "I see it."

"See what?" I asked.

"All that crazy shit you and Nevaeh have been doing. I didn't want to admit it, I thought I was losing my mind... But I see it. That ball of fire in your hand as you took out Molech's tongue. Felix the ghost. It just boggles my mind." he said.

I hugged him, thanking him.

"Don't ever leave Earth yet, because you're my guardian angel. Tell me if you ever do something so idiotic as to get vengeance for Fate and I. Because sometimes even a guardian angel needs protecting." Max said, "I love you, Yule."

"I love you too, Max."

We kissed, sealing our love.

We didn't have sex for a good while, as the intrusive feeling of being raped was fresh in my mind. But slowly… I took him to bed, and he took extra care to my needs, was extra gentle and generous, and made me feel like bliss again. I suppose one bad experience, one bad apple, doesn't really ruin the bunch if you've picked out a really good apple from there. Like my Max. My good apple I got for Christmas.

Part 6: Humilitas

Humility

38

The tulips were blooming, and with them Fate. Fate had come to live in the apartment downstairs, and she seemed much better off. Fate had come in the spring, during time of renewal, regrowth, and rebirth.

And my own fate had come as well.

The crack had grown wider, and wider, over time, and I tried to ignore it for a while... but then a huge chunk of earth cracked to pieces and fell into that hole.

As I looked down into the screaming portal to Hell in my backyard, a giant fissure that opened up, I just hoped nothing would come out of it. It looked terrifying, a swirling vortex of lost souls, screaming in agony, if only faintly because we were so far away from them on Earth.

Felix, Nevaeh, Fate and Max were just as terrified as me.

Felix tried to hide his fear, like a noble gladiator, but he could not resist the urge to shudder with those screams.

Nevaeh held onto her Bible close, warding the pit back with it in front of her.

Fate had a tulip she picked, and she just stared at it instead of the pit.

Max threw some litter into the pit.

"Max!" I said.

"What? It is a giant, horrible hole of satanic trash." Max said.

"Just don't- don't rouse anything to come out of it." I said.

"Oh! Right, yeah..." Max said.

"I need to tell someone about this straight away... Stay away from that thing, alright, guys? Go somewhere else for a while, except for you, Felix. This is your chance to help me fight back Hell." I said.

"I did say I would, didn't I... Well, alright. I will guard the pit to Hell." Felix said.

We waved Felix goodbye, telling him to be careful, and he waved back, then looked down into the pit. We left in Nevaeh's car, while Max took Fate to their mother's house in his car. Nevaeh and I drove around. "Where do you need to go for cases like this, anyway?" Nevaeh said, "Is there some sort of Help With Hell Rupturing Forth group?"

"Sometimes wisdom can be found in the most ordinary of places. Take me to the bar, please." I said.

"...Is this really a time to be getting drunk? I mean, I guess I understand..." Nevaeh said.

"I just need to talk to Thaniel. If the world is ending, I at least want to tell him everything will be alright." I said.

"...Yeah, I guess... We'll all go to Heaven... Whoop dee fucking doo..." she said. Nevaeh dropped me off, and went to go to make peace with her parents, to tell them she loved them, and to tell them maybe goodbye.

Thaniel was really drunk.

I could hardly get a word in edgewise, because he kept explaining how fissures come forth, like when a large amount of force is pressed into the earth, like from a meteorite. Finally I said, "Thaniel. Things are going to get bad... really bad. You need to be safe. I want to tell you that drinking with you has been the best it's ever been. You're a true friend, I mean that."

He said, "Iiiii am? That... means so much! Iffff you haven't noticed, I'm a drunken fool with hardly a friend in the worlddddd... Friends become kinda useless when you get married, and my best friend wasss my wife for so long..."

"Could you take care of my cat, Rasputin, for a while?" I asked.

"Youuu goin' somewhere? Where's that?" he said.

"...I... don't know... I may... have to go back home. I may have to go into that pit. I don't know." I said.

"Weee all go everywhere, don'tcha? It'sssss... just a good time to goooo... Nothing better than a few hundred pages and a talking cat..." he said.

"...What?" I asked.

"Ooohhhh... just this story I've beennnn writing... We all gotta end sometimeeee... I'd end with a kiss. My favorite endddd... Don't let the reader see it comin' though!" he said, grinning.

"...Alright. Well, goodbye, Thaniel. May we meet again." and I kissed him on the cheek. Let his story have a happy ending, when I leave his for good.

He blushed, and said, "I... think of you as my daughter, sometimes... I know you're not, but ever since you told me your parents are all dead... I thought I could help fill in the gap, y'know? When we first met it sounded like you were praying to your father in Heaven."

"Thank you, Thaniel. For the company, the advice, and for being my friend. You are a great father." I said, smiling.

He grinned, slurped down the rest of his beer, and slumped to the side. It looked like he passed out, still grinning.

I shrugged, and went to talk to Mrs. Nestor.

I knocked on her door, and Freckles was already barking in happiness to see me. Mrs. Nestor opened the door and invited me inside, saying she wanted to talk to me.

She had already made tea, and didn't expect me to take Freckles for a walk. She sat me down, smiling lightly, and asked me what I was so gloomy for.

"I… think I want to tell you… but I don't think you'll believe me… I just want you to be safe in the times to come." I said.

"So… it is that bad, huh… I thought our bimbo president would end up killing us… Didn't expect someone else to beat her to it…" she said, sipping at her tea.

"…Huh?" I said.

"Oh, c'mon, Yule. I know you don't belong here. Do you really think I'd let some complete stranger walk my dog, even for free?" she said.

"…You know who I am?" I asked.

"I know you're an angel, if that's whatcha mean." Mrs. Nestor said.

"…How? I thought no one could tell besides demons…" I said.

"I'm not a demon, Yule. Just an old lady. You learn a lot in a long life, where people are supposed to be, where they're not. And you most definitely don't belong here." she said, "Plus I didn't exactly know until you just admitted it…"

I laughed, and said, "As cunning as ever, Mrs. Nestor. Is there anything I can do for you? Before I have to close that pit to Hell that ruptured in my backyard?"

She spilled her tea, and said, "I didn't know *that*. I… guess it couldn't have come at a better time…"

"…What do you mean?" I asked.

"I'm dying, dear." she said.

"…Oh. Can I help ease your passing?" I said.

"Just give Freckles a good home. He's a good dog, even though he's a rabid mongrel sometimes, and I'd hate to see him end up at the pound. I'd ask my son to take care of him… but he and I aren't speaking, no good drunk. You did always want a dog, correct?" she said, with Freckles's head on her lap.

"Yes… but… I didn't- didn't want to have one because of this…" I said, getting sad.

"Don't feel bad, dear. You've been through so much. I have too. Dying is just the rest you get after it's done." Mrs. Nestor said.

"I think of you kinda like my grandma… I know that's weird, but I never really had a grandma before… just a crotchety old grandpa who spit at all the kids. I really do care for you, and I'm glad we could grow from being strangers to being friends." I said.

"Me too, Yule. Please, take Freckles with you, as a guide dog, as a companion, as a friend. I am feeling very tired… and would like to get some rest." she said.

I nodded, smiling, even with a teardrop streaming from my eye.

I took Freckles for a walk, a walk where I knew he would never see his master again. He whined back at the house, as I went crying back home, but I told him and myself it'll be alright.

39

I came back home with Freckles... and Rasputin was sitting outside. Felix waved hello.

"Did you let the cat out?" I asked Felix.

"No. But he's just been staring at me all day... like he wants to tell me something. I swear that if he could talk he would." Felix said.

Freckles whined at Rasputin, and Rasputin hissed at him, which shut Freckles up.

"What's the problem, Rasputin?" I asked.

Rasputin went pawing at the door. I sighed, and let him back inside. I took Freckles with, to show him his new home for a little while, before I have to give him away to Max or Nevaeh or someone.

Rasputin turned to me after lapping up some water, and said, "You aren't seriously thinking of going down to Hell, are you? Just because a giant pit opens up doesn't mean you have to jump into it."

"I don't know... I need to close it, and if I get trapped in Hell for eternity trying to, at least I tried." I said.

"Damnit. You're not supposed to remember things your cat tells you. What if you just took me to the Bermudas and forgot about it?" Rasputin said.

Freckles barked.

I said. "That's not how caring for other people works. You don't let a giant pit stay a giant pit, in case people fall into it. You close it, heal the Earth's wounds, and you-"

"Make restitutions like you're dying?" Rasputin finished.

"...If that's what it takes." I said, crossing my arms.

Freckles whined at me.

Rasputin said, "Shush, you hound. She doesn't need to hear that."

"What? What did he say?" I asked.

"Oh, he just whined at you…. being a dumb dog…" Rasputin said snarkily.

Freckles growled at him.

"What is it, boy? Do *you* know what I should do? Because I'm a little lost." I said.

Freckles smiled up at me, then walked past Rasputin and went into my room. He came back holding a piece of my shield I had kept.

Rasputin said, *"That's* not going to help her… She's already forgotten about the past, anyway…"

"The past?" I said.

Freckles the golden retriever went back into my room and retrieved something else. I don't know how, it's not like he's ever been there before, but he found me the card given to me by Mason gently clutched in his maw.

"You're just being ridiculous now." Rasputin said.

Freckles whined, and went back one more time… and came back holding a lock of Maximus's hair. My one possession in the gladiator pits.

"Freckles! How did you get that?? This- This is exactly Maximus's lock of hair!" I said, gently taking the lock out of his mouth.

He smiled up at me.

"Ok, that could do something. You could make Maximus join you in your suicide." Rasputin said.

"Huh? Oh, no, no, no… I could never coerce another angel out of Heaven! They'd be giving up their Paradise!" I said.

Then a form smashed through the roof, landing in front of me. "There's no Paradise without you." the form said, and Maximus, the real Maximus, got up, dusting off the dust and debris, and stood before me, wings burned off from the fall, halo shining bright.

"*Maximus??* H-How did you get here??" I asked.

"I… heard about it from other angels, of you fighting demons, taking on the forces of Hell in your own capacity, with not a friend on the Earth, but those faithful few. I- know… or I've heard… that you're seeing someone? Is that true? I mean not that it matters! I just- hope- you get enough love. Yes. That is it. I hope that you are loved." Maximus said.

"…Uh. Yes, Maximus. I am loved. Have you come to aid me against the wrath of Hell?" I said.

"Yes! I did… but I really did not like falling from Heaven… Smashing through the roof really hurt, too… But St. Peter, the sly fox, tipped me off how you got out. Really very simple, just walk off that one cloud. I went to look… and he pushed me! Just let me fall back down to you! I suppose I shouldn't have been bellyaching about how much I missed you- I mean, wished to help you in your struggles." Maximus said.

"And you fell to this exact same spot?" I asked.

"Well… I had a sort of pull. Something of the past that drew me here, and I navigated as best I could to that pull. I believe it was you." he said.

I pat Freckles on the head, and hid the lock of hair behind my back. I slyly hid it behind the coffee machine.

"So… How's life upstairs?" I asked.

"Marvelous. It's like the epitome of everything great- Wait. Can I ever go back??" he asked.

"We'll get there when we get there. Let's go talk to Felix." I said, and Maximus, the dog and the cat followed me outside.

"Hello, Castrator. Ever get over that rash?" Maximus asked, glaring at Felix.

"For you, it will always be the Castrator. You look plump. Like you've been feasting on manna." Felix said.

"I haven't gained a single pound!" Maximus said.

"As narcissistic as ever. Well. What do we do now?" Felix asked.

"Anything pop out of there yet, Felix?" I asked.

"Um... No, not yet... but that form that looked like a small fly, because it was so far away in the pit... is getting closer and closer... and it looks like a large dragon." Felix said.

"Classic." I said, "Nevaeh would love this... I'm glad she's safe."

But her car screeched into the driveway, and she got out saying, "Yule! Please don't go in that pit! I kinda thought you would, with your goddamn holy duty and crap... But don't go in that pit! At least not without me!"

And Max's came to a halt behind hers, and he and Fate got out, "She's going into the pit?? I swear to God, Yule... I'll break up with you if you kill yourself! I'd be sore as hell if you tried to jump into a pit!"

They ran up to me, as I explained that I needed to do this, and Fate said, "I want you to be my sister, one day. A real sister. It's my hope. Don't die before that."

I stayed quiet as Max blushed.

And Max noticed Maximus.

"...Who's this, Yule?" Max said.

"Oh this is just Max-" I started saying.

"Maximus. Pleased to introduce myself to you, Yule's boyfriend." Maximus said.

Max glared at him. You could really see the size difference when the two were put together like this... Maximus had a huge frame, and Max, he was just Max.

"Max." Max said, and shook his hand.

They continued to glare and seemed to be shaking their hands eternally, so I took them by the shoulders, broke them off, said, "This is not the time to be passive aggressively fighting each other." and took Max to the side, "Listen, Max, you're the best boyfriend I've ever had… I love you, but I need to leave you… maybe forever."

"What??" he said.

Maximus said, "I will join Yule, take down this pit, and kill Satan if I have to."

Felix said, "Well she'd just get killed pretty quickly with only you. I'm going too."

"What do you mean, Yule?" Max said, "You're going to leave me for Maximus? And then jump in a pit?? Listen, I didn't mean that about breaking up with you! I l-love you!"

"I'm not leaving you for Maximus… I just think I'll never be able to see you again… so want you to continue your life without me. At least you can do that." I said.

"Fuck, no!! I'm not giving up on you! P-Please, just stay with me and my mom for a while! And Fate too! We all love y-you, Yule!" he said.

I felt so sad. I would've loved to spend more time with his family… I felt like this brief relationship was beginning to mirror Heaven…

Then the dragon flew out of the pit.

Black wings in the clouds, wings of death, burst forth from the ground. The dragon roared, cackling, saying, *"St. George could never dominate me forever! I will conquer this world, and bring glory to HELL!!"*

The dragon burned fire on our apartment, setting it ablaze, and flapped gusts of wind at us like a gale of a tornado.

We all flew into the pit, falling to Hell.

40

It was even worse than falling from Heaven to Earth. I'd keep hitting ledges on the side, smashing into them and falling, continuing to go deeper, and deeper, and deeper.

I hit a ledge that held, as my friends continued to fall. I reached out for them as they screamed and fell, but I had hit my head on the way down, and was losing consciousness...

I saw the dragon making Hell for people on Earth in my unconscious dreams.

Mrs. Nestor, screaming as she got out of her house with her husband's rifle, yelling, "I just want to die in peace!! Go back to Hell!" and shooting at the dragon, landing her on her butt from the force of the rifle recoil.

Thaniel, rubbing his eyes as the dragon burned down the bar, after he had just left, and promising to himself that he would never drink again.

All my friends of the past were being thrown into chaos, they were running for their lives, some praying for peace at the sure end of their life.

A hand poked one of my breasts, waking me up. I blinked my eyes and saw a tiny little demon, as when I first saw him, Sax.

He scattered back and hid behind a rock. He said, *"I came back to Hell now."*

I rubbed my forehead, feeling the gash on it. "Sax? Where are my friends?"

He poked a head out from behind the rock, and said, *"They fell to the lower floors. I don't know if they lived."*

"I need to find them. Can you- Will you help me? I know we haven't been best friends or anything." I said, getting up and looking down the ledge. The drop off seemed to go on for an eternity.

"I don't know... I did what you asked, isn't that enough? Can't I suffer in peace?" he said.

"Please, Sax. I can't honestly make a bargain for God... but I will try my hardest to have you released of your suffering if you help me. It'll be a good deed, grander than all your previous misdeeds." I said, kneeling before the little demon.

"Even grander? I did some horrible things... I did go to Hell. Are you sure you can help me? I only came back... because I didn't feel right on Earth. Upset stomach, all the time." Sax said.

"...You're not helping your case." I said.

"You're not helping get your friends back." he said.

"Fair point. I'll see what I can do for you, that's a promise." I said, and shook his tiny hand.

"Then let's go down this path..." the demon said, and jumped off the ledge. I looked over and saw a sort of staircase made of rocks descending down into the pit. I had to jump onto each ledge, but Sax and I continued down into Hell.

We got to a sort of terrace on the ledges, and a little sign made of bones said, *"Welcome to Hell."* I passed it as it cackled at me.

There were caves in the rock, and Sax hopped into the dark. Light streamed from me, an angel in Hell. I burst my halo fire and lit the way.

It was spooky in here, that much could be said about the depths of Hell. It smelled like brimstone in every corner. I thought of all my previous enemies of the past, wondering if they would jump out at me.

A light showed from a cave exit, and I heard… cheering?

I walked out into the light, and saw the arena of my past. The horrible colosseum of old, beckoning me to fight and kill for my survival.

Sax said, *"I'd stay away from Felix this time around. Maybe run?"*

Felix the Castrator stepped forth from the darkness towards me, pointing to me, a challenge.

"Is this some sort of illusion?" I asked Sax.

"The tricky thing about Hell is… No. Everything is real. Everything. You just relive it over and over, until you're sick of dying the same away, and then it changes just slightly, in a worse way, and you wish you had the old way back again." Sax said.

"But I didn't die from Felix before." I said.

"Well you might this time. Watch out." he said.

Felix swung the net at me, but it entangled me.

He had caught me despite my best efforts to dodge, and I had no shield to defend.

But I burst my halo fire and burned the net to a crisp.

"You come at me again, sword bared. Will you ever learn your lesson, pitiful wench?" Felix said.

"Felix! Snap out of it! You don't have to keep fighting in the arena! Remember your home! Your cow!" I said.

He growled, and said, *"I will never find peace until I have conquered every soul in the arena. I will destroy you, and I will make you suffer. I'll cut off your breasts if I cannot castrate you."*

He slashed again, but I remembered his words from when he was in my apartment, I even relaxed, and I parried the small target, deflecting it. I did not want to attack Felix, I did not want to kill my friend.

I parried over and over, deflecting his blows. He was frustrated, angry, furious, he wanted to win his freedom in the arena.

But he would never have it as long as I continued to stand in his way, continued to live.

I let my sword dematerialize, and sang an old Germanic song of peace. I would let him have his peace, my life be damned.

He faltered before he attempted to cut off my breasts, and said, *"That song... It is a nice song."*

"We could always have peace if we chose it. We could've defied them all with just these words." I said, and continued my song. I sang Stille Nacht, or Silent Night in German, and offered my hand to Felix.

He sheathed his dagger, and slowly held my hand, and we sang songs of peace to the booing crowd.

And Rasputin the cat, sitting in the Emperor's seat, said, "Bravo. I'd point my thumb up, but I don't have any thumbs."

He hopped off the seat, and went down to meet us, as the crowd seemed to dissipate. "Rasputin??" I said.

"I thought I'd live through my own worst Hell forever until you switched it up. Human entertainment is garbage." Rasputin said.

"The cat talks?" Felix said.

"I can also scratch my ass with my tongue. Wanna see?" Rasputin said.

"...No." Felix said.

Rasputin licked his ass anyway.

I pet him, and said, "I'm glad you're not dead, Rasputin. You'd think a cat would die pretty easily in Hell."

Rasputin said, "Well, dying is an art, you have to do it right... but it is terrible here. The rats chase *me* in Hell. At least this little one is just sitting on your shoulder."

I looked at Sax who had crawled up to my shoulder, and he said, *"This is a dead end. There are many dead ends in Hell, in fact, your last destination, before you get to it, is just a dead end, and the destination is a dead end itself."*

"We found a few of my friends, anyway. Let's keep looking for the others, guys." I said.

Felix said, "Thank you for relieving me of the arena... but how do we get out of here?"

I looked around, and the exits weren't there anymore. It was just an endless arena. We were trapped here.

Sax said, *"And the roundabouts never end in Hell..."*

Someone was still sitting in the dark chair beside the Emperor's empty one. A voice sitting in that chair said, *"You stayed strong, despite the crushing maws of the arena... Will you be able to survive it forever? Oh... I'm bored... Just fight again or something..."*

I looked to that form sitting in that dark chair, and I defied him, saying, "We will not fight! Let us out of this pit!"

Felix said, "Fight us yourself, coward!"

The dark form said, *"Me? God no. I must ensure my line... my lineage... my status as the son of the Emperor..."*

"You... You were to be my husband, weren't you?" I said.

He walked out from the shadows, and sat in his father's chair, saying, *"This place was always meant to be mine. I WAS MY FATHER'S FAVORITE! Until I met you. Until I was so lovestruck with a winner... a barbarian of the north."*

"We're not barbarians. Just different. I truly did try to love you-" I said.

"YOU NEVER LOVED ME! ALL MY EFFORTS WERE FUTILE!! I had you kill your lover, I had you fight him in jealousy. You thought it was just your own statuses, as indomitable gladiators that brought you to the ring? IT WAS ME." the noble said.

I grew saddened for this lost soul, and said, "...And I still tried. I tried to love you."

He laughed a sad laugh, put his face to his hands, and said, *"And my own efforts had backfired... I spent so much time watching you from these seats... Clinging to a pointless fantasy... and then I killed you... I killed you like plucking a flower from the ground... I should have left you in the arena... Where you could grow on the blood you spilled..."*

"I am truly thankful for your act of freeing me. I would've never had that brief taste of freedom without you-" I said.

"I snatched you up, letting you believe it was me... You were pregnant, and they would not have let you keep fighting... You were pregnant with your lover's seed... and when you were sick after you got to me? Was when I had you kill your child with a brew. I killed your child..." he said.

"I'm sorry, but I was not pregnant... I'm sorry for your actions." I said.

"But... I killed it... I killed it... and I killed you. I killed you when I thought you would truly be mine... I killed you... and I never forgot. Everyone else whom I thought I loved... and I still only loved a woman I had murdered..." he said.

"It was an accident. You had no part to play." I said.

"I made the instrument of your death. It is as if I wielded the weapon myself. I killed you... and no one will know my name for my actions... for loving a gladiator... for killing her child... for killing her... No one will know my name... and I was an Emperor's son..." he said.

I tried to say his name, but I could not remember it. I could not remember my old future husband's name. It felt like it had been stricken from me.

He started moaning in agony, and the blood that had pooled for years in the arena made a sticky mud that sucked us downwards.

Before we were all sucked down deeper into Hell I cried out to him, "I still tried to love you. And you tried to love me. Please remember my name, if anything."

"As your sacred form is taken from me piece by piece, like the cracking of a statue, your name is the one thing that torments me the most." he said, and we were sucked further into Hell.

41

We fell through the mud. I thought I would suffocate to death in that bloody mixture, but we landed in another pit in this huge pit of Hell.

We got up from the piles of skeletons, old fighters in the arena, and tried to look for a way out. It was nearly pitch black, but I burst my halo fire so I could see my friends around me, with Sax on my shoulder.

We walked through the skeletons, over them, on top of them as they littered the floor, and a skeletal hand grabbed my ankle.

"You were meant to die with us. Both of you were meant to die with us." the skeleton said, and arose, clutching at me, trying to bring me down into this tomb.

I sliced off the hands with my sword, and Felix fought the dead men back who had arisen. We needed a way out! The skeletal hands were grabbing me, dragging me down into their eternal Hell.

A dog started barking.

The skeletal hands let go, and Freckles the golden retriever kept barking. He led us away from the skeletons as he barked back at the specters. Rasputin, Felix, and I followed, as Sax clung to the side of my head.

We got out of the chamber to a bridge with lava below it. Freckles had a bone from a skeleton, and gnawed on it. I pet his soft fur. "Thank you, boy." I said.

Freckles smiled a dog's smile to me.

Rasputin said, "The mutt found a Heaven down here instead. A giant pile of bones."

I said, "I don't think, wherever dogs go, that they will truly be in Hell for long."

Freckles accidentally dropped the bone into the lava, but looked up at me happily.

"Let's keep going, guys. Hold hands, Felix, and watch your step here." I said, and we crossed the bridge. Rasputin and Freckles ran ahead, having better balance or at least better faith in their footsteps, and Felix and I held hands, walking carefully over the bridge, almost having to shimmy at one point as it got narrower and narrower.

The hand of Hell reached out from the lava, and grabbed at the bridge, breaking it. We ran for it, but did not let go of each other's hands.

I got to the other side where Freckles and Rasputin were waiting, but Felix was falling, and I held his hand, holding him tight. You'd think a ghost wouldn't be so heavy, but it felt like I was holding the weight of the world.

I heard the Devil in my ear, whispering, *"Let go. You don't have to hold onto the past. You can win this time..."*

I screamed out, and tried to drag Felix up with my other hand.

I slipped from the weight, I felt my hands slipping... letting go of Felix...

But Freckles held onto my pants leg with his maw, keeping me from falling, giving me a little bit more balance.

And I dragged Felix back up.

Felix thanked me, almost relentlessly.

"I won't ever let my friend fall into Hell." I said. He nodded to me, and we continued on into the dark.

All that we could see was what was directly around me. I constantly prayed for Heaven's aid, and the light illuminated the dark, my halo shining bright in my hand. There were caverns everywhere, and it was just endless darkness and shadow. We heard horrible strange sounds come from some directions, and when we followed them there was nothing there, the sound beckoning again from behind us. We continued forward... but there was no forward down in Hell. Every direction looked the same.

Then we found a tulip petal in the darkness, leading a trail of petals.

We followed the trail, until we got to a statue of Calmaog that Fate was crying at. Then she got up from crying, whacked at the statue over and over again, her fists bleeding from pounding at it, and resumed crying.

I went to Fate and told her it was alright. She said, "Look there," and pointed to an engraving on the statue.

It said, *"This is the idolatry you created. The more you try to destroy it, the more it destroys you. You will never have your soul back from the false idols you have raised. Believe in Calmaog, for God will not help you now. Your fate is sealed."*

I told Fate, "You know that's not true. Calmaog was just a despicable rapist."

"Please destroy it. You broke him before. Please break him again... for I am trapped with this statue..." Fate said.

I noticed the chains on her ankles, attached to the statue.

I smashed at the statue with my sword, angry at the wretched monument to a man so wretched, which would only deserve a place in Hell.

But I could not break the statue.

"Please find the others. Leave me here if you have to." Fate said.

Felix came to her, and said, "We will all spend an eternity with you, Fate, before we leave you alone with this evil thing."

"We are all bound to a fate in Hell... and the chains wind tighter and tighter before we are never released..." Sax said, and I noticed he, all of us,

were attached to the statue by chains, even the dog and cat with thick, heavy collars.

I smashed and smashed at the chains, trying to free us... but the harder I fought, the tighter it held.

The statue looked eviler, more menacing, and seemed huge.

I remembered something Thaniel had said.

"If we fear someone because of what they did, then they win. If we laugh at them, then we make them a little bit smaller in comparison."

So I laughed at the statue, just started laughing at it so ridiculously menacing. It was only a statue anyway. I said to Fate, "He sure did have a weird looking penis. Like a mule's head. And boy, when I ripped it off... He brayed like one as well!"

Fate looked at me curiously, but laughed, and said, "And his mother looked like a duck. A duck with a bad hairdo."

The statue didn't seem to change, but it felt just a little bit smaller.

Felix said, "He sure had one big inferiority complex. The biggest thing about him. And even *I* had more balls than he did, with him hiding behind his mother... Well, I've got more man parts than he does now, anyway."

The statue's man parts fell off, and the chains didn't feel so tight.

We continued to make jokes about it, continued to laugh at the thing, feeling just a bit better having some awful thing to ridicule, something that we all feared and hated, and soon the statue was cracking to pieces, simply stone, and we were free.

I suppose idolatry can't take a joke.

42

We left the debris of Calmaog, the only bit of him anyone will remember after time takes its toll, and people laugh the monsters to dust. We all smiled as we continued on into Hell, happy to have our Fate back.

We passed deeper and deeper, and the screams got more intense.

Demons were torturing people in thousands, millions of ways. But it was all the same, really. Endless suffering, and then when the people had been tortured enough, flayed, mutilated, and disemboweled, they got up again as demons to torture the others. Their suffering knew no bounds, and the only way they could relieve it was if they inflicted the same suffering on others.

They turned to us, intent on inflicting their suffering on brand new intact souls.

They swarmed us! Flying demonic creatures, like harpies, snakish monsters, and little demons with pitchforks. They prodded and poked at us as we tried to fight them off, and the only thing keeping them back was my halo soul blazing bright, the one thing they feared, as all fear had been purged of them as demons.

They feared the wrath of God.

I shouted out, as I made my halo burst like a supernova, "Slither away, demons. For God is watching us, and will be watching you not before long."

They crept back into the shadows, as my light lengthened those shadows.

The still tortured souls had a brief respite of peace, but I could not break their bindings, help them up from their suffering, for they were trapped in Hell.

We let them whimper and cry for a second, let them rot and moan, and walked forth, even though it hurt my soul to leave them like that.

One whispered out before I left, saying, *"Please let me repent."*

I kneeled before her, and said, "Go through Purgatory in peace. Always ask for forgiveness, and God will hear."

She said, *"Purgatory... What is that?"*

I said, "It is the place where condemned souls go through penance, before reaching Heaven. You have a chance at penance too."

"No... No. You're lying. You must be lying..." and started crying from where her eyes had been, after they were plucked out by demons.

I could not get anything else through to her, so we left further into Hell.

Sax asked me, *"Would you like to suffer like her? Or suffer a new way?"*

I said, "I don't want anyone to suffer..."

"That woman killed twenty babies in cold blood... and she watched them die. Thus her eyes were plucked out, and she felt every death like those babies. You can suffer like her, if you choose. Just kill twenty babies. Or you can go that way, and find something new. The nice part, I mean horrible part, of Hell is that every suffering is really brand new, tailored specifically to the victim. We take our work seriously here." Sax said.

I shrugged, and we went down the new way.

We were opening doors that kept leading to more doors. Which door had Maximus, Nevaeh, and Max behind them?

"Not even a cat or dog door in these. It's painful seeing places we can't get through, even though we know something is just behind it... with fresh air leaking through the cracks." Rasputin said, as he followed me through yet another door.

"Fresh air? Where's that?" I asked.

Freckles barked, and scratched at this one door. I opened it... and we walked into a spacious, luxurious room, with the windows all blacked out, just darkness to be seen from them. But there were people in here.

Luscious ladies, gorgeous women, scantily clothed and sexily posed... with demon tails sprouting from their plump rumps.

With Maximus eating and drinking from their hands, as they rubbed his thighs, pressed their breasts against his face. His halo had darkened.

One of the succubi saw me, and quickly tried leading Maximus into a room just for them.

I called out to Maximus, and his eyes looked clouded from drink and lust. He looked at me, smiled, and said, *"Yuuuule... C'mere... meet... her."*

The succubus holding his hand hissed at me.

I went up to him, and said, "Maximus. You need to leave this place. It is not right for you."

He waved his hand in the air, and said, *"Iiiii never had so much fun! Not even... Heaven! Had places like thiiiiissss..."*

"That's because it is only lust and gluttony. It is not a real relationship, like you and I had." I said.

"Pfffft... I killed myself for you! And we didn't even have reeeeaaaalll sex! I just pleasured you over and over again..." he said.

"But... you enjoyed it, right?" I said.

"Well... Maybe you can make up for it? C'mon. Come with me and... I wanna say Dusk?" he said, and tried taking my hand and leading me

with the succubus, but I quickly snatched back my hand. *"Suit yourself. Hey, maybe the Castrator... Pffft..."* Maximus said, and started laughing, *"I mean... Never mind. You wouldn't find anything great about this! You've got no balls!! HAHAHA..."*

"And I have never fallen as low as you are right now, Maximus." Felix said.

"...What?" Maximus said.

"You had it all, even when you had nothing. The adoration of the crowd, the love of a real woman, Heaven, and you give it all up for a nameless succubus. I'd knock some sense into you, but it feels like somebody already knocked you so hard it'd be useless." Felix said.

"...Look here! You... Castrator! You've never had the opportunity to be with a woman, the woman you love, and then have to hold back! I'veeee finally gotten my just reward..." Maximus said.

Fate said, "Sometimes attraction can only bring suffering."

"Like death. Having your heart stop for love. Well... I feel it... beating hard again... when I look at you instead, Yule." Maximus said.

The succubus was dragging him harder, but Maximus let go.

"I'm sorry." Maximus said, "I... have only ever really had the living pleasure to be with you, Yule."

"And then you died... I can see why this must be seductive to you." I said.

"Yeah... This is like what I've always dreamed of... but the women... they're all wrong. None of them have your face." Maximus said.

The succubi, seeing that their spell had been broken, lurked away, as I blazed my halo at them.

And Maximus's halo shined bright over his head again.

43

"I know you have a special place for someone else these days…" Maximus said, "But our time together was Heaven in its own way. All of them, the good and the bad. Let's find your love, because I'm sure he must feel the same way that I felt."

"Thank you, Maximus. I truly felt the same way about you. I hope Nevaeh and Max aren't suffering like you all have…" I said.

"These succubi…" Maximus said, "Did not make me feel like I was suffering… but I could not get them out of my head. It was a torment in itself…" Maximus said.

Felix said, "These women only wanted a new toy. When they used you up, made you like them, they would've abandoned you to even worse hells, as they laughed at your fall from grace."

Maximus looked down at his feet. "Thank you." Maximus said, "You all make me feel like there is life in this horrible place. You, Yule, you, Lady of the Tulip, these animals blessed by God… even you, Felix."

"I believe that's the first time you ever called me Felix since we were children." Felix said.

"Yeah, well… You always did hate the name Castrator… It's a shame that it stuck after I gave it to you, and you had to continue down that path." Maximus said.

"I only did what was expected of me... I truly regret not going my own way, after all that time... but I'm glad for the other name you gave me. Felix is a fine name, when I was only called 'slave'. This is Fate, our Lady of the Tulip." Felix said.

Maximus shook Fate's hand, and Fate blushed. Fate gave him the tulip she had kept, which only had one petal left, wilting in Hell. But Maximus took it, and it seemed to cling to that life in his hands. Maximus put it in his hair, behind his ear.

We continued out of this brothel, and walked down a street in Hell. The houses were empty, lifeless, the streets dusty and cracked. It looked partially like our town up above, but every flaw was accentuated, every dark corner darker, and it was utterly lifeless.

And then I saw where Nevaeh would be, where she always said she never wanted to go. I saw the church of Hell, the cross on the steeple turned upside down.

We crept into the church. It was all dark and shadowy, the altar bloodied, and a monument to Satan in the front.

Ee heard a horrible sound coming from beneath a pew.

"Please... help. God. Yule. Anyone... help..." Nevaeh said, in the voice of a little girl.

I saw her reliving her worst moment, ten times over, never-ending, with no witnesses, no one to save her.

I shrieked in anger, and pulled him off of her.

Satan laughed, and vanished in smoke.

I helped Nevaeh up, and she looked small, tiny, helpless, just a little girl. I helped her redress as she was numb to emotions, no crying, no tears, just a blank, empty expression.

Satan whispered around us, *"She'll always be here, you know. She'll never not feel it. You can never take it away."*

I ignored him, and held Nevaeh, just telling her it would be alright.

She stared at me listlessly. I held her hand and led her out of the church…

But there were no doors. We were trapped, like Nevaeh, in this church.

I put my hands on Nevaeh's shoulders, knelt before her, and said, "I know this is a horrible memory. Let's just put it in a box, for now, and we can open it up again later. Let's keep it in the box, and take care of it when we're safe."

"My parents won't love me anymore... God won't love me anymore... Why didn't he kill me?" Nevaeh said.

Felix broke down crying and knelt before Nevaeh too. He said, "Nevaeh. We cannot take it away. It is done with and over, and we can never undo it. But it will always be over, and will never happen again…"

Nevaeh said, *"But why did it?"*

Maximus said, "We are just in a horrible place right now. We all feel your pain, and it is like it happened to every one of us. We will escape, somehow."

Felix was still crying for Nevaeh, and said, "I will not, cannot, ever hurt you like that. Remember our date? We had so much fun! Everyone thought you were nuts talking to yourself like that, but I think we had great conversations, and I even got the waiter to spill that one rich snob's plate all over him! We laughed like nothing else. We can always have time for the future, instead of the past."

Nevaeh smiled, and said, *"Yeah... He'll probably never get that clam chowder smell off his suit."*

"And we can do more things like that for as long as you wish. Let's let the past be, people like Earl, the Devil, stay in that past. Let them rot in Hell, while we spit in all their faces and have our own fun." Felix said.

"Yeah. I wanted to try out this Japanese restaurant, wondering if they make food as good as my dad." Nevaeh said, and kissed Felix on the cheek.

Then she was her normal adult self, and kissed him on the lips, stroked his cheek, and then said, "And we've got things to do... Y'know. Inspiration for my erotic novel. If you're up to the challenge..."

Felix smiled and held her hand, and said, "I always am, Nevaeh."

The church started crumbling, there was no way out, the floor opened up, and we fell deeper into Hell.

44

We were in utter darkness, but everyone could see me, as I led us through Hell.

Sax popped out of my pocket, and said, *"This is a floor for some of the worst scum. If Max is here, he might deserve to be."*

"Nonsense. He's as young as me, and probably didn't have time to do anything truly horrible in his short life." I said.

It was just darkness, and we looked around. It was just a flat, marble floor.

Sax said, *"The lost stay lost here. Forever wandering, while their own mind torments them in worse ways any demon ever could."*

I saw a form that looked kind of like Max, but he ran away from my light.

"Max! Come back!" I yelled out. We heard his footsteps echoing on the marble floor, and I chased him through the darkness, as my friends chased me.

We kept running, chasing him. I was thankful that I was stronger and faster than Max, and nearly caught up with him...

But he turned, and that wasn't Max. It was a demon.

"Leave me alone... Let me die..." he said.

"Oh. Sorry, thought you were someone else..." I said.

"Leave me alone, Yule. You were always laughing at me, hating me, think-ing I was small, inadequate, and a moron... You were always laughing at me..." the demon said.

I gasped, as I looked into his eyes, and they were Max's.

"I'm a demon, Yule. SLAY ME. KILL ME. LET ME MEET MY END..." Max said.

"No. I know you were a human. I've seen your baby pictures!" I said.

"But I am a demon now... Rip out my tongue, my penis, lock me up in a mental institution... Do your justice to me..." Max said.

"Those people deserved their justice! You do not! You were always my sweet and innocent Max! You don't deserve this fate!" I said.

"I always thought you were too good for me... I always somehow knew... and then you turned out to be an angel. I am a demon, a wretch. The only brave thing I've ever done is walk up to you... I am a coward." he said, as he cowered before me. He continued, *"I ran from Fate, Nevaeh, Felix, even Freckles and Rasputin. And Maximus? I let him enjoy his time with the demons... I am unfit to be a human... I deserve to die... I BETRAYED MY FRIENDS AND FAMILY!!"*

Maximus said, "You are in Hell. Perhaps that was your own Hell, to leave the ones you care about. But we have come for you."

He burst out crying, and said, *"The Devil... I am the Devil... I'm a monster... Just kill me and get it over with..."*

Nevaeh said, "Well that shows you you're not the Devil in itself. You'd sacrifice yourself just to get rid of that evil."

Fate said, "You protected me when I went through my worst. That is not cowardly."

Max said, *"But I still let you go to that church. I let you leave. I let my sister get RAPED!!"*

"You did not." Fate said, "You allowed me my own choices. That is what any brother should do."

"I am no one's family, no one's friend... I am nothing..." Max said.

I said, "You are Max. We all love you, we all care for you. You're a friend to every person you meet, you're the sweetest person I've ever met. Who cares if you don't rush to meet your end every chance you get? That's what Maximus and Felix did, and they weren't the best for it."

"But they're an angel and a ghost. I am a demon. Isn't that what I deserve?" Max said.

"You deserve to walk on Earth just a bit longer, and then ascend to Heaven with me. I truly believe that." I said.

Rasputin rubbed against his legs, and Freckles walked up to Max. Max pet them both. Rasputin said, "There. You just did your good deed. You pet the animals, and showed love. Now you don't belong in Hell."

Max said, *"...That was all I had to do?"*

Rasputin said, "Well, that was your tipping point. You now belong in Heaven with the angels, because for every pet you give, your soul is counterbalanced with it. And I know you, you've pet me every chance you can get."

Max said, *"...Huh. I always thought you looked like you could talk. I guess some people just have to show kindness to the lesser beings once in a while..."*

"Only the greatest amongst us can, Max." I said.

He smiled to me, and said, "I promise to never leave you guys again. I will never allow anyone to fall into Hell if I can stop them. I just... was so scared."

Nevaeh said, "Fuck, I don't blame you for running. I would've if I could, too."

I hugged Max as his demonic form dissipated, and he was his old self again.

"Now that we've got Max and everyone back… How do we get out?" Felix asked.

Satan whispered, *"Now it is time for the grand finale. It is time for you to go to Hell, Yule."*

My friends disappeared, and I fell to the lowest pits of Hell.

45

I landed, I died, I landed, I died again. Over and over, I would smash to death on the rocks, and the rocks would smash on me and kill me.

Just like the statue that killed me, but an eternity worse.

I just held onto my halo soul, as Satan tried to rip it away from me, trying to take away my piece of me.

Satan kept whispering while I kept falling.

"You had all that time to make a true difference on Earth. Instead you wasted it, smoking, drinking, fucking for pleasure.

"No one will remember your brief life again. No one will know the name Yule Tidings. Is that even your real name? Sounds like something someone made up.

"We were all waiting for you, every one of us, for as soon as an angel gives up their place in Heaven... there is only one place yet they deserve.

"Hell. Welcome to your eternity, Yule."

I saw all my friends being tortured, with me not able to do anything about it.

I saw the dragon destroying creation, with me trapped in Hell.

But a little demon was clinging to my shoulder as I fell. He said, *"I know this seems bad... but you did get what you deserved, and even had a life to love again for just a little bit."*

"Why-" and I smashed against a rock and died again, "Are-" smash, "You-" smash, "Here-" smash, "Too?" smash.

"Beats me. I never did all the soul moving myself. I was trained for betrayal. And I got you down to the lowest pit. I'm a bit happier with someone else to share it with." Sax said.

"You lied to me?" I said, as I kept falling.

"I'm a demon, Yule. You should've never allowed me that brief stay in your apartment even. Given me mercy. Some people are better off if you just smite them as soon as you meet them..." Sax said.

"I don't believe that. I believe we all need a chance." I said, as Satan nearly tugged my soul away from me.

"You had your second chance. You've given me one as well. And I curse you for it." Sax said, *"You played into the Devil's scheme. You caused me more suffering. It's better to submit, Yule, and serve for eternity. We all serve someone, whether that be Satan or God."*

Satan nearly wrenched my soul away again.

"Just give up... Enjoy the suffering while it lasts forever." Sax said.

I thought... there was no way out. I would be in Hell for eternity now, with Satan and Sax whispering in my ear.

So I gave up my soul. Let Satan enjoy it while he could.

Satan cackled as he held my soul, *"Finally! You are just like me... Betraying your friends, betraying your God... You and I will be eternally locked together, as your soul is mine..."*

"Keep it, Satan. Let it bring you some joy. For as long as you hold it in your hands, it will burn you forever. You will remember the taste of Paradise God gave you, as it is reflected in my soul. You will lust forever after what you cannot have, and suffer all the more." I said.

The soul burned in his hands, as we fell together, but he would not let it go, would stare at its brilliance forever, blinding him and burning his eyes. He would not let it go. He would forever look at my soul, and see God's strength in me, and he would know... that he would never have it.

He screamed out, and threw the soul, far away from him, upwards, to Heaven.

"Go back to Heaven, Yule. I do not want to know what I have given up. Get out of my Hell, and don't come back."

"We're not done yet, Satan." Sax said, and Sax changed, becoming huge, and grabbed Satan as we actually landed, immediately throwing Satan to the farthest reaches of... well, anything.

Sax was a huge demon, larger than ever, and said, *"I always thought it would be neat to be King of Hell... I've lied to everyone, betrayed everyone, and now I've betrayed even the Devil."*

We were on a floor in Hell that looked like it couldn't get any deeper. Sax picked up a little crown on the floor, and put it on his head.

"H-How do we get out, Sax?" I asked.

"Go through Purgatory, Yule. Repent. Purgatory was blocked for so long... But I believe you and your friends will have an easier time of it than most." Sax said. He turned small again, and said, "Thank you for this chance. I promise to change Hell. All those ghosts really should've gone through Purgatory already... But I'm glad I blocked it, and got you all down here, allowing my chance at Satan. Hell would've never ruptured forth, otherwise."

"You made all this suffering??" I said.

"We all need a challenge, Yule. Something to make us feel alive. Go in peace, and feel free to visit. I think I can get most of these everliving shitheads to actually do something good for a change... I changed, and I'm glad you allowed me to. We are all changing, some for good, some for bad, but still everchanging. Keep up the good work, Yule. I will, eternally, be your King of Hell."

"What about the dragon?" I asked.

"Fuck if I care. Not in Hell, not my business. Here's your friends back." Sax said, and opened a door that all my friends walked out of, briefly tortured, but allowed peace by Sax. "Now get the hell out of Hell and go through Purgatory. You all deserve to make changes in the world." Sax said, and showed us the gates to Purgatory that had been hidden behind a large boulder.

Sax moved the boulder for us, just tipping it to the side, even whilst small. I suppose this tiny demon always had the strength to move boulders, to defeat Satan, and even change. The others walked through, I last, and I said to Sax, "Thank you, for showing me mercy."

Part 7: Patientia

Patience

46

Purgatory actually wasn't that bad. Just a bit tedious, having to make amends for *every* sin we've ever done, but I think we were more the better for it. Max had stolen a pen when he was a kid, and had to give pens to every soul there, who were now going through Purgatory because of Sax. Felix, because he had castrated so many people had to give back... er, y'know. He was finally accepted into Heaven, after he made amendments for his sins.

Maximus straightened up and told all the women who he had caught eyes with in the arena that he could not continue giving them their lustful looks. He said he was saving that for someone special, and stroked the tulip behind his ear.

Nevaeh had to write a thousand nice things for everyone she had ever slandered, and Fate... just walked through and had to wait up for our own sins. Rasputin and Freckles followed her, just being a cat and a dog, and really had nothing to amend.

I had to say sorry for every life I had taken in the arena, say sorry for not being a true angel on Earth when they needed me, and even had to pay back that cashier I let give me a wrong pricing on a bottle of booze I had bought. The noble, my old future husband, was doing well in Purgatory, if anything, and I accepted his heartfelt apologies.

"What is your name, by the way?" I asked him, as he was saying his thousandth apology to me.

"Antonelli. I apologize for-" he started.

"Really? I know someone whose surname is Antonelli in the modern day. Maybe they're your long lost kin?" I said.

Antonelli smiled, and said, "I hope so. My family was very long lived and reproductive. Um… excuse me, I have to apologize to my wife whom I never really loved…"

"Go get 'em." I said, and hit him on the arm.

Because more than half of us were living, and had to make amendments on Earth, we were allowed to walk to our front door, now burned to nothing, and do right to the living.

Our house was burned down, the bar was burned down, we had really nowhere to congregate, so we went to Mrs. Nestor's. I hoped she was still alive.

We knocked on the door, our whole group of people, and she opened as Freckles barked happily to her. She smiled and pet him, and said, "Gosh. You're all still alive, too? Well, come in, even the other two angels, and I hope the cat doesn't piss anywhere."

Rasputin mewled at her.

We all had tea with her, and a voice said, "I know my house was burned down by that raging hellbitch… but can't I at least have my old room back, Ma?"

"You know, Nate, that that's my art studio." Mrs. Nestor said.

Thaniel walked in, and was surprised by all the people drinking tea with Mrs. Nestor, his mother.

"I told you about my no good son, didn't I? Well, fucking Hell has come to Earth, and he needs somewhere to mope around in." Mrs. Nestor said.

"Your son is Thaniel?" I asked.

"Thaniel? I always thought that was a strange name..." Mrs. Nestor said.

"Yule!!" Thaniel said, "It burned down the bar, the community center where I had the AA meetings, and everything is fucked!! Can *you* do anything about it?? I always felt like you could do anything."

"You mean that goodhearted girl who you drank with is Yule??" Mrs. Nestor said, "Goddamnit, I should've known. You did always call her a rabbit girl... I thought you thought she was a playboy bunny! I thought she broke up your marriage!"

"No! She's just like an albino rabbit! She's been one of my best drinking gals! And you know me and Sarah really just had our own problems..." Thaniel said.

"I always thought it was interesting your mom had a golden retriever like Mrs. Nestor." I said, "Even on St. Patty's day, when we all met together, you never called each other mom or son."

"Well that's because Nathan had been a ripe asshole that day. I told him not to go drinking like that, but he went on and did anyway." Mrs. Nestor said.

"Ma... you know you aren't the best to judge me on my drinking..." Thaniel said.

"It's for your own good! If you weren't so drunk and hanging around playboy bunnies you would still be married!" Mrs. Nestor said.

"Yule's not a bunny, Ma. Just a very awesome person. I mean, I'm sure playboy bunnies are too... but can you do anything, Yule??" Thaniel said.

"We will try. All of us will try. We've been through Hell and back, and we can still try." I said.

"...You broke up with your wife too or something?" Thaniel said.

"No. I'm an angel, Thaniel. Maximus is an angel, and Felix has just been accepted as an angel. The rest are all living still." I said.

"...The big guy, and the other big guy, are dead? And you're dead? I know a dragon has come forth, but you don't have to keep pulling pranks." Thaniel said.

Max said, "These durastics are just life. Just like you're damn bees... They keep changing. We're all a durastics in ourselves, and well, some of us aren't living durastics... but still far reaching effects."

"...You all... Don't... really get it... It's just... I'm not drinking... and reality still doesn't make sense. I'd ask you all to leave... but... I think I'd just wonder forever then." Thaniel said.

"Just know that God has faith in you too. We'll see what we can do." I said.

Mrs. Nestor said, "Please, take my husband's rifle if you need it. It may come in handy. Nathan? Please get your dad's gun."

"I fucking hated going on those hunting trips... But you hunt a dragon for us, ok, Yule?" Thaniel said, and brought out his father's gun. He offered it to me, and I took it carefully.

None of us really knew how to use a gun, besides Nevaeh, but she didn't want to touch the thing. She still told me to put it in the pit of my shoulder, don't close my eyes, and look down the barrel.

But it still felt like another soul was helping me hold the gun. The old soul of Mrs. Nestor's husband, keeping it from falling from my hands in the sweat of my palms.

We went out the door, and went hunting a dragon, like St. George must've done.

47

We saw it blazing up the town, burning it down. My home… everything was ashes. Felix and Maximus wielded their weapons, Maximus a sword from Heaven and Felix his old dagger, and I aimed at the dragon, shaking.

I shot at it, and maybe because of a miracle, clipped a wing joint. It went roaring down to Earth, and all of us approached it.

The dragon smashed into a building, destroying it, as we crept around it. I aimed again at the dragon…

But it burst fire at me, almost burning me.

I hid just in time, and Nevaeh, Fate and Max hid as well, as Felix and Maximus circled the dragon.

They jumped out at it from the sides! They wielded their weapons and stabbed at it! But the dragon shook them off, shaking them away and whacking them away with its tail and claws.

Whenever I took aim at its head again, the dragon would breathe fire at me.

Nevaeh, Fate and I were crouching out of the dragon's aim… but where was Max?

Max had picked up a steel bar from the debris, and said, "I will never run again."

I yelled out at him, "Don't! Come back, Max!"

But he charged at the dragon, as it was distracted by Felix and Maximus, furiously striking them back and trying to burn them.

And Max stabbed it in the head, rupturing forth blood, as the dragon screamed.

It did not expect someone to boldly attack it, and Max had nearly forfeited his life in such an act.

It tried to burn fire on Max in its last breath, but Nevaeh had tackled Max away, saving him from death.

I threw the rifle to the ground and went to them.

The dragon was dead, and smoldered to ashes being a creature of Hell. Nevaeh's hair was a little burnt, and I kissed them each in gratitude to them and God.

We walked back to… well, there was nowhere to go.

But we found the Italian restaurant still standing amidst the wreckage.

Mike was hiding behind the counter, but I told him we'd like an extra large pizza.

He peeked out from behind it, and said, "F-For here or t-to go?"

"Here, Mike. The dragon is dead." I said.

He breathed out a sigh of relief, and said, "I-I'm the only one lef-left here… I-I'll make a piz-pizza…" and went into the back.

We sat in silence for a while, after all we've been through, but Max said, "Feels like I got my courage back. Holy fucking shit!! I slayed a dragon!"

We laughed, and Nevaeh said, "I never thought you were a dragon-slayer too! Makes me happy."

Fate said, "My brother is the best dragonslayer around! He'd always play as one when we were kids… and who knew he would be one?"

But as they laughed, Freckles put his head on my lap, and Rasputin laid on the table.

I said, "You know we can't stay around forever…"

Max said, "What? You know that's BS! You're here to stay."

But I looked at Maximus and Felix. Felix had a halo now. I said, "We don't belong here. I… love you guys… But we are dead. We don't belong in the living world. We *must* ascend, all three of us, and leave you. But we will always be with you, no matter what you do."

They grew silent, as Max held my hand, and said, "I want to say-"

Mike came to us with the pizza, and placed it gently before us. He looked at Nevaeh and said, "I truly am sorry… that what happened to you happened to you."

"It's ok, Mike. Sometimes we just love other people over time." Nevaeh said.

"I-I just wish- Just never wished- you had to go through that… Suicide sucks. Me and Marie are doing well, and we both felt your pain. I felt your pain… We're thinking of naming our girl that we're having Nevaeh…" Mike said.

"Please don't." Nevaeh said, "I don't want to be a ghost in your life. Name her Yule, if anything. Someone that's brought you true happiness."

"How about Fate? She's made us all feel great, in her own way." I said.

"…I don't really have a clue anymore. I think I'll just proposition Marie to name her after that famous actress we like instead…" Mike said.

We all laughed, Mike smiled, and went to refill our refreshments.

Max said, as we were leaving, "I wanted to say that you will always have a place with us. No matter where you go. I truly want you to stay, and think God will be happier for it."

But there was a stairway beckoning us from the street, coming down straight from Heaven.

I cried, and told Max, "I love you more than anything! I don't want to leave… but my work on Earth is done. None should have extra lives, well, besides Rasputin."

Rasputin licked his fur.

I continued, "I will always love you, Max. And I will wait up for you in Heaven."

He burst out crying, holding my hand, and said, "Please... don't go. Don't go! I always dreamed of asking you to marry me! I wanted to! I thought that would be my greatest dream! Fuck it. Will you marry me? Will you stay on Earth?"

Felix and Maximus were walking to that stairway, but Fate held Maximus's hand, stopping him, and Nevaeh held Felix's.

"We both want you around too." Nevaeh said.

The two didn't know what to say. I wanted to break hands with Max, but I felt like Heaven could wait for a second. I could be damned to Hell if God cared, I could die a thousand times, if I would give my Max up.

But I knew I must leave, and kissed him, a last kiss goodbye.

And left him to ascend up the stairs.

Felix and Maximus followed me, but...

The stairs disappeared, and we fell back to Earth, after the first step.

We were trapped on Earth, whether we liked it or not.

And we liked it a great deal.

We ran to the others, hugging them in delight, for if we were stuck on Earth, we wished to be with them. Fate hugged Maximus, as Maximus kissed her on the cheek, Felix hugged Nevaeh and kissed her on the lips... and I hugged my Max.

I suppose God gives us mysterious choices. Sometimes we're better off with what we're stuck with, rather than what we think we should do.

And I was so happy because of it!

Felix and Maximus were living again, *everyone* noticed them, and it didn't come as much a surprise when Maximus asked Fate to court him.

"Court? Let's just hang out for a while. I think you're... well, *gorgeous...* And I'd like to get to know the real you in a more comfortable setting." Fate said.

"Wherever it pleases you, Fate." Maximus said.

We had nowhere to stay, we were homeless on Earth, but we couldn't have been more happy.

We eventually got lodgings, all of us in a big house we shared, and soon went to the funeral for Mrs. Nestor... as she had died, passing in her sleep from a short nap.

48

Thaniel was crying tears of sorrow, saying he always wished his mother would outlive him. I said, "There, there... That's just ridiculous. We should never outlive our parents."

"But she just had a sort of fire and spittle to her, y'know? I just think it sucks... Excuse me, I've got to talk to my ex wife and kids, mourning the loss of their grandma..." Thaniel said, and left me.

I said a few words for Angelica Nestor, saying she was a great grandmother, mother, wife, a true inspiration to all, that she always had time for me, when I walked her dog and we had tea, and gave me some of the best advice I could get. That we must all live kind and nice and good, even without God or any Heavenly duty, and that she most assuredly will arise to Heaven because she lived through these words. I placed her husband's camera by her coffin, strangely surviving the wreckage, next to a picture Thaniel had in his wallet of the three of them, Mrs. Nestor, Mr. Nestor, and him as a child.

I saw her spirit smile at me, with her halo, wave me goodbye, and she was escorted to Heaven by an angel, Mr. Nestor himself.

Thaniel and I were smoking cigarettes outside, and I said, "So... Nathaniel Nestor. That's a rather catchy name. Why didn't you sign your book by that? Nathaniel Hamburg just doesn't sound as nice."

"I took my mother's maiden name when my dad and I had a falling out. This was after I first started writing, too, and I just cemented it with that. I never wanted to be like him... My parents were always fighting, and one day him and I got into an argument instead, and my dad and I just could never see eye to eye after that. Beats me how they stayed married for so long." Thaniel said.

"Maybe some people just try to fix what's broken, instead of throwing it out. But maybe they really did love each other, and the fights were like the occasional stall in the car in a great road trip." I said, and puffed on my cigarette. "Did you know Max proposed to me?" I said.

"Really. I'd think about it before you get married so young, but heck, it feels like you're even older than me sometimes. I suppose just follow your heart." Thaniel said.

"I'm letting him out of it, but he gets really excited whenever we talk about it... I don't want *him* to make any mistakes he'll regret. I nearly got married before... and then had my accident that broke the marriage up." I said.

"Right... So what was that about being an angel? I think I'd believe it now that I've seen a dragon rise forth... and then be defeated by you and your friends." Thaniel said.

"It's crazy how people still don't believe a thing like that happened, when it happened in our own backyard. I don't think you should worry about me being an angel. Just have hope that truly great miracles can happen. I wish I could do more miracles in the world... I wish I could change everything." I said.

"You've done all you can for now. Just have patience, and things will change for the better." Thaniel said, and flicked his cigarette butt, "Well, see ya, Yule. Please stop by and visit. I'll be staying in my ma's house for now. Thanks for letting me keep Freckles. I wish me and my ma sorted out our differences long before she passed… but the dog reminds me of her."

"He's a good boy. Well, later, Thaniel." I said, waved him goodbye and we each walked back home, our new homes on Earth.

49

Nevaeh was fidgeting at her typewriter that managed to survive the destruction, in her new room in our new house, and said, "I've had to rewrite the whole story of Hanatrix, and I think it's a lot better this time around. Good thing I practically memorized the entire story. But... I'm just shy of fifty chapters..."

"Well, it doesn't have to be any round number. Just end it with a happy ending." I said.

"Eh. Hanatrix loves a ghost that came back to life, that's a eunuch. Shame I can't give Felix his balls back... but I think he's just used to not having any, y'know? Wouldn't feel right or something. Maximus and him aren't getting drunk and making up another silly contest, are they?" Nevaeh said.

"They're arm wrestling right now, and they've been locked together like that for ten minutes so far." I said.

Fate was sitting on Nevaeh's bed, and said, "Maximus is sooo nice, and gentle, and sweet. You wouldn't expect it from a big person like him, but he truly is an angel like you. Although... he cries out in his sleep sometimes, remembering our trip to Hell."

"Yeah, I think we all still have nightmares from that... But they're just dreams, memories of the past, and you shouldn't worry about them.

I wonder where Satan went? Y'know what, best not to speculate. You gals wanna watch a movie with me?" I said.

They said sure, as Nevaeh ended her story on a kiss.

We watched a really funny movie, that was a little cheesy and the romance plot was over the top and sappy at times, but we enjoyed it anyway as Felix and Maximus continued to never beat each other at arm wrestling.

Max walked in, said that he'll take on the winner, and snuggled up with me on the couch.

Rasputin curled up on our laps, and we just enjoyed each other's company.

Life was good, and it would stay good. The demons all went back to Hell as the afterlife finally stabilized, and the ghosts went through Purgatory.

It went on like that, for a good while, all seven of us, three angels, three humans, a cat, all mortal now.

Well, maybe not the cat, but I'm not exactly sure.

Rasputin said, "And they all lived happily ever after."

I kissed my Max, and we continued our own lives, our own story, knowing that there is never really a true end to love and life.

www.ingramcontent.com/pod-product-compliance
Lightning Source LLC
Chambersburg PA
CBHW060249100726
47907CB00003B/818